CURSED FATE

BLOOD FATE SERIES
BOOK I

GRACIE STONE

WILLOW
HOUSE
Publishing

For every reader ...
May you find the
love of your life.
May it be eternal,
ethereal and
all consuming.

Love is an undeniable magic, transcendent of time, and the only emotion that ever drives humanity forward.

— GRACIE STONE

CURSED

FATE

PROLOGUE
LEWIS - LONDON, 1724

L ewis staggered from the Old Cheshire Cheese, spilling into Fleet Street, feeling more drunk than he was. The brown wooden door slammed, rattling the pub's lamp sign. Rounding the corner, he mulled over every word Defoe spoke moments ago, explaining the entirety of his work, *Robinson Crusoe*. Struck with the overwhelming fantasy of jumping ship on an adventure, he turned into the dark alley that made his walk home a little shorter.

He shouldn't have left Denver to fend off those women by himself, but daydreams trapped him in his head, imagining penning out stories and traveling to far-off places. Imbued with enough whiskey to drown a sailor, his brother would most likely pass out before he would do any further damage to their reputations. Gentlemen of their age, in the heart of the city, must make proper, smart choices. It was all too easy to be branded for the worse, landing a man in dire need of lodging and well-paying work.

Shadows encroached on the alley. Lewis spun back. The tang of rotting garbage and the ever-creeping fog of the streets of London wove through his senses. The slick cobblestone underfoot met the seemingly narrowing grimy sides of the buildings on either side of him. Collar up, he shoved his hands into the pockets of his coat. Sobering somewhat, he walked on, picking up his pace.

The moon was long into its descent into dawn as Lewis's clipped footsteps echoed through the long, narrow space. The city's night scavengers trawled through the trash, hunting for any morsel to be snatched up. A cat screeched, fighting over a find with another. The garbage toppled over, tin and litter scattered across the stones. Head down, he turned to check behind him.

Two men in top hats and tails stood at the entrance between the two buildings, as if deciding whether to enter the putrid space. Lewis turned back, assessing the distance between himself and the far end. Just about halfway. Wrapping his coat around his body tighter, he walked faster.

A whisper and a chuckle right behind him shot shivers up his spine. He spun around.

Nothing.

He turned back, smacking into the chest of a man with a top hat and dark coat. The man's riding boots shined so well they managed to reflect the dim light the narrow street offered up. Immediately, Lewis stepped back, mumbling an apology. How had the man gotten there so fast?

Lewis nodded and moved to step around him. The man blocked his path, and his gut plummeted. *Should have gone the long way home.* Denver would never let him hear the end of it if he got robbed in the backstreet he'd been told to avoid on so many occasions.

"I don't have anything worth your while, mister. Let me pass," he said, meeting the man's darkened gaze.

"I'm not after your treasures, boy," the man drawled back, his accent strange, his movements almost imperceptible.

"Then what do you want?"

"Your soul is all, young'un," a voice whispered from behind.

Lewis flinched, spinning around. The man's face, fiercely pale, was a stark contrast to his eyes. Dark but lined with crimson. What on earth? An iron grip slid around his wrists, and he struggled against them, heart pounding. The man's eyes in front of him lit up, angling his head as he studied Lewis's face, his gaze traveling down his neck, where it stayed.

"Whatever you want, just tell me," Lewis choked out.

"I don't think we will. Will we, Thomas?"

"Doubt it, Edward. Not our style." A strange European accent rolled off his tongue.

Edward leaned in, smelling every inch of his neck. When he stood back up, his eyes were completely black, his mouth opened, canines stretched past his otherwise perfect teeth as he tilted his face to the moonlit sky. A raw growl left his throat.

Vampire.

Lewis stood frozen; every breath far too shallow to be of use. The vampire lowered his head and met his gaze. A savage smile ripped across his face as he lunged, sharp teeth sinking into Lewis's fleshy neck.

Lewis scrambled to stay on his feet, blinding pain surging through his body like fire.

Moments later, he lay on cold cobblestone, gasping for air, his entire body consumed by a raging current of agony and cinders. Motionless, he allowed his eyes to drift shut. *This is what dying feels like.*

At least he wouldn't have to put up with Denver's lecture about the consequences of back alleys one more time. The sky moved overhead, stars tracking across the slim space between the buildings, keeping their own time.

"You can't leave him here to die," Thomas uttered. "Sloppy gets us hunted down, like last time."

"Are you suggesting resurrecting this one, Tom?"

"At least there would be no evidence. The Council would use anything to take us out; we can't afford sloppy, and you know it."

"Fine. But next time, I say we toss them into the Thames."

"Excellent plan, man, now finish your work and let's head back before the good folk of London start to rise."

Edward knelt by Lewis, leaning over. With the flick of a small blade, he made a cut across his wrist, which he held over Lewis's face. Red pearls of blood bloomed at the site, falling one by one onto Lewis's mouth. Startled by the warm, wet drops, he jerked, mouth gaping. Drop after drop hit his tongue.

"There's a lad. That should fix you up."

"That's enough, Ed, let's get out of here."

Edward studied the vacant stare of the young man underneath him briefly before rising and following his comrade into the shadows. Satiated, they made a swift exit.

Motionless, Lewis lay on the cobblestone, stunned.

·))) · ● · (((·

S oftness touched Lewis's cheek. The golden haze behind his eyelids signaled dawn had stolen the night's darkness.

"He has been bitten," a warm voice said.

A woman.

"Let's help him inside." Another coaxed, older, rougher.

Lewis struggled to his feet, cracking his eyes open. A woman, around the same age as he, stood before him. Her long brown hair twisted to ringlets around her neck. Her face held a thin smile, her blue eyes burning into his. A hunched woman appeared at his side. Taking him by the arms, they led him to the end of the alley and into a door on the side of the building.

Barely able to stand, with fire coursing through his body still, Lewis let them lead him into their dim-lit home. The heavy door clunked shut behind him. The aroma of herbs crawled its way into the air. The front room was small, with coats lining the wall by the entrance. Through the closest open door was a kitchen. To the left, a hole in the floor that sunk into a winding, dark staircase.

"Better put him downstairs, my girl." The hunched woman nodded to the steep treads. The descent was precarious. With every limb still raging from the attack, Lewis, desperate to lie down, faltered. If he could only lie down. Once inside the dank little basement, the woman lowered him onto the floor. Hands white-knuckled around his arms, he rocked, trying to drown out the fire ravaging him with each breath.

﹥﹥﹥﹥·◐·﹤﹤﹤﹤

L ewis shifted on his seat, aching bones creaking in protest from hours of sitting on the frigid, hard floor. The cold air of the stone basement tangled around his shivering limbs. The clothes he wore from the night before were tattered and ripped, filth coating every inch, as if some unholy force had dragged him through the London sewers for miles.

He had no idea where his brother was. Knowing Denver, he was probably held up in some woman's parlor, enjoying himself. He laid his head back, wincing, as a thumping ache coursed through it, and met the slimy stone wall. God only knew what had been kept down here before him. If the rancid, stale air was any indication, death had followed the occupants of the small space and stayed.

Hours later, the women upstairs had not allowed him to leave the confines of the locked basement. The sounds of the city going about her business tumbled in from outside. His body jerked, changing. Splintering hellfire came and went, worse each time, as if rising to a pinnacle of some sort. Smoke from burning herbs drifted down through the gaps in the floor, twisting its way down the spiral stairs.

Hands trembling over the bite on his neck that throbbed constantly, he called out, voice raw from breathing through the bouts of pain, "Hello?"

Thudding footsteps overhead made their way down-stairs. The woman his age stopped on the last tread as she studied Lewis's condition. She held a small vial in one hand, amber liquid moving between its walls as she stepped off the staircase.

"I have a proposition for you, young man."

"What do you want? Since you are not willing to help me, let me go, so I may seek proper treatment."

"Ah, if only it was that simple."

"What are you talking about? I need a doctor, woman."

She took a long stride, stopping short of where Lewis sat twisted on the cold stone. "You are in no position to make demands. You either help me, or I let the poison in your blood take its full effect."

"What do you want?" Lewis ground out, annoyance long having taken hold of his manners.

"I require a certain person taken care of. I want him to cease to breathe. And I need you to do it for me." She held his gaze, her otherwise elegant face set in stone in anticipation.

"You want me to kill someone?"

A smirk spread across her face. "You catch on quick."

"No!"

"So be it. Enjoy the last of your human hours. I am sure the agony will be much more enjoyable than accepting my simple task."

She spun on her heel and swept up the stairs, skirts trailing the treads behind her.

"Wait!"

The woman paused, the liquid in the vial between her fingers sloshing. "Changed your mind?"

"What will happen to me? How can you cure me if it is poison those thugs have left me with?"

"The poison from the bite you received will change you irreparably. This vial contains the antidote. Do one simple task for me and you can have it. And if not? Let's just say you will have a long, long time to mull over your choice, centuries even."

"Nobody lives that long; you're making no sense."

"Do you accept my request or not?" she snapped, hand tightening to white around the small vial.

Lewis slumped against the wall. He could never bring

himself to kill. It wasn't a choice at all. He would die here in this grimy, cold cellar.

"No," he choked out. "My answer is no."

"Pity ... You are about to become very familiar with hell."

Lewis watched as her skirts ascended the spiral passage, each footfall softer than the last. The blood in his veins thundered through his ears, heat swallowing him whole. Helpless from the agony, he slid down the wall, head hitting the floor. Writhing, he screamed, waiting for his heart to stop and save him. A ringing inside his head deafened him. Every muscle in his body spasmed. Blood filled his mouth where his teeth grit down hard.

The breath in his lungs stalled.

Weak heartbeats slowed to a still.

The ringing faded and the room around him brightened.

Lewis staggered to his feet.

The scent of dried blood on his shirt flooded his senses and his throat caught fire so damning, he gasped for air. Wild with hunger, he lunged up the stairwell. Smashing a palm into the small wooden trapdoor, it flew from its hinges. The grey-haired woman stood startled. Grabbing up a bunch of herbs, she stepped backward. The pungent stench coiled up his stomach.

Witches.

What in the Lord's name? How did he know that? But the instinct awoke in his gut and told him to get far, far away.

The younger woman was nowhere to be seen.

Rushing the front door, Lewis fell into the alley. Loud, it was all too loud!

"Anjelica! He turned!" the hag called from behind him.

"He won't get far, mother; I have placed the curse of the moon over his soul. His days are predefined."

Lewis stumbled over his own feet, adjusting to a strength he had never possessed before. Seconds later, he stood by the Thames.

Surrounded by beating hearts.

A burning thirst in his throat.

CHAPTER 1

SAMMIE

CASTLETON, 2024

Flame licks my palms. No heat. The stench of smoldering hair and charred flesh coils my stomach. My little brother lies burned at my feet, moaning in agony. Quick breaths steal my clarity and blur my vision as my hands tremble. Fists balling, the fire snuffs out with a hiss. Smoke leaves my hands as I uncurl them. Leaving my unharmed, creamy flesh as it was moments before.

"No, Jackson!"

The ground by his side bites my knees as I sink.

His moaning stops.

I roll him over; his face is mangled by pain and fear. His terrified, widened blue eyes stare at me. Singed hair falls from his head, away from his arms like dust.

Ash.

What have I done?

His chest is almost still. Wrapping an arm around his small

shoulders, I sit him up, hoping he will wake up and this is another one of his little-brother pranks. His head lolls.

Screams rip from my throat.

"Momma, help!"

Jackson stirs and grabs my arms. His eyes close, and he goes limp, his head falling back.

No. Please no.

"Momma! Daddy!"

The back door to our old house flings open, slamming behind my parents. A second later, Mom drops to my side. Dad stands frozen, gaze drifting from me to Jackson.

"What happened, Sammie?" Mom utters, her hands wandering over Jackson before the healing light she carries glows from her palms.

"He wanted to practice with me. We—"

We were literally playing with fire. How can I tell her that?

"What, honey?" Dad says.

"Training my fire. He wanted to be a moving target. I never thought I would be able to get close, but he—"

He stopped, tripped. Too busy pulling inward with my eyes closed, when I opened them and shot the flame, I realized it was too late. He wasn't moving anymore. And I watched as the fireball I sent swallowed my sweet, always joking little brother.

Releasing my hold on him to Mom, I stand. Sobs spill from her in a torrent. Staggering a few steps away, I lose my stomach on the grass. Dad hovers.

Jackson's lips are grey; his chest is still. The light in his eyes dulled.

He's gone.

My body shakes violently, and bile rises again.

Dad homes in on me. "This is all your fault, Sammie. If you learned to control your power when we asked, this never would have happened!" He stalks toward me.

"I-I—" I stumble backward.

"He's dead! You murdered your own brother!"

A raw, agonizing scream pours from Momma as she slumps over my little brother's body.

*B*eep Beep Beep Beep Beep ...
Jerking from sleep, I slam a hand on to the alarm.

God, I hate that dream.

My phone pings.

> Hey sis, have an awesome first day of college! Wish I could be there too, the parentals are driving me nuts already. When are you coming home again?? Jackie.

Ping.

Mom.

> Enjoy your first day, sweetheart. We are both so proud and excited for you!

I throw the covers off and sit up, resting my feet on the polished wooden floor. The girl I share my room with is still asleep. Her side of the room looks like she dragged it kicking and screaming from Dracula's castle—it couldn't be drearier if she tried. No color. No personality. Only grey and shades of ombre black, everywhere. *Hello, Wednesday Addams.*

Moving to my dresser, I pick out something colorful, some underwear, my toiletry tote and towel, and wander to the door. Closing it gently behind me, I traipse toward the sound of running water, greeted by tendrils of hot steam as I round the hall and into the bathroom. Girls chatter over the dividers of their showers. I smile. I'm going to like this place.

Twenty minutes and one steaming-hot shower later, I am dressed and back in the room. I fiddle with my pendant necklace, taking in the first day of my new chapter. Excited would be an understatement. Wednesday is awake, donning her accessories for the day, which consist of a black watch, an evil-eye necklace, and a bone ruched into a thick bracelet. Gothic vibes, eat your heart out.

"Morning," I chirp in her direction.

"Hey." She glances up.

I wander over and offer her my hand. "Sammie. We didn't have a chance to meet before."

"Truly," she says.

"Yeah, I fell asleep. Wiped out from unpacking, you know," I offer.

She rolls her eyes at me. "My *name* is Truly."

"Oh! Sorry, I thought you didn't believe me. Wonderful to meet you, Truly."

"Yeah, well," she says, brushing past me.

She walks through the door without closing it. *Well, that went well. Ugh.* I groan and check my phone again. Nothing from Serena. That's not like her. We have been best friends since the age of thirteen. She gave me the necklace. She wears the matching one. I don't think either of us ever take it off. Like, ever.

A knock on the wall next to my open door startles me back to reality.

Standing with two brown bags and her megawatt smile, she wiggles the bags. "Morning! Hungry?"

Serena.

Instantly, my arms are around her shoulders.

"Air, girl," she chokes.

When I've had my hug, she plops the bags onto the floor.

"What are you doing here? I thought you'd be halfway around the globe by now in some tiny country with no real toilets or electricity?"

"Well, apparently, my mother developed second thoughts about that."

We walk to the bed, and she hands me a brown paper package as I sit. Sweet cinnamon pastries are nestled in the bottom, the scent wafting up turning my mouth to liquid.

"Oh, what are you going to do now?" I ask, biting into a cinnamon roll.

"She made me apply to, like, six colleges. She got it into her head that if employers find out you took a second gap year, you will forever be branded lazy or a hippie or something. I don't understand half the thoughts that woman comes out with. It's not like we just graduated. After working for my gap year, I was so looking forward to a whole twelve months of fun and freedom. But I don't want to go back to waiting tables and odd retail shifts, either."

"I don't know, I'm ready for this. Working and having money is good. But I want to learn and travel and explore the world, when I have a degree, preferably. What does your dad say?"

"No input, as usual. It doesn't feel weird to you, going to university late? We're almost twenty ..." she says, biting into her roll.

"Well, I have another month or so until then. But I think it's kind of the norm these days, and besides, we worked hard for this. What programs did you apply for?"

"S'pose I should check out the whole higher-learning thing, if it keeps Mom happy and off my back." She jumps from the bed and walks out the door. She bends over and pops back up, tray in hand.

"Coffee?"

"Absolutely!"

We walk arm in arm to my first class. Serena tells me she is going to check out enrollment here. I try, unsuccessfully, to contain my enthusiasm. The door to the lecture hall opens, and I file in with the crowd of excited first years. The room is huge. Seats tower upward, their burgundy fabric and folded-up bases making the entire place seem so sophisticated.

Suppressing a squeal, I ascend the carpeted stairs between the rows, sliding into a middle row before dropping into a seat and setting down my satchel full of notepads, pens, headphones, laptop, and three of each piece of writing equipment I could find in the store before fleeing my hometown of Burlington. Castleton is the only college close by that offers an archaeology program I liked. And to my complete excitement, they accepted me.

The hairs on the back of my neck prickle and rise. I still, fingers clasping the pen and highlighter I snatched from my satchel, raising my gaze from the stationery to the source of the feeling. Staring at me, stone-faced, mouth a thin line, is the professor.

He stands behind a long desk, hands gripping the edges, eyes burning into mine. Distain is etched over his face. His neat blond hair parts on the side, flopping over his face to one side, his dark brown eyes set in his square face, jaw tense. Goddess save me, he is smoking hot. *Sammie, no! Lecturer, he is your lecturer.*

Heat floods my cheeks.

My heart thunders as I hold his gaze.

"Right!" He claps, face turning from looking like he swallowed something vile to happiness in a split second. Did I see it change? Focused back on my notepad and pen, I shake my head, willing my stupid heart to slow down.

"My name is Dr. Lewis Sullivan. You can call me Lewis or Mr. Sullivan. We will be spending the next ten weeks together, so let's go over some house rules, as I know this is your *first* college class."

I look up a moment later, hoping to zone out on the slides as they scroll across the hall's enormous projection screen. The students around me absorb every word as he explains what Introduction to Cultural Anthropology entails. Excitement gathers after we are given the rundown of the subject and assessments for this unit.

My phone pings.

Shit!

It echoes through the huge open room. Fumbling in my things, I silence my phone and rest it on my lap. One new email. With a tap on the notification, the email pops up.

My stomach drops. My scholarship, that was approved before I enrolled, is suspended pending further documentation.

No, no, no. I can't lose this spot. And without the scholarship, I can't be here. I close my eyes and groan. The room falls silent.

"Is there something you wanted the rest of the room to know, Miss—?"

I snap my eyes open. He gestures for me to fill in the blank, his face back to stone. Swallowing, I glance around the room. Other students stare at me, scowling, as if I have robbed them of something precious by interrupting their first-ever lecture.

"Williams."

"Well, Miss Williams?" He keeps his face straight and runs a hand through that gorgeous hair of his.

"No, nothing to share."

"Very well; you don't mind if we return to the content, then?" he says, raising an eyebrow.

"Fine by me," I say, a little too chipper, and his eyebrow drops.

Magnificent. Now he hates me. How is he old enough to be a college professor, anyway? He's like, what? Twenty-five, maybe twenty-eight or something?

The lecture ends and Mr. Sullivan packs up and walks out like a man on a sinking ship bailing to the last life raft. Gathering my things, I shove them back into my satchel. I have to see the Chancellor and sort out my scholarship. Let's pray to the Goddess it's a hiccup and nothing huge.

Sunshine explodes all over my face as I straggle outside behind the rest of my cohort. I double-check the map of campus on my phone and head in the direction of the administration building. Past the front doors, the secretary greets me.

"I am here to see the Chancellor about my scholarship," I offer.

"Yes. Samantha Williams?"

"Yep."

"Through this door"—she points to her left—"down the corridor, last door on the right. He is in a meeting but will only be a few minutes if you want to wait outside."

The corridor is long, and every step I make echoes. The door to the Chancellor's office is cracked open. I lean against the wall and pull out my phone to check my messages. Nothing. Turning on the photo app, I glance over my appearance, brushing my curly blonde hair behind my ears. Face is fine, no leftover cinnamon roll. I shove it back into my bag.

"... to swap classes with Judith. The students in the group I have are more suited to her approach." The voice is familiar, so I peek between the door and frame.

Mr. Sullivan.

He wants to swap us out? Because of me?

"At this stage, that is not an option, Lewis."

"But the cohort is more suited to her, sir."

"The answer is no, Lewis. Whatever you think you have discovered, you will have to handle it as a professional. We all come across students that test our limits. This is no different."

He *is* talking about me.

Footsteps thunder toward the door. Do I flee now and come back later or stand my ground? Undecided, I hover, facing back down the hallway.

The door bursts open. I spin and slam into Mr. Sullivan's chest.

Shit.

My backpack slips from my shoulder and hits the ground, spilling the contents across the polished floor.

He hovers for a moment, taking me in. Rigid, he stares at me before stalking down the corridor. I gather my belongings and stand, brushing the non-existent dust from my knees.

"Arrogant ass," I mutter.

He stops dead.

How did he hear that?

His hands ball to fists, uncurling and slamming into his pockets. Breath firmly held, I can only hope he doesn't stalk back here and ream me out for disrespecting a faculty member.

He turns back, looking me over, then disappears through the door.

CHAPTER 2

LEWIS

After my last lecture for the day, I toss the laptop and notebook into my backpack as fast as I can without drawing attention for inhuman behavior. How could this happen? And with a witch, for heaven's sake. This tiny town always makes Denver and me feel so welcome, and I let my guard down.

For the first time in over fifty years. Last time Anjelica found us, it cost my brother his mate—and almost his life. Never will I permit that to happen again. Nothing is more important than staying out of her reach. Nothing.

Hitting the light switch off, I shove the door open and walk into the brisk Vermont fall outdoors. Gold and bronze leaves dance over the ground, partnered by the ever-cooling breeze from the north. The campus's large oaks scatter their leaves like glitter. The scent of the coming first snowfall laces the crisp air.

A minute later, I round the sciences building and into the parking lot. The 1968 black Mustang I bought the day it released sits waiting, hood up and chrome rims glinting in the fading rays of the afternoon sun. The only thing I love more than my brother is this car. Unlocking the driver's side door, I crack it open, throwing my backpack into the passenger's seat.

The comforting sound of the deep rumble of the engine drums out the noise in my head. Thoughts of being found and having to flee settle somewhat as I turn down University Drive. Turning the wheel, I wind through the houses and then down Main Street. People are walking, huddled in their coats and warm boots, anticipating the first fall of snow that I can smell days earlier than they can. It's coming, a few days away now.

I roll to a stop at the last set of traffic lights before Vermont Route and twist the knob on the radio, filling the car with static until I hit the right channel. Old jazz plays over the aged speakers, still sounding like it did the year I first listened to it. A small smile grows across my face.

We had been living on street food, as Denver, my older brother, called it. His name for the criminals the cops couldn't catch but we could. And way too much whiskey. A time when we felt like this life we lead could actually do some good. Until it ended all too soon. She found us again. So, we ran and hid, again.

The light turns green. As I sink my foot onto the accelerator, the car growls to life, lighting up the asphalt. It turns to a solid roar as the needle hits four thousand revolutions, bounces, and falls. I roll the window down and let the cold air tunnel into the car, tousling my hair.

With a tap on the breaks as my next turn comes up, I swing her around in a drift at seventy miles per hour onto Blackridge Road. The asphalt snakes through the forest, narrowing to one lane. Our road. Out of sight, out of the way.

Rolling to a stop before the garage, I see Den's pickup is already here. He must have gotten off work early. Did they run out of trees at the sawmill in the middle of the Vermont dense timber? The lumberjack life suits my big brother. He needs the physical work to level out his overthinking mind some days.

Grabbing my backpack and shutting the car door behind me, I jog up the steps to our oversized house. The Manor, we used to jokingly call it when we first moved in. It stuck. Pillars on either side of the stair treads are aged with wear that the previous owners couldn't afford to fix. Almost too rundown to be livable when we arrived, it gave Den something to occupy his mind after all he lost in New Orleans. His mate.

I still remember the expression on his face when their bond snapped into place. Shock mixed with annoyance, quickly swallowed by tenderness. She was younger than him. And human. He'd been standing inches from her, leaning from a ladder to change the blown kitchen light.

The overwhelming sensation almost knocked him off

the ladder. Den was a different man after that. Zahli consumed his thoughts. Keeping her safe and making her feel loved became his entire personality. She used to joke that his overprotectiveness would be the end of her.

In the end, after the moment he eased off after her begging for a little less overbearing and a little more trust, she died within days. She didn't know the lengths that our enemies would go to hurt us.

We lost her to Anjelica.

Never had I seen fear like I did in Zahli's eyes that night. The worst day of both our lives. We swore that would never happen again.

On the porch, his muddy boots lay scattered beside the front door. I turn the knob and push the door open.

"Den?" Hanging my pack and then coat on the hooks by the door, I unzip the bag, sliding the laptop out. The foyer is as grand as the porch and fully renovated inside. The old-world aesthetic Denver enjoys so much is like a warm hug coming home.

"Living room, brother."

Computer in one hand, I detour to the study, left of the foyer, to plug it in to charge. The green light on the side of the machine flashes and I leave it, walking to the living room. My big brother sits spread out on the lounge chair that appears small under his sprawling frame, whiskey glass in one hand, head resting on the back of the sofa, eyes closed.

"How's school?" he asks, eyes closed still. A soft smile spreads over his stubbled jaw.

He loves asking me that ever since I started back teaching literature, archaeology, or whatever positions in relic-type subjects I could find.

"Fine. A small incident with a student."

Den opens his eyes, and his mouth stretches to a grin.

"Not that kind of thing." I frown as I pluck a tumbler from the drinks caddy by the lounge. Glass chinks as I pry the crystal from the throat of the canister and pour an inch of the amber liquid into one for myself.

Denver sits forward, his brows imitating mine. "Well?"

"One of my new students is a witch."

"That's impossible; there are no practicing witches here. I checked, *thoroughly*, before we settled on this location, remember?"

"Yup." I swirl the contents, the amber liquid sloshing up the crystal wall. Anjelica's reach back then had been extensive. The smaller and more isolated the town, the better. The city is my preference, but when you are trying to outrun the devil herself, choice is not a luxury you have.

Denver meets my gaze. "So, change classes, and hope she doesn't realize what you are. Witches would love nothing more than to out us."

"Tried; the Chancellor won't budge."

"Fuck."

"Tell me about it." I slump into the armchair opposite my brother, studying the bottom of my glass. "You know what, I am tired of running. Let her find us. Three hundred -odd years is more than enough for any one soul to be dragged through hell."

"You don't mean that, Lew; we have come close in the past, we will figure this out."

"We are not moving again; she doesn't control us anymore. We're done."

"It's not that simple, Lewis." His voice is a raw growl. He's only trying to protect me, but I will not be the reason the only person I care about gets a shadow of a life.

He plonks his glass on the drinks trolley with a crack. "What if we stay put and she turns up on our doorstep? Your time would be up."

"Not necessarily. I still have a number of moon cycles to go."

"Have you found anything of breaking the curse yet?"

"Only that it requires an elemental witch. And what witch is going to go up against a coven leader who is centuries old and holds influence and connections almost everywhere?" I scrub my hands over my face.

The research I have been doing into breaking the curse Anjelica put on me the day I turned consumes my mind. Especially since my three hundred years ticked over. The moon cycles she wove into the spell are dwindling. We should have started hunting for a way to break it the day that bitch execrated me, decades ago. But staying alive seemed more urgent.

"So, pull out of teaching and let's go find someone willing to help," Denver says, standing.

"You think I haven't already scoured the country? I have!"

Denver's head tilts to the side and his mouth thins to an angry line. "You can't give up, Lewis."

"It's not about giving up. We have run out of time, and there is no one left who would be able to do what we need them to do. Anjelica made sure of that."

"Women and their grudges," he grunts.

"I need to feed." Making my way toward the foyer, I pluck a parka from the rack, not that we feel the cold. But if someone sees me out in the night forest without warm clothing, it only adds to the questions. The last thing we want is people taking notice.

"Wait, I'll go with you." Den appears by my side, throwing on a flannel jacket and a dark scarf. Always the lumberjack. We have become good at playing the part, after decades in various roles and lives.

We hike past the last of the homes toward the nature reserve closest to our home. The tall pines and thick undergrowth are home to much wildlife and the larger animals that we hunt on the regular. The bouquet of timber and damp earth calms my soul.

A heartbeat after we leave the highway, Denver picks up a trail and takes off, his movements faster than any human could focus on. I track in the opposite direction until I come to another trail, but this one isn't animal. I crouch, touching the ground indented with a boot print large enough for a man. That scent again.

So familiar.

Caution waxes through my core. A stick snaps deeper into the woods, the odor of deer reaching my position. The thundering in my veins turns my throat to fire. Without warning, I charge toward it. It can't outrun me, but I let it try, for a little while, to send its blood pumping. The flavor is always so much richer. I sprint past trees, faster and faster. Brush and bark are collateral damage as I close in on the fawn beast . . . can almost taste the warmth of it.

Three strides and I am around it. I plunge a fist into its still-moving chest and it buckles toward me, weight lifting off its back feet. I slide backward a little but hold my ground. A second later, I rip my hand from its trembling body. It crumples to the forest floor, its heart quivering in my hand. The fire in my throat flickers upward.

Holding the now-still heart above my face, I squeeze every last drop from the four chambers into my open mouth, tossing it to the ground. Stepping to the limp beast as the life dulls from its eyes, I sink my teeth into its soft neck. Copper warmth satiates the burning, easing it further until it subsides. Every last drop drains from the beast, and I won't need to hunt for another few weeks.

A twig snaps underfoot mere feet from where I kneel. That familiar and unwelcome scent finds me again. I rise and wipe my face clean with my sleeve. The heat in my vein's gone, my vision turns from reddened to crisp in seconds.

Snap.

Closer—the scout is closing in on me. There's more than one.

Dirt and debris fly from under my boots as I spin around, searching between the pine trunks. The shape of a man comes into focus around four hundred feet away. He is mostly hidden by a dark robe. Shadow scout.

Fuck.

If they are here, they must have followed us. But we have taken out their type before. I pretend to be unaware of their presence and turn back in the direction Denver went. Here's hoping they are only hunting me. Pulling my phone from my jeans pocket, I text Den, asking his location. He replies with a drop pin, deeper in. Heading off in that direction, I'm slower than normal, allowing the scouts to follow.

Moments later, I find my brother, kneeling satiated beside a mutilated bear. He turns when a stick snaps under my boot, and I raise an eyebrow.

"What? It put up a fight." The bloody grin on his face coaxes one from mine.

"Fun's over, brother; two scouts popped up on my six."

"In that case, let's have some fun." Denver stands and cleans his face and hands. He inhales, long and slow. I do the same. They are not far away. Denver shoots me a side glance before taking off toward them at speed. My vision struggles to keep up with his hulking frame and agility. First, we split up, as we always do. Next, we appear from either side.

Last, they die screaming.

Two fewer witches in the world.

CHAPTER 3

SAMMIE

L ate again . . .

Mr. Sullivan stands behind the lectern, hands white-knuckling the sides like a tornado is about to rip him from the ground. His gaze floats across the filled seats of the auditorium, returning to me every few seconds. If it wasn't for the scowl on his face, I would think he enjoyed staring at me.

Five minutes late—that's not *bad*! This place is huge; my last class was on the other side of the campus. I practically ran to make it here. It's literally five past noon.

My phone vibrates.

Serena.

> Girl, guess who got accepted to Castleton University?!

Goddess! Yes!

Sliding the phone onto my thigh, I tap out a reply.

> Yay!! This is going to be so much fun!
> Maybe your mom is right? ;)

Ugh, maybe. Gotta go and fill out some
more forms. Pick you up in 30.

> Okay.

The room goes quiet. With a movement that would bore glaciers, I shift my gaze up. Every set of eyes is homed in on me. Including Mr. Sullivan's.

Shit.

Sullivan's eyes, laced with annoyance, burn into mine, and I force a smile.

"Miss Williams?"

I wriggle on the seat. "What's the question?"

"Are you done?"

Knuckles white around my notebook, heat flushes my neck and face. "Ah, sorry, yep, all done."

Dropping my attention to my notes, I wait for the lecture to resume as normal. When nobody speaks, I raise my focus back up. His dark brown eyes bore straight through me, fire lacing his icy stare. My stomach flips as warmth pools in my belly. Seriously? Why can't I be attracted to the average guys, instead of a professor who loathes me? I clear my throat. "Is there something else?"

Chuckles spill from behind me. Mr. Sullivan holds our

connection for a moment longer before pulling his attention back to the slide show lit up behind him. That countenance is what people refer to as quiet rage. He sure does send those kinds of vibes my way.

Another long and painful twenty-seven minutes later, we are dismissed. Well, not all of us. Mr. Sullivan waves me down. Maybe I should apologize. I can talk my way onto his good side, right? Since I can't afford to fail any of my classes, having a professor who hates me isn't going to bode well.

I make my way down the soft steps and fall in beside the lectern, waiting for him to finish packing up his laptop and notes. His tousled blond hair falls over his forehead for a second, and he brushes it away. Swallowing, I try to squash the butterflies in my stomach that insist on taking flight. Hands around the strap of my satchel, I wait, rocking back and forth on my heels.

He finishes his packing and walks toward me. Hands in the pockets of his cargo pants, the polo shirt he wears is more casual than I have seen him in before. *Focus on his face, Sammie.* His mouth is a thin line over his square jaw, and his brown eyes all but drill me into the floor.

"Tardiness is unacceptable in my class, Miss Williams."

I step forward, taking a long breath.

His jaw clenches, and he all but flinches backward.

"Sorry. My class at eleven is on the other side of campus. I've tried to be here in time." A blush swallows my neck and face, and I pull my hair away from my skin, letting it fall over one shoulder.

He stills, nostrils flaring.

"Are you okay?"

He swallows and his chest heaves for a second, like someone punched him.

"Mr. Sullivan?"

I move toward him; his face twists in horror, like he's seen a ghost. Or something else really bad, because his face is torn by something like disgust and fear. He wavers on his feet.

Dropping my satchel to the floor, I hold out a hand. He staggers back a step, gripping the lectern.

"Do you want me to send for help?"

He shakes his head, his face too pale.

"No," he rasps.

"What is happening? Are you having some kind of episode?"

"No."

"Are you sure you don't want—"

"No, Miss Williams, please"—he raises his head—"just go."

"I can't leave you here like this; what if you're having a stroke or something?"

He shakes his head again.

With a sigh, I pick up my bag and move away from him. He pulls in a deep breath and releases the lectern. Making my way toward the door, I glance back at him. His disheveled hair, his lax stance, his arms hanging by his sides, his chest heaving, his eyes tracking my movement.

His face returns to a normal color by the time I reach the door. It opens, and Serena runs right into me. "Hey, you okay? You look flustered," she asks.

I turn back to check on Mr. Sullivan. He stiffens, eyes widening and settling on my best friend.

"Are you sure you're okay?" I ask him, brows lowering.

"I said get out," he snarls.

"Jesus! Cool your jets, man; we're leaving," Serena bites back, wrapping an arm around my shoulders and leading me through the doors into the sunshine.

I stare at the heavy door as it closes with a thud. What's up with him? I hope he will be okay. He isn't my favorite person in the whole world, but I wouldn't wish him ill. Not with a face like that. I suppress a groan at my overactive attraction to my professor and lean into my best friend. I so need lunch. Depleted blood sugar is messing with my sanity.

We settle in at a table at the campus cafeteria and Serena orders for both of us, chili fries and chicken wings with sodas. She plops back onto the seat opposite me and pulls out her phone.

"So, I have classes on every day except Fridays at this stage. When are yours?" she asks.

"Every day except Wednesdays."

She rolls her eyes. "Trust our days to not line up. Ugh. Also, you're moving in with me. That big old house of my grandma's is lonely, babes. And the commute from home is too far."

I laugh at her. "Ah, thank God, another night with Wednesday Addams and I am likely to set myself on fire."

She is always thinking of the fun things, never the serious things, like plans or goals. Her journal, the one she showed me in senior year, is full of doodles and daydreams. She's always drawing sketches of a guy dressed like Mr. Darcy, or some other regency type.

Mine, in true Sammie style, is set out in a logical layout of career waypoints and challenges I want to accomplish over the next ten years. Everything I want to do prior to thirty. Jackson calls it my dirty-thirty bucket list. Like he doesn't have his own catalog of things to do before he graduates, the dork.

To practice and regain the use of my magic is my number one non-academic project this year. But that is something I can never share with Serena. Apart from the basic Wiccan routines my parents have, she doesn't know about my magic, the power I inherited from my grandmother. The ability to bend and control the elements.

Grandma once told me that a *great* witch can not only control the elements, but they can command them to appear at will. I almost perfected that the day Jackson got hurt. Stopped trying after that. Just because you have the ability to do something, doesn't mean you should.

A girl around our age drops our order onto the table between us. Serena gives her a snarky smile. Stomach grumbling, I dig into the chili fries. The spice and salt make my mouth water, and I grab another handful, loading them onto a napkin in front of me. She gnaws away at a chicken wing, absent-mindedly scrolling away on her iPhone.

The hairs on my neck rise, and I look up from my food. Mr. Sullivan sits a few tables over, tapping on his phone, his jaw tensed, a hand shoved into his hair. I stare at him while I eat, one fry at a time. He obviously recovered from whatever that episode was that affected him before. His coffee cup sits by his laptop. He drops his cell onto the table and swipes up the cup, downing the contents.

Feeling silly for staring for so long, I return to the food. I guess he's embarrassed I saw what happened to him. But I should make sure he's okay. Despite the unwelcome reception from him almost every time we are in the same space, I still feel like I want to be around him. And with that slightly insane thought . . . "Hey, I'll be back in a sec, I need to ask Mr. Sullivan about our midterm."

Serena glances up from her iPhone and mumbles something. I doubt she heard me. Standing, I grab my stuff, wiping a hand over my mouth to make sure no chili fries are hanging from my face. Mr. Sullivan stares at his cell. But I can tell from here, he isn't really looking at what's on the screen.

When I make my way to his table and stop a foot from where he sits, he turns his head; his deep brown eyes find mine. The breath leaves my chest. I try to clear the stone lodged in my airway but fail.

"Samantha?"

Drawing in a ragged lungful of air, I huff a small laugh. It's the first time he's used my first name. His voice is raw with the word.

"Ah, I wanted to make sure you're okay? You looked pretty pale before."

He stands, moving into my space. "I'm fine. You shouldn't worry about me." His aftershave slams into my senses, his breath falling onto my face.

"Okay, I—"

"You what?" His head tilts to the side.

"I think we got off to a wonky start, and I wanted to apologize. To start over. Usually, I'm a devoted student. Guess there is a settling-in period or something."

He steps back to the table and gathers his things. "Or something. Don't be late again."

Ass.

Something like a smile peeks on one side of his face before it disappears, and he turns and heads for the parking lot. He strides toward a black vintage convertible Mustang. If my brother could see that, he would lose his mind. Jackson is obsessed with vintage muscle cars.

He unlocks the car, tosses his backpack over to the passenger seat, and slides into the driver's seat. A heartbeat later, the engine roars to life, and he backs out of the space. I track my gaze with the gleaming V8 as it rumbles to the university's exit. The rumble intensifies as it gains speed, disappearing down the winding road toward Main Street.

Serena comes to stand beside me. "Sweet ride."

"Yeah."

"Whose is it? And the real question—is he hot?" she jokes.

I turn and stare at her, unable to find the words to answer. Not sure which way to go with this.

"Can college professors be hot?" The words almost choke their way out and, for the umpteenth time today, crimson flies up my neck, filling my overheated face.

She winks at me and shakes her head. "Girl, professors are off-limits. For the love of all things holy."

As I groan into her shoulder, she chuckles at me. Every time one of us has a crush, we navigate it together. But this time, he is out-of-bounds. Off-limits. Not in my league. Forbidden. Both of us would lose our spots at the college.

A full-price program isn't something I can afford. Plus, Castleton is my first pick. Whatever this physical response to Sullivan is that has me riled up, it stops now. No more trying to make him like me. No more unnecessary interactions.

No more Little Miss Sunshine.

Just study.

I'm here for an archaeology degree.

Nothing more.

CHAPTER 4

LEWIS

I slam the car door and make my way through the small parking lot of the sawmill. The buzzing and constant whine of machines chewing their metal teeth through the woody flesh of the recently cut and dried lumber spills out. Do the trees of the reserve stand horrified in witness to their brethren being slaughtered, length after piney length?

Making my way around the back, I head to the cutting shed where Den makes the slabs that are used for more refined applications, like dining tables and sideboards for the cultured people of Vermont. Sawdust floats through the air, making its way from the machine to the outdoors in steady waves like rhythmic exhales.

"Den?!"

Despite his earplugs, he can hear me, unlike his human work buddies. He hits the round red stop button on the side of the long cutting machine, and it whines to an eerie halt. After letting the dust settle a little, he pushes his safety glasses into his hair, the dark blond hair coated with sawdust.

"Lewis, here to pick me up for our date tonight? You're a bit early, brother." His face lights up with a grin. Always the joker.

Lowering my brows, I step closer to the behemoth machine and run a hand over the tight grain of the freshly cut hardwood slab. I look back to Den, and his face falls. Swallowing, I turn to face him, leaning against the deck of the saw, arms tight over my chest.

"What? What happened?" Denver tilts his head, eyes narrowing.

"Something," I choke out, as if reliving the moments I stood in front of Samantha with that overwhelming feeling so deep it vibrated through the marrow in my bones. Like nothing I have ever felt before. The shock of it still renders me speechless.

He steps closer. "Lewis, are you alright? You look like you saw a ghost."

"I—"

"You what? Weren't you at school?"

I shake my head at the phrase he insists on using.

"You weren't at school?"

"No, I mean, yes, I was at work. Teaching. Then I asked one of the students to come see me after class. And she—"

"She what?" His eyes widen.

I track my gaze past his shoulder to the forest teaming

with tiny, harried heartbeats and aging wood. "My—It snapped," I breathe. He looks confused, but as my focus stays on his, confusion melts to understanding and his mouth gapes.

"With a student? Hang on . . . not that witch?"

I nod.

"No," he mutters, shaking his head. He turns around, running his hands through his hair. If my body wasn't numb from everything that happened, I would be doing the same. Instead, I stand rooted to the spot as my brother runs every likely scenario through his head.

The fact that interspecies mating is almost impossible, and absolutely forbidden.

That witches have been the sworn enemy of vampires for the last four hundred years.

Samantha is my student.

That despite our species being enemies, physically, I will start to yield to her.

Lastly, the fact that I have no fucking choice whatsoever.

"We can move on, again. Distance will make it easier for you to ignore the bond," he says without turning around.

Do I want to ignore it? I definitely don't want to move again. First, it was Anjelica constantly chasing us, now this, an unwanted, forbidden mating bond that would only see both her and me in deep trouble with the Council if we act on it. I know practically nothing about her. I pull my arms away from my chest and let them hang by my sides. "No."

Denver turns and studies my face. "Why?"

"I don't want to make a decision too soon. We worked so hard to get to this point, where we are finally not running. I am not going to give that up so easily. And nor are you."

"You don't understand, Lew, you can't stop a mating bond. It has a life of its own. You will be fighting it constantly. It will dictate your *entire* life."

"I won't let that happen." Schooling my face like I have more experience than the man who went through it, I clench my teeth.

He shakes his head again, scanning the shed as if what he needs to say is tucked away between the piles of timber and web-covered rafters. "Fine, but if you start acting on the bond, we reassess everything. I will not let what happened to me in New Orleans happen to you and this Sarah girl."

"Samantha. Her name is Samantha."

"Brother, let's call her Sarah for now." He grins and slaps me on the back. He doesn't want me to start getting attached. Like that's going to happen. The last thing I want to attach to is a goddamned witch.

I huff out a laugh, and we walk to the parking lot. His pickup is parked a few cars down from mine.

"There's a game on tonight; let's go and forget this little hiccup for a while, hey?" he says.

"Catch you at home," I say, sliding into the driver's seat of the Mustang. Hands gripping the wheel, I stare at the old shed that my brother calls home for ten hours a day and wonder how on earth we are going to get out of this one.

Of all the things to threaten our peaceful existence that we fought so hard to have, it's a girl. A curly blonde, brighter-than-sunshine, twenty-year-old girl, with blue eyes that could drown the ocean. I groan and let my forehead hit the wheel between my hands.

This is going to be harder than I thought.

·)))·◉·(((·

The halftime whistle blows and the crowd shuffles around, half heading for concessions, half for the restrooms. Den and I sit in our seats, three rows behind Samantha and her friend who appeared in my doorway yesterday, the one with the familiar scent I couldn't place. They sit, laughing and chatting, watching the players as they take a break, hydrating themselves even in the crisp, cool air that the night dragged in.

Moments later, the crowd files back in, fresh snacks in hand, bladders drained and anticipation high for the Spartans to take this home game to the win. They have been on a great streak, finishing out last year with a hefty score gap. They had won three-quarters of their games, both home and away. The green Spartan mascot is painted across the center of the football field. Green-and-white oversized foam fingers wave around.

The crowd roars as the players run back onto the field in

a long line. The whistle blows and the roar ebbs to a cheer. I home in on the two girls three rows ahead of me. Samantha is leaning into her friend, saying something louder than one normally would. She points to one of the players, and her friend's face splits with a grin.

"—he is a freshman, god above he is *hot*." Samantha fans her face, like she is some southern belle needing vapors after the sight of a man. My body tenses at the sight of her looking at the muscle-bound jocks on the field below the grandstands.

"A much better choice than that moody professor of yours, Sammie." Her friend laughs.

What the . . .

Samantha shifts in her seat and pulls her gaze from her friend. Her heartbeat turns rapid. What the hell was that?

Apparently, I am not the only one affected by this bond. She didn't seem affected back in the lecture hall. Denver's hand slaps my shoulder. I turn to face him, now acutely aware I've been staring.

"Lewis." His face is screwed up with concern.

"You catch that?"

"Yup." He glances between Samantha and me, his mouth pulling into a thin line. "This is going to be harder than we thought. You want to go home?"

"No, we should stay for the rest of the game."

He grunts but turns his attention back to the players, and we follow along as the Spartans close in on another touchdown.

After the final whistle blows, we make our way to the parking lot. I try to avoid any of my students. Denver's cell rings and he picks up. After a few short words, he taps the screen and shoves the phone into his jeans. "Mike. A small fire at the mill, I gotta go. I'll see you at home."

He takes off at a jog down the street in the direction of the mill. I know he'll run as soon as he is out of sight. It will only take him a matter of minutes to get there. The crowd filters out, cars pulling out full of players and families riding the high of the latest win.

I open the car door and slide into the seat, sinking the keys into the ignition before turning over the engine. I let her rumble at an idle while I search the radio for something halfway decent. After finding something more contemporary than my usual jazz or old-style rock, I shift the stick into gear and roll past the stadium gates.

Bouncing blonde curls walking along the sidewalk alone into the darkness catch my attention. Tensing against my will, I pull over and wait, hoping for the feeling to pass. The further she walks away from me, the harder the feeling burns.

Ignoring the sensation, I shove the car into gear and drive down the street. She shrinks in the rearview mirror. What kind of friend lets her walk home alone in the dark? Three guys leave the stadium gates, turning in her direction on the footpath. One wolf whistles. I slow the car to a crawl, and she ducks her head and quickens her pace.

None of my business.

I train my eyes on the road in front of me.

"Look at that ass," one scoffs.

"I'm more interested in the front," another growls.

I check the rearview mirror.

"Quiet, you idiots, before someone hears. Then we all miss out." The third smacks the guy beside him up the back of the head. They pick up the pace, like lions stalking prey.

None of my business.

My insides twist with rage and blood thunders through my veins. I push the car faster, the distance between me and her growing. The twisting intensifies, and I slam a hand on the wheel. "Sweet Jesus of all saints."

I slam on the brakes and fling the wheel around. The low rumble of the Mustang turns to a roar. The three guys stop, standing in awe of the car. I fly past them, catching up to Samantha. Planting my foot on the brake, I bring the car to a screeching halt alongside the sidewalk. Startling, she stops and turns to face the noise beside her. Her bag bumps at her side, her hoodie dropped over her arms in front of her.

I roll the window down. "Get in."

My voice is harsher than I intend, and she looks around as if searching for another option before landing on the three guys behind her. Her face scrunches, and she chews on her lip.

I tighten my grip on the steering wheel.

"I don't bite," I growl, nodding my head toward the guys. "But those three do." I make a mental note to sort them out later. Besides, there is no way I am letting her walk home in the dark with Anjelica's scouts hanging around like unwelcome vermin.

She hovers, shifting from foot to foot for a moment. "Fine," she says, walking to the passenger side. I lean over and open the door for her. She grabs the top of the door and opens it, sliding onto the seat. Her scent hits me instantly.

I use every muscle in my body to temper my instinctual reaction to her. The fire that uncoils in my core sends heat through my veins. Close proximity to her after the snap of the bond is like a special kind of torture, knowing I can't act on it.

I can't touch her.

I can't complete the bond.

Her heart rate is too fast. Its thumping right beside me sends a need so visceral through my body that, if I didn't know better, I'd think it could literally kill a man.

Samantha stares out the window.

"Where do you want to be dropped off?" I manage to rasp.

She glances at me, heat flushing her neck and face, before staring at her hands. "16 Willow-Lane Avenue. Three blocks from here, north of Main Street."

"Right."

I shift the stick into drive and let the car float down the street at a steady pace. Samantha keeps her focus outside the car. We make a right onto University Drive, and I turn the music up a little. The corner of her mouth peaks.

She glances at the dash, not me, and clears her throat. The action tenses the muscles in her neck. The creamy flesh moving over her thundering veins sends the blood from my head to my core.

Not one for small talk, then. At least not since our last encounter. I decide silence is a better option and head right onto Main Street. We pass the pizza joint, and she looks into the establishment, as if trying to see who is inside. I take the next left, the only street north of Main Street, and back off the gas. The rumble slows a few miles per hour, and I search the curb for the sign for her Willow-Lane Avenue.

"Next right," she says.

I spin the wheel, and we roll into a cul-de-sac with six houses. Sixteen is the last on the left, and I pull over and shift the stick, letting her idle. We sit in silence for a moment. Samantha opens the car door. The breeze tosses her scent at me again, and I grip the wheel harder.

Samantha steps out of the car and grabs her things. Hovering for a moment, she shoves her backpack over one shoulder and holds the hoodie in one hand. I keep my eyes straight ahead, not trusting this stupid bond not to rouse more unwanted instinct.

She leans down, her curls falling over her shoulders and framing her face. Those ocean-blue eyes meet mine. Her thundering heart sets my veins alight. It's nothing like my normal thirst; this need is something deeper, more colossal. Entirely too devastating, should I act on it.

"Thanks for the lift, Mr. Sullivan." A smile tugs up on her lips, and something flashes through her eyes.

The breath in my lungs disappears. I stare past the windscreen at nothing, and she shuts the door. Pulling away from the curb, I turn the wheel sharply, sending the Mustang around the cul-de-sac. I keep my attention on Samantha, rolling past as she walks toward her front door.

I roll down my window. Another scent so wrong, so familiar, finds me in a heartbeat, and I hit the brakes. Samantha looks back at me, her face tight.

Three hooded figures step out of the shadows from behind the trees by her house. Her face slackens. Her heart thunders at a rapid pace. Standing frozen, she lets her hoodie fall to the ground, palms open by her sides.

Shit.

This girl is a goddamn trouble magnet. I push the door open and appear at her side in the space of one heartbeat. Her eyes wide, she stares as if gauging the distance from where we stand to my car on the other side of her street.

The three hooded figures hesitate before closing in on us both. Samantha turns her head, shock etched over her face. I keep my focus on the three men in robes. The same uniform as the last two Denver and I encountered. Shadow scouts. Low-level witches doing someone's bidding.

"Stay out of this, Lewis," one of the scouts growls.

He knows who I am.

That is not good.

They stop short of where we stand, two of them moving to flank us.

"I will do no such thing." I stand rigid, waiting for one of them to make their last move.

Samantha's head swivels on her shoulders. Looking from the three scouts to me and back around again, confusion etched in every feature.

Every muscle in my body tenses, ready for what comes next. They make a move for her, they're dead. They won't even have time to realize their hearts have been ripped from their chests on the way to face-planting into the grass.

A cackle spills from the shadows as another hooded figure steps into the dimness of the waning moon's light.

This robe is red.

Fuck.

Holy Christ.

"How entertaining. Lewis and his latest prey." Her words are like snakes up my spine.

Hands curling to fists, I move closer to Samantha. Behind one of the old oaks, another figure stands, also hooded, female. It's as if she is simply observing . . .

Snapping my gaze back to the red robe closing in, I push Samantha behind me.

"Hello, Anjelica."

CHAPTER 5

SAMMIE

M r. Sullivan is completely still at my side, hands balled into fists. I'm not sure he is even breathing. The woman stares him down. They obviously know each other, and not in a good way.

"Step aside, Lewis. This is none of your concern. Coven business." Her focus leaves his stony glare, meeting mine. What coven business? Our family hasn't been part of a coven for generations. Not after they started warring with each other over territorial power.

I step forward. "I'm not part of any coven. I have no idea what you are talking about."

Mr. Sullivan grabs my hand, stopping me from moving any further. I glance back at him, then to where our hands are joined. His jaw grinds, his grip on my hand tightening.

"Leave her be, Anjelica," he snarls.

Why is he protecting me? I don't want his protection.

Or his hand on mine, for that matter. I rip away from his hold and fold my arms across my chest.

"Whatever it is you think I've done, I assure you, I haven't." I hesitate, not wanting to say too much in front of my professor. "I haven't practiced *anything* in years. It barely exists anymore."

I tilt my chin in defiance as she studies me closer before huffing out an indignant laugh. And I sincerely hope she understands I am talking about my magic, the non-existent magic.

"Regardless, I will be keeping an eye on you, girl." Her minions close in.

Lewis—Mr. Sullivan—steps in front of me. My focus glazes over, burning into the back of his head. For a split second, I wonder what it would be like to run my hands through his gorgeous hair.

Oh my Goddess, Sammie.

"I have no idea why you are getting protective over this one, Lewis, but remember your expiry date," Anjelica coos.

"She is a friend. Leave her out of your sick games, witch."

Oh.

Another witch. And Mr. Sullivan and I are so not friends. He tolerates me, and I him. His time is almost up? What's that supposed to mean?

"Three moons left, Lewis. I'm sure you remember the price you paid for betraying me."

"It's not like you gave me a choice. And I don't need a reminder."

I turn over in my mind what could have possibly happened between them. Anjelica looks almost a decade older than Lewis—Mr. Sullivan. Maybe some college thing? Did something happen at work? Who holds on to vendettas these days, anyway?

"Stay out of my way, boy, or I will shorten what little time you have left." She scowls at him before turning, flinging her robe around with her. Ten out of ten for dramatic flair. But who wears robes anymore? The three minions traipse after her, casually glancing back, as if to warn us that we have triggered some deadly game. The eager maleficence on their faces makes my skin crawl, sending goosebumps awash.

Mr. Sullivan steps away, turning to face me. "Are you okay?"

"I'm fine."

"You should go inside."

"Yep." Spinning on my heel, I walk to the front door. Fumbling with my bag, I find the keys and slip one into the lock, twisting it. Shoving the door open and stepping inside, I look back. He stands, watching me. A heartbeat later, he is in my space, on the threshold of my house, as if he can't come any further.

His jaw works like he is trying to find words to say something. I hold his gaze for a moment before slamming the door. An actual second later, his car roars down the street. I push the curtain back on the window by the door. How? I didn't even hear him walk across the street.

The curtain falls as I release it and lean against the window, closing my eyes. Now coven witches are coming after me, accusing me of using my magic. I haven't tried seriously since the incident with Jackson. And it's mine to use, my power to hone, however I see fit. I remember Grandma telling me those exact words at the age of seven. She had been so excited when she found out I had inherited her powers. Her type of magic. Elemental.

After the incident, my parents stopped encouraging my magic, despite my grandmother's pleas. Not long after my tenth birthday, she died. Mom blamed her magic for her death. Said it had gotten out of control and consumed her and tore her apart. She had tried to harness all four elements in one spell. To do that and survive is rare; at least, that's what Dad said after the funeral.

My thoughts wander back to Mr. Sullivan. The way he felt the need to protect me. Embarrassment coils in my gut, and I groan. If witches are going to turn up confronting me, I need to be able to protect myself. Tomorrow, I will try again and make a plan to coax back my powers and learn to control them. Grandma's grimoire contains all the spells from her lifetime. I need that book. And I know just where to find it.

It's the strangest feeling, sneaking into your own home. The basement window of our stone plantation home on Whately Road in South Burlington gives way easily, and I lower myself through the small space, feet landing on the cool stone floor.

Dankness and dim light fill the small storage space my parents hardly ever visit. Boxes of my grandma's things line one wall. I pluck the flashlight from my back pocket and click the button. The spear of light reaches the boxes, and I run it over each label. China and utensils. Clothes. Miscellaneous. Books.

Bingo.

I place the small light between my teeth and tug at the packing tape on the side of the box. After a few attempts, it curls under my fingers. I rip it up slowly to reduce the tearing plastic noise. Flinging it to the ground, I open the lid. All of Grandma's books, from her cookbooks to her journals, are stacked neatly inside the box.

I pull the top books from the stack and run a hand over the well-used, well-loved books she worked with every day. Breath catches in my throat, an ache growing in my chest. I miss her. Her love, her hugs, her food. Her laughter. The way her and Mom would work through problems together. No problem existed that those two couldn't handle.

"Hey Grandma," I whisper to the dust-covered possessions, so carefully boxed and stored. I pull more books out, searching for the brown leather tome she completed over her lifetime of witchcraft. With only three books left, I toss aside the smaller books, revealing the large brown book I have known my entire life.

Her grimoire.

I pluck it up, blowing the dust from the soft, worn cover. The gold-embossed symbol, the **pentacle** glitters even in the dim light. Resting my forehead on top of it, I breathe through a wobbly smile. It still smells like her.

After a handful of long moments, I pack away the books I pulled out and set the tape over the lid the best I can. I turn off the light and climb back through the window before tiptoeing my way across our front lawn.

"I've been wondering when you would come home for that," a soft voice says.

Breath caught, heart racing, I turn back.

Mom sits on the front step, dressing gown wrapped around her body tight.

"Momma, you scared me."

"Your dad would not approve, Sammie."

"I know. But it is part of me. Of who I am."

She smiles and stands. I walk to the steps, ascending the treads until I am one below her on the five. Her face is soft but pained. No doubt she is thinking about her mother.

"I will be careful, Momma," I whisper into her chest. She kisses the top of my head, arms wrapped around my shoulders.

"I know you will." She releases me, and I walk down the steps. "Sammie?"

I turn back. "Yeah, Momma?"

"Next time, use the front door. You scared the living daylights out of me, girl."

I smile at her. She shakes her head and walks back inside, clicking the front door shut behind her. I drop into the driver's seat of my car after tracking back to the block where I left it, feeling a little silly for thinking I had to break into my own house to get the book. But if Dad had found me, I never would have left with it. I hope Mom doesn't feel like she betrayed him by letting me take it.

Eager to try something small and dig into the dormant magic I haven't touched for years, I pull over. Rolling behind the nearest gas station, I make sure to park in the shadows. With the engine still running, I open the book. The front pages are covered with names. Our family tree. The next is adorned with the Wiccan Rede, the last line as familiar as my own hands.

If it harms none, mote it be.

I turn the page; it creaks with the movement. The first and easiest spell. I read over the phrases I haven't seen for more than a decade.

Spirit of air and wind,
May you feel my light.
Come to my mind,
Bend to me with all your might.

I hold out my palm and chant the passage over and over, watching the space above my palm intently. Wisps of air brush against my upturned palm. I repeat the phrase, pulling from my core, energy, and light. A small spiral of air twists above my skin, and I gasp. It shatters and disappears like fog dissipating under the heat of the morning sun in fast forward.

I huff a small laugh and close my hands around nothing. Closing the book, I place it on the passenger's seat. Hours later, I pull into the garage of the small blue home Serena and I live in. The house her mother owns, that we get to stay in for the entirety of our college careers. I turn off the engine and walk inside.

The sun is coming up behind me—my first all-nighter. And it had nothing to do with college study. I pad through the foyer and up the stairs to the right, rounding the banister to the first door on the right. Without bothering to change, I collapse into my bed, hand still gripping the grimoire.

Shadows close in around me. Mr. Sullivan stands on the edge of a cliff, shrouded in mist. The woman from last night stands at his back, a dagger piercing between his shoulder blades. He stands at the very edge, the wind tossing his hair about. He is wearing a blue sweater, dark jeans, black boots, and his usual black leather banded analog watch. He is looking back, his brown eyes burning into mine.

I can't breathe.

I feel tethered to him.

As if, if he falls, so will I.

Anjelica raises a hand, and he drops to his knees.

He closes his eyes.

She glances at me, and a smirk splits her face.

She removes the dagger from his back and presses it against his throat.

Bile claws its way up my own.

No.

Lewis opens his eyes and finds my gaze.

I drop to my knees.

She is going to kill him.

The haze around us shifts with the breeze, and the moon's full light illuminates the rocky ground.

"Your last moon, Lewis. Anything you would like to offer up?" she hisses.

"Go to hell, Anjelica."

"Very well."

The blade slashes its way across his Adam's apple, and blood spills down his neck, the muscles working as his breathing turns shallow.

The scream that flies from my mouth splits the air, rattling through my skull.

My vision narrows.

My palms burn.

The tether between us tugs hard. Pain swallows me whole and I collapse to the ground.

A second later, Lewis hits the ground, face-first.

My heart stops. Chest on fire.

I bolt up in bed, rapid shallow breaths burning their way from my chest. I press a hand over my mouth to strangle a cry.

Lewis was bonded with me. Like the stories my grandma used to read me about witches she had known long ago. Bonds between two witches.

Lewis is not a witch; I would have felt it.

But in the dream, we were bonded. I shove the blanket off, too hot from the sun pouring in from high up the window. Hard velvet touches my hand.

The grimoire.

Lewis's face floods my mind. What is he?

Mr. Sullivan?

Lewis.

The tug from my dream is still there but faint. Hours after I used my magic purposely.

As if every part of me is waking up.

Holy shit.

CHAPTER 6

LEWIS

Wednesday. Samantha's day off. So why is she here in the campus library? The last few days have been torture, my every thought consumed by her, Anjelica, and the threat that is so raw that it makes my head spin. Watching her in class is like staring into the sun. Staying away has been like an endless night.

My phone pings. Den.

> You know you're a stalker, right, brother?

> Shut up.

I tap the reply button.

Pressing the lock button, I shove the phone into my back pocket and lean back on the shelving in the modern history section that conceals my position two rows down from where Samantha sits on her laptop at a study table.

For the first time in decades, I have missed a lecture. This bond is driving me crazy.

Every time I had a go at Denver when his bond snapped comes flooding back to me. Now I feel like an idiot. I have minimum control over myself; every decision is murky. Nothing is clear unless she is in my sight. This got intense, fast.

I close my eyes, and her blonde hair and sweet face disappear from view. My gut flips. I open them as she leans into the screen in front of her. How is first-year content that interesting? I need to get closer. I slip from behind the shelving and move to the aisle behind her. If I could be sitting next to her, I would be.

What the hell?

I lean into the musty stacks and pretend to read a text on ancient languages, the book mostly concealing my face. From over her shoulder, I read the text on the website filling her screen. Mythological creatures of recent times. It's alphabetical. She is scrolling past the Ms.

A large brown leather book sits to her right. If I am right, it is a tome or grimoire of some sort. How did she find *that* in the library? I haven't seen one of those for around fifteen years. Her fingers brush over the trackpad of her laptop and hover as she reaches the Vs.

What is she looking for?

She's a smart girl. And if she's looking for something about me, she is about to find it. Running a finger downward, a quarter inch shy of the screen, she traces the list of traits for the vampire. Her breath stops as she leans back from the screen and sits frozen in the chair. I wish I could see her face. I mean, I could walk over and pretend to have bumped into her at the library. I do work here.

I replace the book on its shelf and adjust my backpack over one shoulder before running a hand through my hair. I step out of the stacks to where she sits. "Find anything interesting?"

Samantha jumps and turns in her seat, one hand grasping her necklace, the other falling onto the brown book beside her. I glance at it. A grimoire. I meet her wide-eyed stare as her volumes of curls bounce and settle over her shoulders. Her scent hits me. The tug in my core turns to a low heat.

"Mr. Sullivan. Ah, didn't see you there. Sorry, you—" She runs a gaze over my face, pausing on my mouth. Is she actually looking for fangs? "You scared me."

"Sorry, Miss Williams, that wasn't my intention."

She swallows, eyes traveling across my body. I track mine to her screen.

"So? Research for another class?"

Huffing a shy laugh, she slams the laptop shut.

When I raise an eyebrow, she blushes. "Not class, then?"

"Well, kind of. I'm examining traits of some mythological creatures. Sort of a side project of mine."

I pull out the seat beside her and dump my bag on the table. "I can help. I have a fair bit of knowledge in that area."

Samantha stares at me; the dark irises of her pupils dilate as her heart rate speeds up. The tug and fire in my core intensify, and I lean away a little, hoping to drown it out.

Sheepishly, she turns back to her laptop and opens it. I lean over toward the screen, and she picks up the brown book and shoves it back into her bag before looking back at me. "You don't have to help me. I haven't been all that receptive of your help."

I suppress my response and focus on her screen. "What have you found so far?"

"A bunch of information on vampires," she says, her eyes drifting from the screen to meet mine, "and most of the sources agree on the major details, such as lifespan, abilities, and sources of food."

"Uh-huh, and what details didn't line up for you?"

"Well, there is a note about how they mate, for life. One source says this is solid fact, the other . . . a little more vague."

"From all the information I have come across, they do in fact mate only once, and it's for life."

She turns to face me. "Where did you find that?"

"An older source than this. It isn't in public circulation."

"Oh," she utters, bringing her silver necklace to her mouth and pressing it between her lips.

My hands tighten around the back of the chair and the edge of the table.

I count her breaths, forcing my own.

"I guess it's all speculation, since they don't exist," she says, dropping the necklace and turning to face me.

"I guess—" I utter, watching her lips part, her chest rise and fall. Her pupils dilate further, and she swallows. My heart thunders in my skull, and I inhale her again. Fire explodes in my veins, a slight burning at the back of my throat. Shaking my head, I clear my throat. "What about witches?"

She stills.

"What about them?" Her arms fold over her stomach.

"What traits did you find on that species?"

Her gaze drags back to the screen and her hand trembles as she scrolls down a little further to W.

"Do they mate with *only* their own kind?" I ask.

Her breath stops and she doesn't answer.

"Samantha? Do they?"

"It is rare for them to mate with other species," she mutters.

"That's what I thought. Is there anything else you need help finding?"

She shakes her head. I force a smile and stand, picking up my backpack, shouldering it quickly. "See you in class, Miss Williams."

She nods, still staring at her screen. Her heart is racing so fast, it is the only sound that registers until I clear the heavy, wooden library doors.

Too close, Lewis.

Far too close.

)))·◖●◗·(((

I bite into the soft roll of my venison-and-salad lunch and try to savor the flavors despite the blandness coating my mouth. Samantha and her friend sit a few tables down, eating and chatting. She hasn't noticed my presence yet. She plucks the necklace from her chest, like she did in the library earlier today.

This time, it is surrounded by a soft glow. As is her friend's. The necklaces are identical in every way. She leans into her friend as they talk quieter, the pendant brightening on the chain. The light it gives off is so minimal it would be imperceptible to the human eye.

"He just appeared. Then he had the answer I had been looking for, about the species mating. It's only hearsay, since it's all myth, but it's freakily accurate, right?"

Her friend's brows draw down and she shakes her head. "There is no such thing, babe. Maybe you should concentrate on your actual subject content. You need to keep that scholarship, remember. As for the professor, girl, he is way, *way* out-of-bounds, and if you ask me, a little creepy. Besides, if they catch you two, you get kicked out and he gets fired. Please tell me you're not thinking about him?"

She leans away from Samantha and the pendants dull. Odd.

Her face reddens slightly, but I doubt her friend even notices. "No, of course not."

I train the growing smile from my face, flattening my

mouth back to a thin line. Samantha's gaze drops to the table, and she shrugs, as if not wanting to commit to the statement either way.

"So, are you coming to the frat party this Friday? Jonas invited me, plus anyone I wanted to bring. You in?" her friend asks.

"Yeah, sure," she mutters, fixing her focus to her lunch but playing with it mindlessly.

Over my dead body is she going.

Sweaty, horny, barely adult males, all looking to sew whatever it is they are apparently allowed to sew. Oats. There will be no fucking oats anywhere near Samantha.

"Well, I have class. See you at home, babe." Her friend stands and walks away without looking back. Samantha sits, stirring the contents of her paper cup with a wooden spoon. Her heartbeat fills my ears again. This time steady and strong.

The pendant dulls to the silver it faded to in the library. Samantha pulls the brown leather tome from her bag, flipping past the center and stopping at a page toward the back. She leans over the book on the table, her hair falling around her face.

Ping.

I pull my cell from my pocket.

Den.

We have a problem, brother.

What's up?

Anjelica hasn't moved on. I think she is still tracking your little blondie.

Her name is Samantha, Denver.

Okay, she is still keeping tabs on SAMANTHA.

How do you know?

I tracked another of her scouts down this morning after you left. His scent had lingered at her house. By the time I caught up with him he was back in the forest. He wasn't very talkative and now he's mute. Silent as the grave 🔪

What would she be tracking Samantha for?

Lew . . . maybe she is more than just a green witch???

What are you talking about?

I traced her family tree a little closer, her grandmother was a higher-level witch. Not sure what type. The details were pretty vague. No photos either. Might be worth having the conversation with her about it?

No way, leave her out of this.

Brother . . .

No, Den. Not happening!

I am aware being bonded to a low-level witch is worse than a slow death but at least ask. Maybe there is a reason your bond snapped with her? Maybe there is more to Little Miss Sunshine than meets the eye?

She is absolutely like watching sunshine. Like the dappled kind that filters through the sheer white curtains on a warm day when she is quiet. Like the blazing burst of dawn's light when she smiles.

The light to my darkness. Urgh . . .

Lewis? Where did you go?

What, Den?

Stop thinking about sunshine. 😏

I may hate witches, but this is different. She's a student. And, from what I can tell, a non-practicing Wiccan. She's basically human. Does she even realize what she is? She certainly doesn't act like any witch I have ever met.

Shut up, brother. And the answer is still no. I am not dragging her into this.

She's just a witch, Lewis. What does it matter if you lose the bond to her anyway?

What is that supposed to mean?

The Council would never allow it. You know this. Use her for her magic and move on.

God, you are an absolute ass sometimes, Denver. She is not something you can use and throw away when you're done!

Not even if it breaks your curse? Think about it, Lewis.

I tap the lock button and throw my cell back into my backpack. If Anjelica is keeping tabs on Samantha, I am not letting her out of my sight. I don't care what type of witch she is. And hell will freeze over before I let my brother or anyone else use her up and toss her away.

Denver is trying to stay practical and uninvolved, but I draw the line at stabbing my mate in the back like she is worth nothing. No matter what it may cost me later down the line. Samantha is mine to protect, whether she likes it or not. I glance to her table.

She is gone.

So, every fact I have found about vampires matches Mr. Sullivan. And it doesn't scare me one bit. He's not what I would call your typical professor. For starters, he is way too young to have that job, which points to him being much older than he looks—trait of a vampire, check. The way he shows up or is in places long before he should have gotten there. Vampire trait, check. He's always put together, check. I have only seen him eat like once, check.

Serena is at her part-time job today, so I have the entire house to myself until around lunchtime. I sit up on the bed and fling Grandma's grimoire open to the dog-eared page on vampires. She has written out in her elegant cursive facts about vampires, their origins, lives, food, interactions with witches. Turning the page, I find an envelope, sealed with dark-red wax. I slip it from its nestled spot between the pages and turn it over in my hand. The wax seal is intact. There is smudged writing on the front.

Sammie.

I slide a finger under the flap of the envelope and still. What would Grandma have needed to hide in her grimoire for my eyes only?

A thought flies into my head. Did she intend this for when I came of age? Witch powers come to their true capabilities when females turn twenty, males twenty-five. Twenty is just over a month away for me. I drop the envelope back into the book and slam it shut.

If I am supposed to come into my full power in a few short weeks, I should be honing my skills, not ignoring them. Images of my little brother lying burned in my mother's lap make my stomach twist. I walk into the hallway, down the stairs, and out the back door. The grassy backyard is lined with old trees that pre-date the house itself. I comb through the knowledge of the basics my grandma taught me years ago as I sink onto the grass.

My phone pings. Serena.

> Be home in a bit for lunch. Your special chicken sound good?

I ignore the text and lie on the grass. The sunlight pierces the canopy of ancient gnarled evergreen trees and I raise a hand and play with the light that dances over my fingers. Closing my eyes, I imagine light, then fire spinning in my hands. It's been years since I wanted to try my magic properly. I sit up, eyes still closed.

Something tugs inside me every time I think of Anjelica's words. What does she want me for? Nothing about what happened the other night feels good. Despite what happened with Jackson, I at least need to be able to defend myself.

Heat burns my palms, and I snap my eyes open. A flicker of amber fire sways over my palm before snuffing out.

Holy crap.

Examining my palms one at a time, I sit up. Turning over my hands, I pull in a long breath and rub them together. I hold them out over my lap again, and this time, keep my eyes open and imagine fire dancing above my hands.

Nothing.

Willing it harder, I slam my eyes shut and try again.

Nothing, again.

My heart sinks.

Still broken.

Just like I thought. I have no idea where to start. Knowing that rips a hole in my chest. The dream about Lewis runs through my mind, the mist, the knife at his throat, that woman Anjelica standing behind him as he kneels at the edge of the jagged rocky cliff. My hands tremble.

Why am I having this dream at all? I have no connection to Mr. Sullivan, apart from the student-teacher relationship we have. Most of the time, he only tolerates my existence in his classroom. The only time he's been more than uncivil was the time in the library. That was something else.

Something intense.

With him so close to me, I couldn't think straight. But he offered up information on vampires. Heat rushes my neck as I remember the fact that I shared a personal project with him. And he is the reason I decided to delve into the existence of species other than my own.

His too-fast movements. Being in one place at one moment, another a second later. The fact that he heard me call him an ass in the corridor that day outside the Chancellor's office.

I shake my head and return my focus to the powers I have neglected for years.

Sitting on the grass, legs crossed, I place my hands on my knees and exhale. I send my mind deep into my center, willing the energy from the earth under me to rise at the same time. Tingling washes from the tips of my fingers, into my palms, and past my wrists.

> *Fire, earth, water, and air.*
> *I bring you release.*
> *Bend to my form,*
> *Meet me here.*

Warmth speeds over my palms. I keep my eyes closed, imagining a lick of flame coiling around itself above my upturned hands. Heat hits my face. I open my eyes. Two identical flames dance above my palms, no heat touching my palms. I smile and chuckle. It snuffs out.

Crap.

The front door slams. Serena. I curl my palms and rise from the grass, making my way inside. She wanders down the hall toward the kitchen, dumping her satchel on the sofa as she passes the living room on the left and plops onto a stool at the kitchen counter.

"Hey, how was your shift?" I ask.

"Killer. My feet are aching."

I pull the fridge door open and take out the leftover special chicken from the night before and turn back, placing it on the counter. She scrolls on her phone, not looking up. Grabbing ingredients for a garden salad, I place them next to the chicken before hunting for a chopping board. Every downward slice of the knife in my hand is heavy. I toss the sliced tomato into the lettuce and pluck an avocado from the wooden bowl in the center of the kitchen island.

Memories of my magic swirl in my mind. But every thought I have of trying again ends with the image of my little brother, burned. The tang of his burning hair and skin.

A knot forms in my stomach and my hand stills on the knife as I reassure myself. *He is okay. He is okay now.* I finish the salad and place it on the table as Serena looks up and leans on the island, opposite where I am working.

"Hungry?" I ask.

I turn my back to her and pull the fridge door open. I lean down, reaching to the back of the cold space, feeling for glass bottles. The cool square bottle that holds Mom's homemade dressing touches my fingers. I pull it out and make my way to the table.

"Yep, starving," she says, moving to her seat at the wooden dining table, next to mine. I pile salad onto her plate. She grabs the chicken and serves us each a generous portion.

"What have you been up to this morning?" Serena stares at me, fork loaded.

I grind my teeth and release a breath, trying for nonchalant and failing. She doesn't need to know about any of this. My suspicions about Mr. Sullivan, my connection to the supernatural world, or the fact that I have been pining away for my lecturer since the first day on campus.

"Nothing. Study and research for an upcoming assignment. You have started yours, haven't you?"

"Ah, no, not likely. That one will be a last-minute job," she says. Her eyes narrow at me, but she goes back to her lunch.

Serena shovels salad and chicken in like it's her last meal, and I chuckle.

"What?" she says around a mouthful, surprise written over her face.

"Nothing. Glad you enjoy my cooking. But you should try to chew a little before you inhale your entire plate." I scrunch my nose up at her playfully.

After finishing lunch, she brings the plates and cutlery to the sink while I pack away the leftovers. Serena retires to the couch while I wash up. My mind slips back to the fire that danced over my palm only hours ago. Elemental witches have control over all elements, including water. Water can't hurt, right?

I wave my hand above the sink, watching as the water sloshes side to side. I wonder. Hovering my hand over it, I concentrate on an upward movement. Inhale. The stretch of air in my lungs steadies my mind. Exhale . . .

Water hits my overturned palm, and I crack one eye open. A small stream rises from the sink to meet my hand. I hold my breath and turn my hand over and open both eyes. A sphere of water floats above my palm for a second before bursting over my hand and returning to the sink.

I glance over my shoulder. Serena is cuddled up on the couch on the furthest end, engrossed in whatever regency show she's found to stream. Turning back, I hold two hands over the sink. This time, I keep my eyes open, suck in a deep breath, and will the water upward. It bobs in place for moment, and I set my shoulders back, forcing breath out fast. A torrent shoots past my hands like a tornado, rising almost to the ceiling. I gasp and pull my hands back, hiding them behind my back.

Crap.

The water plummets, spilling over the sink, countertop, and floor.

Dammit.

I grab a towel and clean up the mess.

"You okay over there?" Serena says. Her brows lowered, she peers over the back of the sofa at the mess over the counter and floor.

"All good, just dropped a plate in the sink and it splashed everywhere," I lie.

That was close.

·)·)·)·❂·(·(·(·

The internet put up a good fight, but I have found a home address for Mr. Sullivan. It's about twenty minutes from here. Gathering Grandma's book and my phone, I shove them into my satchel. I call out to Serena, telling her I'll be back in an hour.

I fly out the front door before she can offer to ride along and hit the unlock button on the keys. The car beeps and the blinkers flash. I pull the driver's door open and am down the road heading for Main Street before I have a chance to change my mind.

He lives north of town. I turn onto his road and slow down as it disintegrates into twist and turns. The afternoon light splinters through the trees to my left, casting shadows across my path. The tall evergreen pines that flank the road tower ominously above. A dead-end sign creeps past on my right. He must be the only house up here. My hands sweat under a tight grip on the wheel, and a cool chill runs down my spine.

I can't even turn around, the road has narrowed so much, with no room on the sides to maneuver a vehicle around. My only option at this point is to keep going until I reach his house or a place to make a U-turn. My clock on the dash flicks over—almost twenty minutes have passed. I'm going to end up at his house. I slow the car, hoping I haven't made a huge mistake. Apart from stalking a member of the faculty, I am potentially walking into a vampire's lair.

Okay, that is a little dramatic. Mr. Sullivan doesn't exactly scream 'I live in a sordid lair of darkness and death.' But I would be stupid to be unafraid. I round a turn, and an enormous home comes into view on the opposite side of a small lake. The tires crush over gravel around the lake until I roll to a stop short of the front of the house.

A lump tightens my airway, making each breath forced as I pluck out my phone. As if that will save me now. I check—no missed calls, no messages. No requests for me to return to safety. I let the car idle but shift it into park.

The home is large and sprawling. Like something you would find in one of those luxury-home magazines where the house is been handed down from generation to generation. Or, maybe in this case, one generation has lived here that long.

I open the notes app on my phone and scroll the few notes I made about vampires. Somehow, I neglected to add defenses against them, should one find themselves in a position of wanting. Ahhh. What the hell am I thinking? I should leave . . .

BANG!

Something hits the roof of my car. I yelp and clutch my phone to my chest. A shadow moves across my window, clearing to what looks like flannel and khaki. A man leans down, peering in through the window. His features are similar to Mr. Sullivan's, but his face is longer, older. His hair is slightly darker but the same. He motions for me to roll down the window. I keep my eyes on his, trying to assess whether that would be a good idea.

"You lost?" His words are muffled against the glass.

A smile pulls up on his face, lighting up his eyes. Not a serial-killing vampire then? I press a finger on the window button and it lowers with a whir. I force the breath from my chest and try to plaster a smile on my face. I'm pretty sure he can smell fear. Ugh.

"No, I'm not lost."

His eyebrows shoot up and he steps back, letting me open the door. I grab my bag and step out of the car. "I am looking for Mr. Sullivan."

He tilts his head. "You one of his students?"

I nod.

Something like recognition blooms over his face and he turns, walking toward the house, looking back to wave me on. I follow a few paces behind, taking in the huge house. The windows, the multi-peaked roof, the pillars that adorn the front porch like something out of *Gone with the Wind*. He opens the door and nods for me to follow. I climb the stairs but hesitate before the threshold.

"Come on in, we don't bite," he says. The kindness in his eyes is deceptive, I am sure of it.

"Okay, thanks."

The moment I cross the threshold, I am struck by the grandeur of the home. Wood panel and ornate trim, arches over doors, a hearth the size of my car in the living room, visible from the foyer. The floor is marble, polished. Brass hooks hold coats and scarves. Paintings hang from the walls, and the back of the large living room is flanked with dark shelves, packed with books. Twin sofas hug an expensive looking rug.

Movement stirs in the room to the left.

"Lewis, visitor," the man says softly, waving as if to say he's done his part and I'm on my own and walks toward the sofas. I wait in the foyer, still in awe of the old-world charm of the wood-paneled interior of the grand home.

"Who is it, Den?" Mr. Sullivan says, but his brother's voice was too quiet for a human to be able to hear from another room.

Another trait, check.

I shift on my feet. Maybe this is a bad idea. My far-too-young professor appears from the room that I now realize is an office, papers in hand. He looks up and stops in his tracks.

The rattle of ice in a glass echoes from by the hearth. I

glance to where the man sits on the sofa, curiosity plastered over his face, his focus solely on Mr. Sullivan. He tilts his glass toward me and says, "Samantha."

Mr. Sullivan's mouth opens and doesn't close. The door moves wider with the breeze.

I grip the strap of my bag, forgetting what I came for. "Hi."

His pupils dilate as he steps back, going rigid. A chuckle drifts from the living room. Mr. Sullivan collects the papers into one hand, his jaw feathering.

"What are you doing here?"

CHAPTER 8

LEWIS

Every single fiber in my body is on fire. I am going to pummel Denver into the ground for this one. Why the hell did he let her in? He bloody well knows who she is. And that I am trying to ignore the bond, and this is making it almost impossible. I glance at my older brother, now settled on the sofa, whiskey in hand. The smirk over his face sees my brows lower. He's enjoying this.

Samantha clears her throat and I drag my focus to her face. Her hands are almost white around the satchel strap running over her shoulder.

"I'm sorry to just show up. It's probably not what students are supposed to do. But I was working on that project you helped me with the other day, and I—"

"You thought driving to my house was appropriate?" My words come out far harsher than I intend. My annoyance is at my brother, not her.

Samantha stiffens. Her gaze darts around the small space, heart rate climbing at an astonishing pace. Fuck.

I take a step back, hoping a little distance will hamper the need that pushes through me when her heart takes off like that.

"I'm sorry; I should go. It was stupid." She walks toward the door.

Denver appears before it far too fast and turns to face her, his hands behind him closing the door with a gentle thud. She gasps and looks from my brother's face to mine.

She's scared.

Enough.

"Let her go, Denver." The words are a low rumble that translates to a warning. I don't want her here. And when she steps back toward me, I brace myself as her scent works its way through my senses yet again.

"Samantha, is it?" he asks.

"How do you know my name?" she says to him before looking at me directly. The realization that I have told my brother about her lands and her mouth parts. Her heart kicks up again.

Denver smiles at her, this time in a friendly way.

"Lewis told me about you. Said you had an interest in the supernatural, which is something we also take interest in."

"Oh." Her voice is soft, understanding, but a little too innocent.

"Come in, I can help you with whatever you were

needing for your project. Denver may have some more information for you; he is a keen study of everything Wicca and vampirical. You have five minutes."

Her brows shoot up, and she bites her lower lip before nodding. I lead her into the living room. I gesture for her to sit, and she sinks onto the sofa, still gripping her satchel. Finding the furthest point that is still socially acceptable, I sit. Denver swaggers into the room, plonks on the sofa opposite her, and leans back, lacing his fingers behind his head.

Samantha pulls the bag from her shoulder and pulls out a notebook and pen.

"What species are we looking at for the project?" I snap.

She glances between us. "Vampires, still."

"What is it that you need to know?" Denver asks. "We have comprehensive insight on the species." He leaves the part out where it is from personal experience.

"Well, researching their physical traits, I found some inconsistencies." She is looking at her notes intensely. I shift in my seat, thinking back to the moments that I shared with her, combing through them, hunting for anything not human enough to keep me conspicuous. "What did you find?"

Denver throws me a look—his 'it's now or never' face.

"Well, for starters, some sources refer to their speed, some do not. Some online sites claim that they can move about freely in the sun, while older documentation from more historic sources claimed they were strictly creatures of the night." She looks up and stares right at me. I swallow past the lump in my throat that forms with the speed she is referring to, fighting the urge to growl at her.

I open my mouth to enlighten her, and Denver leans forward. "Speed is accurate, daylight is not a problem, and while we like to get out at night, it's not essential. We form mating bonds, only once in our supernatural lifetime, and it is rare for interspecies bonds, but not impossible; other species are usually aware of our presence unless their abilities have been dulled for whatever reason; and we can only be killed by some kind of unnatural interference or silver dagger to the heart. We can't enter someone's home unless invited in or else we shatter to a million pieces. Is there anything else on your list?"

I can't drag my gaze from her stunned face. Denver said *we*.

Fucking hell, Den.

"How old are you both?" she says softly.

So, she picked up what he put down. Just great.

Den glances at me. "Around three hundred years, give or take a decade or two, depending how you calculate it."

Samantha simply stares at me. I swallow hard. That seems to be all I can do right now, unless you count the threadbare breaths that slip past my lips.

And then she shifts on the sofa, with a small huffing laugh. "Have either of you... I mean, are either of you mated?"

"I had a mate, her name was Zahli, it was fifty years ago

now." Denver's shift on his seat but then recovers. "What *I* want to know, Samantha." He clasps his hands together in front of him. I am literally unable to move my body at this point. He sighs, as if all the rehashing is tiring to someone who rarely tires. "What kind of magic do you practice?"

"I—" She swallows and shakes her head, glancing at me before shifting on the sofa. Her heart pounds faster, hand reaching for her pendant.

"Green. Kitchen. Psychological. Elemental?" Denver's words have turned short. He is trying to figure out if she wields elemental magic. And I know all too well he will use her up to save my miserable existence.

She shifts her shoulders back, her eyes drilling into his. "I don't honestly remember. I wasn't encouraged to hone my skills after the age of eight."

Transparency it is.

I shift closer to her. "Time's up."

Denver catches my movement and leans closer to her. The bounding in my veins intensifies. He is testing my resistance to the bond by being in her space. Prick.

"Fine. My initial take on you was vampire. The least I can do is give you as much."

Well, shit. I didn't expect that. Her persona far exceeds her age.

"I have been studying basic Wiccan magic my whole life, but after an incident with my brother, I stopped practicing." She lets go of the pendant and wrings her hands together.

"If you're practically unmagical to the point of being human, why is Anjelica keeping tabs on you?" I ask, hoping she will know something that connects the two.

"I have no idea who that woman is. Or her friends."

"Anjelica is one of the most powerful Wiccans to have lived across multiple centuries. Her magic keeps her young. She is able to harness all four Wiccan practices, including elemental."

"What does that have to do with me?" she asks.

The last person I want to be vulnerable around is this almost-witch . . . but if there is a chance she can help?

I look at Denver but decide the truth it is. "She asked something of me a long time ago that I could not fulfill, and as punishment, she cursed me. She gave me a limited number of months to live before the cycle of the moon would end my life but never told me how long I have, mostly to keep me in endless torment. What better punishment than to live centuries, terrified every moon is your last. Anyway, the only way to break the cycle is to use a spell, one that harnesses all four elements in one moment."

"Lewis and I have been scouring the earth for centuries trying to find a witch with that kind of power. But every time we were close, that particular witch either went missing or died," Denver says.

"You think she thinks I am an elemental witch, and that's why she is keeping tabs on me?"

"It's a theory. But if you tell us you're not one, then we have no choice but to believe you," I say.

"I'm not; at least if I had been, I'm not anymore. I lost my ability at the age of eight. It's not something you can simply turn back on."

I sag into the chair and stare past her. Partially relieved it's not Samantha, and I don't have another reason to have to be around her, partially devastated we still have no solution.

"Look"—she pivots on the seat to face me—"I'm sorry I can't help you. Thank you for the information. I should be going." She rises and pulls her satchel back onto her shoulder.

I stand and walk behind her to the door. "You cannot breathe a word of anything we have told you today. Not even to that best friend of yours."

"I understand. And I won't."

Curiosity supersedes my aversion to witches as I ask, "What's the end goal for your project?"

"Not sure, actually . . . I kind of started it when I—"

"When you met me?"

"Yeah."

"Why?"

"Um, I . . . I just felt compelled to." She blushes with a shrug and runs a hand over her face. If I didn't know better, I would say she feels the bond, too. But I am not about to bring it up and sure as hell am not going to put her in danger by being bonded to me.

Council aside, if Anjelica knew about the mating bond, she would use it to hurt me, and it wouldn't end well for Samantha.

At all. Images of Zahli, Denver's mate, limp on the asphalt, the light gone from her eyes, her body twisted into inhumane angles, flood my mind. I shove my hands in my pocket.

She is studying my face, hovering by the front door. Sunlight streams through the windowpane by the door, filtering through her hair. It shimmers golden when she makes the smallest move.

"Well, if that's everything you need."

"Oh yeah, sure, I'll get out of your hair." She opens the door, and I fight the overwhelming pull to follow her. Then she disappears over the threshold, leaving me staring at the door. Minutes later, her car engine whines to life and rolls down the gravel drive. I close my eyes and let my forehead thud onto the door.

"Oh brother, you have it bad."

"Shut up, Denver," I drawl into the wood.

"At least she's pretty?"

I snap my head up and spin around. Before his next heartbeat, my hand is at his throat. A smile pulls over his smug face as he waits for me to sort through what I just did. Fuck.

I drop my hand and step back. Denver chuckles, slapping me on the back. "It could be worse, little brother; she could still hate you."

I am pretty sure she still does. But that's the most civil conversation we have ever had, and about the most unhinged topic on the planet. At least she can hold her own in that department. Despite her being the only witch we have ever had in our home, and most likely the last, Denver warmed to her quicker than me.

After what happened to Zahli, I never thought he would look at another witch again without wanting to rip their throat out. I really must be a mess if he is playing matchmaker. I'm officially screwed. How can I survive the rest of the semester in the same room as her with this bond pushing me to the edge every other minute?

"You look like you could use a run," Denver says, grabbing his coat from the hook by the door.

And some.

Maybe feeding again will temper the animalistic tendencies I have around Samantha. It can't hurt to try.

We are bundled up and out the door before the sun starts to lower in the sky. This time, I take the lead, streaking through the forest at a pace so fast, even Denver struggles to keep up. Birds flee branches as we run past, leaving a wake of broken timber behind us. Past the first ridge, we climb higher, not slowing. I reach the peak and stop.

Denver slides to a halt beside me. The sun slips over the horizon, and the stars begin to stud the sky behind us, one by one. From our high position, most of the reserve sprawls out in front of us. The gushing creek winds its way through the tall pines and grey stones.

I run a hand through my tousled hair and loose a sigh.

The weight of everything reaffirms its grip with every deep inhale.

"We will find someone, Lew," Denver says.

I force a smile and meet his gaze. I want to believe him, I do. Perspective is a wonderful thing, and up on this ledge, it hits me. I've had more than three lifetimes to enjoy what I was given the day Anjelica let me turn. And how have I spent it? Running in fear, wasting months searching for something that may not be able to be found. Maybe that is the real punishment in the end.

Centuries of fear and chaos. Not the end. Not the expiry date she set for me. And the kicker . . . To have found my mate weeks before my time is about to come to an end is fucking tragic. And I don't want to leave my brother behind.

But I have also waited longer than any other man on this earth to find what Denver had with Zahli. My entire life has been one desperate choice after another. I have wasted the precious gift she inadvertently gave me. For that, maybe I don't deserve a mate. And that is the worst burden to carry.

I return my focus to the now orange and pink hues of the fading daylight. The image of Samantha's face, her blue eyes, her soft curls framing her face. Her soft pink lips as she chews her bottom lip. I groan and sink to my knees. Denver slaps a hand onto my shoulder, and I scream, burying my fingers in the dirt, palms pushing into the sparse grass.

I am a fucking idiot.

CHAPTER 9

SAMMIE

Bass reverberates through my chest, rattling my heart between my ribs. I'm pretty sure the speakers are about to explode. Serena hands me a red cup. Its pale yellow watery contents slosh as she releases her hand. I take a sip.

The bitter taste of cheap beer coats my tongue and lips. Ugh. I place it on the small table holding snacks behind where we stand, waiting for some classmates of Serena's. I could think of so many better ways to spend my Saturday night, but here we are.

"Come on, girl; at least have one drink and try to have fun." Serena bumps into me, her megawatt smile plastered over her pretty face, her long dark hair curled and around her shoulders. The dress and boots she is wearing are not even warm enough to smother out the goosebumps that line her skin, but she doesn't seem to notice. I pull my coat around myself tighter and inch toward the bonfire in the center of the party.

In the midst of someone's enormous backyard, with dustings of a failed snowfall, hay bales line the grassy area, holding up dozens of chatty students. A giant pile of firewood sits beyond the circle of hay bales by the tall fence lined with shaped topiary plants sitting in white rock. A wooden platform holds the DJ, and in front of it is a wide dance floor made of polished wood. Someone's gone to a lot of trouble for this party.

The house behind me is impressive, with its original historical features well-preserved and painted grey with white trim. The homes in Castleton are well-kept. It is so lovely to see heritage remembered and honored.

"You look like you would rather be anywhere else but here," a guy says, stopping at my side, drink in hand.

I turn to face him and offer a smile. "That obvious?" I chuckle.

His green eyes find mine, and he runs a hand through his dark hair. "Did you want to dance?"

"Oh, god no. Sorry."

He laughs, throwing his head back a little, and takes a sip from the beer bottle in his hand.

That came out wrong. "I mean, I don't dance."

"Oh, so not just with me, then?"

"If I danced, you would be a contender." I try to fix my mistake and wish I hadn't the instant the words leave my mouth. As handsome and fun as he might be, whatever is happening here is awkward.

"Noted." His smile radiates happiness. Still, all I want to do is make space between us.

"Excuse me, I need to find my friend; I have her things." I pat my oversized pocket where Serena's keys and purse sit.

"Enjoy your night." He tilts his head. "I didn't even get your name."

"Sammie." I force a smile and turn to leave.

"Declan, in case you were wondering," he calls after me, holding his hand above his head in a casual wave.

I wasn't.

I wander back inside to find my best friend talking with three guys. She's always been more outgoing than me, but she doesn't date. Ever since we were old enough to talk about boys, she wasn't interested. We were thirteen when she moved onto my street, back in South Burlington.

She'd been in a bad place when her and her mom moved onto the street. Something about her friend back in her old town getting sick; I'm not sure, she wouldn't talk about it. Still, she leans into the conversation with the three guys she is chatting with, each of them intently listening to what she is saying. Like they are mesmerized.

I walk over and stop by her side. She cuts off the last word and swings an arm over my shoulders. "As I was saying, boys, this is my bestie, Sammie."

Three sets of eyes settle on my face. Heat floods my entire body, leaving my stomach in a tight coil. I wish I didn't have to do the outgoing thing when I am around her, especially with guys. I hate it.

"Just telling the guys here about your beef with Sullivan."

My mouth gapes.

"I—" I huff a half-hearted chuckle. "I don't have a beef with the professor." I shake my head as the words come out, as if that will reenforce the sentiment that I am not at odds with a member of the faculty.

If only they knew what my actual sentiments were toward Lewis, I doubt I would even be here, flanked by three guys in what is starting to feel like a matchmaking setup by Serena.

"I totally saw him call you out like three times already, and we are only two weeks into the semester," the guy on my right says, his blue eyes lit up with self-assurance that plants him on my avoid-at-all-costs list.

"Well, to be fair, I used my phone in a cell-free lecture hall at the time," I say, the words weaker than I planned.

"Like, who doesn't take their cell to class? He must be like some ancient relic to think students are going to not have their phones turned on in class. It's 2024, for god's sake. Not the 1900s." He laughs, nodding as his friends agree in unison.

Heat coils in my gut. Their disrespectful tone and behavior are everything that is wrong with these parties. These people. Young guys have always annoyed me. They're never interested in anything past the next score or party. All fun and no future. No ambition.

I sigh and turn, walking away to the exit. I would rather sit on the front steps in the frigid air and wait than listen to this diatribe.

"Hey, babe," Serena calls out after me. Her footsteps quicken as she catches up to me, grabbing my arm. "Where are you going?"

"I'll wait outside; this is not my scene. I'm done."

"You're joking, right?" Her tone is flat, her face twisted in annoyance. She can stay as long as she likes; I brought my book.

"Nope, take your time. I'm quite content with hanging out in Velaris, thanks. No teenage idiots in sight."

Groaning, she walks back inside. I make it out the front door and find a place on the porch—the swing. Two large navy blankets lay draped over the back, and I lay one over the seat of the chair and across the back. I wrap the second around my shoulders and settle into the seat. I pull out my novel and open it where the bookmark sits, leaning back into the warmth of the thick wool blanket.

Disbelief thoroughly suspended and the rainbow bridge about to be overrun by the enemies of Rhys and Feyre, my blissful existence is disturbed by two guys. Both reek of alcohol as they swagger on unreliable legs in my direction.

"Well, what do we have here?" the one on the left says, slapping the second boy's back. He teeters on his feet and looks like he is about to lose his stomach on the porch, but he straightens and staggers over, stopping inches from the porch swing. I grab my legs and tuck up tighter in the seat.

"You look like you want some company," he says, leaning down. His putrid hot breath hits my face, and I suppress a gag.

I slide the bookmark between the pages and close the book, resting it on my lap. Maybe if I am polite, they will leave me alone.

"Come on, girl, we can show you a good time," the boy on the right says, trying to wink, but looking like half his face is paralyzed.

I grimace and shake my head. "No thanks, I'm good."

"Huh, that's what you think. The nerdy ones always think that."

"We can show you, you'll see," the boy on the left slurs and grabs my arm.

"Hey, get off me." I try to pull my arm from his grip. But his friend pulls the blanket from around me and I almost slide from the seat. "Stop it, leave me alone!"

"You won't be saying that in a few minutes, girl," one slurs.

"We are gonna rock your world," the other says, tracing a finger over my cheek and down my jaw. I struggle in the grip of the guy still holding me and try to reach my bag to hit him with. It's too far away.

Shit.

"I promise, this will be the best night of your life," the guy holding my arm says.

"I am not going anywhere with you two."

"Sure you are. It won't even take that long." One snorts. The other starts laughing. They high-five in front of me and turn back. "Come on, don't be a killjoy."

I grab my pendant, heart hammering in my chest, bile rising. The silver between my fingers warms. There is no way I want them to lay a finger on me. I could try screaming, but the music is so loud no one would ever hear me. They most likely thought of that.

Shit. Shit, shit, shit.

I struggle in the boy's grip again; he's too strong.

They drag me across the porch and to the front stairs. Nobody else is out here. Everyone is either inside behind the curtain-obscured windows or in the backyard.

No one is coming.

Digging my heels into the ground, I close my eyes. Hot tears well up before streaming down both cheeks. How is this happening? Every shallow breath burns. Straining against their hold, I lose my footing as we descend the steps. A car door opens. I open my eyes, pushing backward with my feet as they try to push me into the brown station wagon.

Shit.

No, no, no, no.

"Take your hands off her." The low voice is raw, almost feral. But feminine. Serena.

One of the boys whips around, letting my arm go. He

swaggers to where she stands. Her eyes are laced with fire, drilling into his. Her hands are balled into fists at her side.

"Now we don't have to share." He grabs her arm.

She tracks her gaze to his grip before meeting his eyes. Her eyes dilate, the pupils almost blacking out her irises altogether. "Take your hands off me, now."

He straightens and removes his hand, stepping back.

Serena steps into the second boy's space. His focus swings from her to his stunned friend.

"I said, let her go," she growls. The blackness is completely swallowing her brown irises now.

Like his friend, he straightens and lets go, moving out of my space.

"Get in your car and drive home. Don't make any stops. Don't talk to anyone. Go home, go to bed, and when you wake up, you won't remember a thing about this party or the people you met."

"Yes, ma'am," they say in unison.

Her eyes are fire-loaded. I move away from the car, and the two still-intoxicated boys hop into their car and drive away.

"What the hell?" I ask.

Serena stares at the car as it disappears before turning to face me. "Are you okay?"

"I'm fine. What just happened?"

She sighs and motions for us to go back up to the porch. I follow her lead and sit beside her on the swing. She plays with the belt on her coat for a moment before she says, "How long have you known you were a witch?"

My breath catches and my mouth gapes for the second time tonight. What?

Serena tilts her head, resembling a momma with a little kid who's been caught stealing from the cookie jar.

"Most of my life." My words are a strangled whisper.

She nods.

"You have magic, too?"

"I do. But it's not something that I use very often, and I definitely do not tell others about it."

"So, you are a witch, also?"

She wraps her coat around her body and ties the belt over it. "I guess you could say that."

"What is your power like? I mean, what type do you have?"

Her eyes narrow and her brows lower, concern wrapping her face.

"What? What is it?"

"I'm not like you, Sammie. Not all sunshine and rainbows like you, girl."

Huffing through a nervous laugh, I fold my arms over my chest. "What do you mean?"

"I am a shadow witch. But I don't practice, at least I haven't for years, dark magic. I haven't wanted or needed to."

A shadow witch—those are the ones who are keeping tabs on me. That's what Lewis and Denver said. From the way they spoke of them, they were bad. And not in the way that vampires and witches generally hate each other.

"Can you—" Do I want to know the answer to this next question? I have to ask.

"Can I what, girl?" she says, running a hand through her long dark hair.

"Can you sense other species? I have trouble with it because I haven't been using my magic for so long. But can you?"

She stares at me for what feels like an age, her mouth a thin line, her face like stone. "You mean like your vampire professor, Mr. Sullivan?"

My breath stops.

She knows.

She knew.

CHAPTER 10

SAMMIE

Icy tendrils whip around Serena and me as we wait for our families to emerge from the growing amount of traffic pouring into the university grounds. Family Day. Every student has the chance to show their families around the grounds and have them meet their professors. Despite enjoying my newfound freedom and college experience, I'm so excited to see Mom and Jackson. It feels like I have been away from my family for months, not a handful of weeks.

Mom's car appears in the procession of cars. She pulls into the northern parking lot before finding one of the few spots left. Jackson is already eagerly looking through the window, head swiveling on his shoulders as he takes in the enormous, tall old buildings and the extensive grounds.

Dull green grass is dusted with white from last night's scattered snowfall. The lanterns on the poles dotted around the paths and through the manicured lawn areas are still on. Music blares from behind the main administration building, which is adorned with a bell tower. Mom and Jackson leave the car, wandering in our direction.

Jackson spots us first and sprints to where we stand, flinging his arms around me in a huge bear hug. How did he grow so much in a few short months? For a senior in high school, he is the typical lanky, tall teenage boy, but I swear he got bigger. I giggle and he lifts me off my feet. Show-off. The smile that spreads over my face lights to a cheeky grin then melts to something more somber.

"I missed you something fierce, Sammie. It is not the same at home without you."

I dot a kiss on his cheek, and he blushes. I remember Serena is by my side.

"Sorry. I missed you, too, little bro."

"Did you get taller or something, Williams? I'm pretty sure the giraffes are going to need shrinks if they see your height." Serena punches his arm.

He chuckles and the heat intensifies on his neck. She shakes her head at him. Mom arrives and wraps me in a tight hug.

"Hello, my love. How's this only been a few months? An entire year's dragged past, I swear."

"I know," I whisper into her hair. The familiar feel of my mom's arms around me and her smell swallowing me brings a prickle behind my eyes. She breaks away from the hug, holding me at arm's length, her gaze running up and down me. "You look so grown up. You just"—she squeezes my arms—"you both look so well. You're thriving!"

"Thanks, Mrs. Williams," Serena says, before she goes back to scanning the parking lot for her mom's Volvo.

"Should we wait for Serena's mom?" I ask.

"No, you guys go. I'll text when she gets here and come find you," Serena says, not taking her eyes off the fast-filling parking lot.

"If you're sure," I say, nudging her arm with my elbow.

She drags her focus from the sea of cars and meets my eyes. "Yup, go ahead; she won't be long."

"Okay, well. First, you have to come and check out the gorgeous old buildings. We can start with the administration building," I say, waving toward the large red brick structure with a bell tower across the green lawn. Jackson huddles into his coat and walks beside me, bumping shoulders every so often. Gosh, I missed him. His sweet face and bright blue eyes are lit up with wonder as he flicks the light brown hair from his eyes and shoves his hands into his pockets.

"You coming here next year, too?" I ask.

He glances at Mom before returning his focus to me. "Dunno, maybe."

"You haven't thought about it yet? You're a senior."

"I'm aware. Trust me, the parentals haven't let me forget it since the minute you left." He rolls his eyes, and I laugh.

Mom chuckles. "Your dad and I want you to have the

life you want, and that starts with knowing which direction you want to go in."

"You have told me this already. I will pick something, I promise."

"You'll figure it out, Jackie," I say and swing an arm around his shoulder, attempting to ruffle his hair, but he is taller than I am used to, and I end up hanging off him by one arm. He raises an eyebrow, rooted to the ground.

"Anyone ever told you you're super embarrassing?"

"Only you," I laugh and remove my arm from his shoulder and straighten his jacket. "Luckily, you recover well. Come on." We approach the wide steps. "The inside is even better than the outside."

·)·)·)·●·(·(·(·

Half an hour later, as we are wandering around campus, heading for the lecture halls, Serena and her mom catch up to us.

"Hey, Mrs. Stewart!" I hug her, and she pats me on the back. Serena's mom has always been a little awkward, almost robotic. Serena laughs, saying the alien abduction triggered it and she's never been the same. But the love she has for her mom shows in their every interaction. When she was thirteen and they first moved in and we met, Serena and her mom weren't that close. As we got older, they became much closer after her dad left.

"Hello, Samantha, it's good to see you girls so happy. I am thrilled, this place is wonderful."

"We love it. Mom, thanks for the nudge." She leans into her mom's side. Mrs. Stewart plants a kiss on her forehead and Serena closes her eyes like she is breathing her in. Despite arguments over when she should start college, they have such a special bond. I adore both of them. They are family. "What's inside this door, Sammie?" Jackson says, pushing the door to Mr. Sullivan's lecture hall open.

"No!" I jump toward him and grab his hand. The latch slips from his hand, but the door drifts open. I reach to close it.

A hand grabs the side of the door, opening it fully. Standing in dark jeans and a navy sweater is Lewis, a welcoming smile spread across his face. He looks so different when he smiles. He's stunning. Butterflies fling from the pit of my stomach, and I look anywhere but his face.

"Welcome, come in. This is the lecture hall most first years use for our archaeology and literature classes. I'm Lewis. Feel free to look around." He nods for us to enter, and Jackson wastes no time striding across the front of the room, arms wide.

"This is so cool." He sits in a burgundy velvet chair in the front row and leans back, making himself at home. "Imagine the things you're gonna learn in here, Sammie."

Lewis's focus is solely on Jackson. He forces a laugh and

walks to where Jackson sits. "I'm not sure your friend Samantha shares your enthusiasm."

Jackson cocks his head, staring at me. Lewis turns to face us. Mom looks at me with an expectant look, as if I need to explain that accusation. I have no control over Lewis's opinion of me and less over the myriad of thoughts that will be burying their way into Mom's brain with a statement like that. Her brow crumples with concern.

Now my heated stare burns into Mr. Sullivan's brown eyes as I shake my head. What an ass!

"I am properly enthused for every class I take, Mom; please don't worry."

"Okay. You don't want to lose your scholarship, Sammie. That's not an option for us."

Heat floods through my neck and face. I can't believe we are having this conversation in front of Mr. Ye Olde Worlde Mansion here. "I won't, I promise."

Mom visibly relaxes, and Serena's mom interrupts, "How many students attend most lectures, Lewis?"

"Anywhere from fifty to one hundred and twenty. The attrition rate as the semester progresses is acute."

Mrs. Stewart laughs and nods. "I am sure the novelty wears off for some."

"Sometimes it is more of a time constraint than loss of appeal. But still, numbers often dwindle toward the end of semester."

"It is a lovely lecture hall. I'm Samantha's mom, this is her brother, Jackson."

Lewis shakes her hand and then my brother's, and I stand stunned at the complete stranger he's become. Talk about turning it on. Urgh.

"Okay, well. That's quite enough embarrassment for one morning. How about we grab some lunch?" I say, guiding my mom and brother from the lecture hall. Serena and her mom trail after us as I hold the door for them all. After they are all outside, I turn back and catch a glimpse of Lewis. The happy facade falls, and his eyes burn into mine.

What the hell?

This man runs hot and cold.

"Samantha?" he utters.

I hold up a hand. This is the only day I have to enjoy my family and I'm not wasting a second of it on Mr. Moody.

"I'll see you tomorrow in class, Mr. Sullivan."

"Please, don't call me that. It's Lewis."

His words are cut off by the closing door. I hurry to catch my family and don't look back.

))) ● (((

The mouth-watering aroma of pepperoni on an extra-thick crust with extra cheese sucks me into a trance. The five of us sit in a middle booth at Third Place Pizzeria. Jackson sits next to me, avoiding eye contact with Serena. It's almost hilarious.

I think he fell in love with her the day she moved onto our street. He was, like, ten? Whenever he wasn't busy with school or sports, he'd be trying to hang around or get our attention. I always thought it was because he loves to be annoying.

Turns out, he's lovesick over my best friend. I worry for him. He isn't going to get out of this crush unscathed. For starters, she is my best friend, she is older than him by five years, and she doesn't date. It's not looking good for him, even with his recent growth spurt.

Serena is busy chatting to Mom about her shifts at the only other takeout joint in town—the rival diner, Mikey's. She works Saturdays to help fund her college career. Although my parents can't afford to pay for college, they do help with my living costs. So I can focus on studying and not add part-time work to an already full-time study load.

The waitress arrives with our entrée and five pizzas, disappearing to return with a tray of drinks.

"God, I am starving," Jackson grumbles.

"Of course you are, giraffe." Serena tosses a fry at him from the entrée we selected, and he ducks. Mrs. Stewart gives her a look, and Serena flattens her grin, mischief still lining her eyes.

I pluck a slice from the pizza pan, the dough hot on my fingers, and I take a large bite. Oh. My. God. This pizza is epic. I moan, savoring the flavor and texture of the gooey cheese, soft, fluffy dough, and earthy sauce. If I died now, I would die happy. I let my eyes drift shut, as if that'll make the moment last longer.

My phone rings, vibrating on the table.

Dad.

I should answer; he'll be so bummed he couldn't come.

I swallow and pick up my phone. Mom points to the door. Her table etiquette doesn't allow for phone calls at the dinner table, and I guess that rule extends to the pizza joint. I slide from the booth and answer the call, heading for the door.

"Sammie?" Serena calls from behind me.

I turn back, still moving toward the door.

"Say hi for me!"

"I will."

The door to the pizzeria sounds, followed by the swoosh of the door behind me. I turn back. My face hits a wall of navy sweater and heady cologne. "Shit."

My hand falls from my ear, Dad's voice sounding through the speaker. Lewis stands, like a wall, in the doorway. He is looking down. Rigidly still.

I track to where his gaze is pinned. My palm is flat against his chest. I gasp and stumble back a step. "I—" Forcing air into my lungs, I hang up the phone. "Sorry, I didn't see you there."

"Walking backwards will do that." His tone is flat, like his expressionless face.

I move, trying to get past on his left. Another customer squeezes through the door, pushing me into the open door.

"Ouch."

The static face of Lewis turns feral, his fists curling. Um, okay?

"I'm fine," I say, annoyance sharpening my words. I move onto the street; the wind blows past me into the pizza place, and Lewis shudders. His behavior, even for a vampire, is kind of getting weird. Shaking my head, I remember why I came out here. I hit Dad's number and relax when he answers.

"Hey, kiddo. What happened? I lost you there for a moment. Service bad at that place?"

"No, it's fine. I accidentally hung up. Sorry, Dad."

The doorbell chimes again. Lewis walks past, pizza boxes in hand. He studies me as he moves past, his expression back to nonexistent.

My patience for his moody bullshit . . .

It just ran out.

CHAPTER 11

LEWIS

E ach bite into the slice burns my mouth and it may as well be tasteless. My body is still in a frenzy from the close proximity to Samantha. Having her touch my chest could have seen me go a few rounds in an Olympic sport of self-control.

I'm pretty sure if she hadn't huffed her way past and left when she did, I would have burst into flames.

We sit under one of the only park lamps, at a picnic table. A guy in a hoodie lingers by the edge of the park. He walks aimlessly for a few minutes, and I return my focus to the food.

"Why the long face, brother?" Denver says, lifting a slice over his head to lower into his waiting mouth.

"I ran into Samantha again."

"Doesn't that happen on a daily basis?"

"She touched me. I almost lost it, Den." My words fade to a whisper, and he stops chewing.

"Shit." He drops the slice back into the box. "You okay?"

"It's not me you have to be worried about. This bond is driving me insane. Every time she comes too close, it feels like I'm teetering off a goddamn cliff."

"Been there, done that, brother; you can't let it overwhelm you, you won't be able to control yourself if you do."

"What happens if you—" Heat rises in my chest. Merely thinking the thought turns my body to fire.

"If you what?" He cocks his head to one side.

"Hypothetically, if we were mated and the bond was honored. What happens when you, you know, consummate it?"

Denver's face cracks with a grin, and he raises an eyebrow. "So, you have thought about it. Who would have known my brother, the practical one in the family, has thought about something *he* wants for a change."

"No, that's not what I mean. I haven—"

"Oh, yes, you have, Lew—your face looks like a tomato right now." He tosses a piece of pineapple from his pizza. I dodge it, and he chuckles.

"I thought about it once, okay? What you and Zahli had was nothing short of incredible; a chance at having that isn't something you ignore. But it's not up to me, is it?"

He picks up his slice and takes a bite, chewing slowly like he is processing the words.

"Even if it was with a witch?" he finally says.

As if summoned, Samantha drives past, Serena in the passenger seat. Their dinner must be done. Only two heart-beats . . . Her family must have accommodations in town. I drop my gaze to the pizza. Any other witch, and I would immediately say no to this bond.

But Samantha . . . There is something about her I can't pin down, something drawing me to her. She's not the closed-off and self-absorbed type like the rest of the witches I have run into. Even when she is letting me know in no uncertain terms that I am her least favorite person, I respond to her. She pulls me in like the tide calls to the sand.

Timeless and endless. Like if we made the connection, it would be transcendent.

"Earth to Lewis." Denver is holding a hand in front of my face. His fingers snap as I jerk and return my eyes to meet his.

"Man, where did you go?" He chuckles. "I don't think you're going to have a choice with this bond, brother; you are well and truly ensnared. I hope Samantha survives long enough for you to get past the connection phase."

"Zahli did, and she was human."

Denver forces a smile. "Yes, she did."

Castleton may be a one-horse university town, but the pizza is the best I have tasted almost anywhere. I bite into a fresh slice.

My brother picks up the wandering guy's scent. He stills and tilts his head. The muscles in his neck all but pop.

I scan the park, finding the guy tracking across the grass toward the street. He walks down the street, turning into the first cul-de-sac. Samantha's cul-de-sac. I swallow my bite of pizza, dropping the slice back in the box.

"Give him a minute, Lewis."

That street is a dead end. If I don't hear a front door, voices, or a car, and he doesn't return, I'm going to investigate. The seconds drip by like molasses. Denver settles back to his dinner.

One minute.

"So, saying she does survive the joining, the consummation. You would be willing to be mated to her as she grows old and inevitably leaves you one day?" Denver asks.

"I don't think there is any way around that particular issue. At least, not one I'm willing to agree to." I lower my brows as Denver raises one of his.

"You wouldn't consider turning her?"

"No, she wouldn't understand what she is agreeing to; how could she?"

"Well, I guess you will have to live without her, then, in say sixty, seventy years."

Two minutes.

"I don't know, Den," I say, scanning the park and the street one more time. "How do you even approach something like that when emotions are involved and this unrelenting, very impractical bond?"

"You take one day at a time, Lewis. That's what you do."

Three minutes.

I shove a hand through my hair, my gut twisting like a burly sailor has gripped his calloused hands around it.

"He didn't come back," Denver says.

Leg jumping from my toes, I scrub my hands over my face and groan.

"Lewis, his scent hasn't faded; he's still close."

Four minutes.

I jump from the bench seat and run. A second later, I am standing in her front yard.

Everything is quiet.

Chill descends in the air, vividly reflected by moonlight on the sluggish, drifting fog. The low cloud is my only indicator it's cold—I don't feel it. I walk to her porch and hesitate mere feet from the front door. Frozen on her front porch, I study the entrance, the front door ajar.

They wouldn't leave it like that. Witches are careful. It is not in their nature to be careless. Someone else has left or forced the door open. I am not welcome, nor are they. For me, entering means turning to marble, followed by the shattering of my centuries-old body. The only thing left to do then is sweep away the millions of shards. I've never come close to that, in all my decades, but I have witnessed it, once.

Samantha could be in trouble, but I hesitate, weighing my choices. I imagine her lying on the floor, hurt or worse. The breeze shifts the door, opening it further. Moonlight bounces off the wooden floor, illuminating the foyer. In the half-light, I track dirty footsteps. They must be from the hoodie guy.

I barge through the door.

"Samantha?" I say quieter than I feel I should, not wanting to scare her. If he lays a finger on her, he is a dead man.

Relationships between vampires and witches are forbidden. I know the penalty for acting on this bond. It spells death for the vampire, magical binding for the witch. No prolonged life through witchcraft, as Anjelica has done. No healing spells or remedies. They are stripped of their essence and left to rot in the darkness of their own minds.

I pause, closing my eyes, trying to analyze his scent.

Not human.

Not witch.

Definitely not vampire.

For all I know, Samantha may be able to protect herself. But the thought of her having to try makes my insides curl. So, I will protect her. For all the bond is worth, at least I can give her that. Until the day she tells me to leave her be. To let her live her life, without me in it.

I am lucky I haven't experienced an emotional connection with her yet. Denver says that's when everything gets harder. A lot harder. A mating bond is one thing. But falling in love as well is something nobody comes back from if they lose their mate. Denver survived, only through the grace of God and a few not-so-legal practices.

I stride through the front room, following the steps of

the intruder. They are easy to find. Dirt and debris trail through her home, up the stairs, and right to a bedroom. The door is closed.

Silence thunders down on me.

I grab the doorknob, ready to shove the door open. Every part of me is almost seized up. The shuddering in my body from entering without invitation takes hold, and I know what comes next.

Shattering.

Everywhere.

With the last of my mobility, I shoulder the door open. Samantha stands in the en suite of her room, readying for bed. Completely oblivious to who is in her room.

In the corner of her room, hoodie guy stands in the shadows, keenly aware of me. I catch his scent, strong in the small space. My breath stops in my throat.

Demon.

Without permission to be in her house, I edge closer to my messy end. Flipping between calling her name to save myself or disturbing the intruder, I make a split decision. I can't help her if I break into pieces.

"Samantha." My voice is changed, my face almost marble. She moves, swaying, as she picks up a toothbrush and paste. Her hips and waist twist with the beat. The slow tones of music pulse. She has earbuds in, concealed under her volume of curls.

"Samantha!" My entire body solidifies to marble, and small cracks ripple across my cheeks. She spins back on the spot, with wide eyes, studying my frozen body and my face.

Her hand claps over her mouth as she gasps, as she rushes from the bathroom, grabbing a robe. As she pulls it over her body, her eyes land on the guy on the other side of the room.

"Lewis?"

"I can't—" My jaw grinds.

"Come in!"

Slowly, I regain mobility. When my focus returns to the corner of her room and not her, she realizes something is wrong and tracks my gaze to the silhouette standing in the corner of her room.

"Lewis," she breathes.

Lewis. Not Mr. Sullivan.

"Stay there." The cracks in my face seal, like treacle being poured through a sieve. I itch to take him out in one impossibly fast maneuver he will never expect. He sways from foot to foot but doesn't move. Samantha closes the robe over her chest as if protecting herself with her thin shield. Her breathing quickens, and I take a tentative step toward the corner of the room. My body is all but free.

His gaze swings from the door to the window, as if deciding which way out is the best. Wringing his hands, he shifts on his feet. Most likely regretting this decision. He has two options: the window next to Sammie, or the door behind me. If I were him, I would throw myself out the window. But I doubt he realizes who he's in the room with, in this dim light.

Samantha shuffles toward me. I guess she figures I'm the lesser of two evils.

"What do you want?" she says, her voice strong, but her arms fold over her chest, hands gripping her goose fleshed skin.

"The Council wants to know what is happening with you two. Interspecies issues."

"What's that supposed to mean?" she snaps.

"Pretend like you don't know. But him showing up here confirms our suspicions."

I step closer to the guy; his heart is thundering in his chest. His fists curl and he leaps toward Samantha. She drops her arms and raises both hands. Flames flicker in her palms and smolder out.

He makes his move. Demons may not be as quick as vampires and lack any magical powers, but they are trained mercenaries for the Council. And they train for one thing—assassination. This one looks particularly green. His unsure footing and awkwardness close the gap between him and Samantha. If she is going to defend herself, now is the time.

Now, Samantha.

"Samantha," I growl.

She looks at me, her expression turning from annoyance to fear. Prickles of heat course through my body. The demon is inches from her, and she turns back, raising her hands.

Nothing happens.

She yelps and staggers backward.

I fly at him, taking him by the neck with one hand, the other bending his arm behind him, and shove him through the open window. We hit the ground, me on top of him. He whimpers. I grab his head and rip it sideways. The Council should have sent a better man if they wanted to have the upper hand.

A dead demon is all they accomplished here tonight.

The Council, zero.

Lewis and Samantha, one.

CHAPTER 12

SAMMIE

Students file into the lecture hall, and I hang back. I used my magic in front of Lewis last night. My gut churns thinking about the epic fail to protect myself. Readjusting the bag over my shoulder, I suck in a long breath and step inside. He is busy setting up his laptop, and he looks flustered.

It's not like him to be running late for one of our lectures. Usually, he stands and takes note of every single student as they walk in and find a seat. Not today. Today, his hair is ruffled, his clothes creased like he either slept in them or didn't go to bed at all.

Do vampires sleep? I have no idea.

His jeans and light grey sweater look like they need an appointment with laundry day. Something is up. I have never seen him like this before. He is usually painfully punctual, his dress neater than most guys in their twenties, and he would be rigid, waiting, as if his patience for the humans is waning thin.

The wind changes, sending leaves spiraling in through the door as it slams shut. I wince and pin my focus on the rising seats of the hall. From the corner of my eye, I see that at the front of the room still, Lewis has stopped. Hands still on the laptop. I ascend the steps and walk through a row of seats to the middle. My spot.

From some reason, being higher than Lewis makes me feel like I have at least some semblance of control over what happens between him and me. The fact I can't control my reaction or response to him undermines the fleeting sense of security every time we are close.

I pull my notebook and laptop out and set up before returning my gaze to the man behind the lectern. He brings up the PowerPoint, starting the lecture. After a slow forty minutes of Lewis fumbling through a process that he usually has down to the second, he waves us all off. I pack up my things and wait for the room to empty a little before leaving my seat. At the bottom of the stairs, I give him one last look. His gaze is focused on the students leaving the hall, so I head for the door.

"Samantha." His voice is raw.

A pang of guilt impales my gut. I feel responsible for his current state; at least a little, anyway. I turn back, letting straggling students pass me as they walk out the door.

Then he's in front of me. He swallows, and I force out a breath. I don't understand why, but the previous evening has both of us rattled. Me, fair enough. But I don't understand why *he* is so upset.

"About . . . last night," he says, meeting my gaze.

His brown eyes tighten, brows lowered. Oh god, I don't want to talk about the many ways I epically failed to do even the simplest of magic.

"I don't want to talk about it, Lewis."

"You're not safe in that house. You need to leave and find another place to live."

"What?! No way, Serena and I are perfectly fine where we are."

"No, you are not. It was too close. The guy was a demon, Samantha. They don't pop over for a friendly visit. They work for the Council."

"I—" Breath leaves my chest and doesn't return.

"Like I said, you need to find another place to live. Something more secure and unknown. They will keep sending more, until they achieve their goal."

"What? What goal? What are you talking about?"

"The Council uses demons as assassins. They will keep sending them until the job is done."

"What job, Lewis? What are they supposed to be doing?"

My gut sinks, acid crawling through my veins. Does he mean they are trying to assassinate me? For what?

His jaw clenches. His hands, which were hanging by his sides, lift to fold over his chest. "You really want to find out?"

"Why?" The word is little more than a breath.

"Why, what?"

"Why are they sending demons to my house?"

"Because of involvement with Anjelica I'm guessing." His gaze hits the floor.

"What involvement with Anjelica? I saw her once. What is going on, Lewis?"

"Anjelica has been at odds with the Council for centuries. They track almost everything she does and who she is involved with, which is you and me. Me because of the curse she put on me, you because she seems to think you are going to be useful to her and has been keeping tabs on you."

"Oh."

"So, you need to find somewhere else to live, at least for a few weeks."

"No. I'm not leaving Serena; she's a witch, too. Who's to say they won't hurt her by proxy?"

"They won't."

"Why not?"

"Anjelica is not interested in her, is she? You have to listen to me."

I shake my head and grip the strap of my bag. "I don't have to do a damn thing you say. Stay away from me and maybe the Council will, too."

I spin and stalk through the door. Arrogant ass. Telling me what to do and where to live. I march down the path littered with rust-colored leaves. A hand grabs my arm, and I stop, spinning back around.

"Samantha, stop. You don't have to like me. You don't even have to believe me. But please, do this one thing." His face is etched with worry. Those brown eyes burn into mine. I look down to the hand gripping my arm, and he releases his hold, dropping his hand to his side.

"Why? Why do you care if the Council has some ridiculous vendetta out against me? I haven't even heard of them until the other day, for god's sake!"

His eyes widen. "Your family didn't educate you on the laws we live by?"

"Obviously not." I roll my eyes at him.

"Samantha, please." His words are laced with annoyance.

I move into his space, inches from him. "And what if I do as you ask? What becomes of my studies? What about Serena?"

"You don't need to move too far, but somewhere you haven't lived for weeks, so there is no scent to follow."

"I'll think about it," I say, inching closer, if only to make him squirm.

He goes rigid and his face falls to indifference. He looks past me, fixing his focus beyond where we stand.

"Why do you care so much, Lewis? Do you do this for all your students?"

His brown eyes are laced with something like fire when they meet mine. "No."

"No, you don't care? Or no, you don't do this for all your students?"

"The latter, Samantha."

His smell, sandalwood and cologne, envelops me. Butterflies frenzy around my stomach, and my heart flings against my chest. I try to think of something sarcastic to respond with, but words clog my throat.

"I can hear your heart racing." His words are gravel.

"I—" Breath catches in my throat, most likely slamming in the unsaid words. I swallow and suck in a breath. "So can I."

I can hear my own heart racing? *Urgh, Sammie.* Heat flushes my face.

"You should get to your next class."

I nod, not trusting my words anymore.

"I'm going." I stay rooted to the spot.

"You will find another place to live?"

It's not that easy. I gave up my spot in the dorms; I highly doubt I could get it back. "Maybe."

"Not maybe!" He grinds out. "You have to do this; it's not optional!"

My brows lower, heat coiling in my center. "I don't have to do it because you say so, you arrogant ass, this isn't the 1950s!"

He moves into my space. The veins in his neck thunder and his chest heaves. "Do it, Samantha."

"Huh. And because you told me to, I'm not going to." I turn on my heel and stalk off. I half expect him to grab me again. The thrill of his hand on my arm gives me a heady rush. But nothing comes, and I glance back.

He doesn't call out.

Doesn't move from his spot.

>)))·◉·(((·

Serena shifts on the bed, tucking her feet underneath her. "Where the hell would you even move to? And are you sure he is right? I mean, I have lived by the laws my whole life and never heard of a demon coming after a witch." "Well, there was one in my bedroom, and it attacked me. So, I am inclined to believe Lewis." Despite the fight I put up about being told what to do, I know he is right. I couldn't even hold my own against one demon. If he is right, more will come. I am not sticking around to find out.

I can't rely on my magic to save me. It's not like I have a live-in vampire to be my bodyguard. The thought takes off on its own, creating more scenarios than I would care to admit. I shove the last of my clothes into my bag and grab the pile of books from the desk.

"Please, don't do this. Don't leave. If another demon comes, we can handle it together," she begs.

"I am not putting you in danger because I have some demented shadow witch stalking me."

The second the words leave my mouth, I regret them. I haven't told Serena about Anjelica and hate that she might assume because I called one shadow witch demented, I think she's that way, too. I *so* don't think that about her. She is my best friend. I grab the pendant on my necklace, rubbing it as I bite down on my lip. She stands and grabs my hand around the pendant, stilling it.

"You have a shadow witch stalking you? Why didn't you tell me?" Her face is a mix of hurt and annoyance.

"I didn't have time to think about it. And it wasn't a big deal until last night, apparently."

"Sammie, girl, who is hunting you?"

"Anjelica someone . . ."

Serena goes rigid.

"What? Is that bad? Is she dangerous?" I grab her shoulders and tilt my head.

"Yes." She removes herself from my grip and sinks onto the bed. I sit next to her, not taking my eyes off her. "Did she do something to you, too?"

Judging by the look on her face, it's not good. Serena breathes through a few shaky breaths before turning to face me. "I know her."

"You have had contact with her before?"

She huffs a strangled laugh. "You could say that."

"What do we do?"

"If Anjelica is after you, there isn't much you can do, Sammie. She is the most powerful shadow witch on the planet."

"Surely, someone else must be a match for her powers?"

"Maybe. Only an elemental can defeat a shadow witch.

An *epic* elemental witch." Her eyes bore into mine. A warning, a plea.

"She is after Lewis, too." The words are all but a whisper.

"I know."

I search her face. She knows about Lewis's curse?

"You know about Lewis?"

"I know about the curse." She hesitates, dropping her hands in her lap and setting her focus on the door to my room. "Word gets around about that kind of thing."

"Oh."

She is quiet for a time. I mull over the new information. Serena knows Anjelica and about Lewis. About the laws. She is a shadow witch. I am an elemental witch. Only an elemental witch can cure Lewis and take out Anjelica, who's a menace to all species. What if I could train and fix both problems with one solution?

If Anjelica is gone, Lewis is safe. All other witches and vampires she has preyed on would be safe. The Council would have no reason to send around demons to take out anyone associating with her.

"Promise me you will keep your head down and stay out of her way," Serena says.

Why is everyone telling me to run and hide? Their absolute lack of faith in me is starting to grate. I pluck my bag from the bed and lift the books from the desk. I will find another place to live. I will keep to myself. But I will not sit by and let some self-absorbed, too-big-for-her-boots bully of a shadow witch hurt my friends or my family. If she thinks she can manipulate me, she has another thing coming.

I stalk out of the bedroom, march through the front door, and toss my bag and books into the car. I twist the ignition like it's Anjelica's scrawny, ancient neck and sink my foot onto the accelerator. The car peels from the curb and flies down the street.

Game on, bitch.

CHAPTER 13

LEWIS

The knock at our door comes after dark. As far as I know, we are not expecting any visitors. As I reach the door, her scent hits me, even with a wall of wood between us.

"Who is it?" Denver calls from the kitchen.

When I don't answer, he walks to the front door, stopping short at the sight of me trying to fight the instinct of the bond with every muscle in my body. Some days it's worse than others, and after our conversation today, it's driving me insane.

"Answer the door, Lewis." Denver's words mean business. His warning for me to get my shit together. I run a hand through my hair and ignore the blazing fire in my core, the fire lacing my veins. I grab the door handle and open it.

Samantha stands with her back to the door. Not the best position when she literally knocked on the door of a house with two residing vampires. She turns and her face twists into a frown, hands in her pockets, a bag on one shoulder.

"So, turns out, there is nothing free to rent—no apartments, no houses, no rooms, nothing. Everything is full because of the college influx." She chews on her bottom lip, waiting for a reply.

Denver appears at my side. "Come in, Samantha."

She smiles at him, and I step aside numbly. Denver glances at me, his face still carrying the warning he has given me my whole life: 'be nice and behave.' At this point, I am barely holding it together. I have no choice other than to stay rigid and at least four feet from her. I force the vision of her scared face into my mind, and the intense embers crawling along my skin ease.

"Are you okay?" she asks as she walks past. The hair blowing around her shoulders drops as Denver shuts the door.

"He's fine. Are you okay? What are you doing here?" Denver says.

Samantha looks at me and back to Denver. "Lewis told me I couldn't stay in the house with Serena; the Council could send another demon. And I couldn't find anywhere else."

Denver's eyebrows shoot up, and I wince. I haven't had the chance to tell him about the outcome of last night yet.

"A simple text, brother; that's all it takes," he grinds out, shaking his head before turning back to Samantha. "You stay here. I won't have those morons interfering with every facet of our lives."

I grit my teeth, tensing my jaw. *Our* lives, as if Samantha is a part of it. I am trying my hardest to keep her out of it. It's for her own good.

She meets Denver's gaze and her face blooms with a small smile. "Thank you. Someone was tailing me. At first, I thought I was imagining things. But, an hour later, the same guy was still always a block behind me. I don't understand how Anjelica can invest so much into someone she knows so little about, or why the Council would be in our faces for associating with her."

"The Council?" Denver says, lifting an eyebrow.

I catch his eyes and shake my head so subtly Samantha won't notice.

"Ah yes, the Council, always butting in where they don't need to." He forces a smile, which is definitely not for my benefit, and gestures for Samantha to follow him as he walks into the living room. She follows and looks around the room, her face lit up with awe despite this being her second visit here. I follow them at least four feet behind and stop short of the sofa as they sit on opposite chairs.

"Did you see what the guy looked like?" I ask.

She looks up and her eyes dilate, her heartbeat quickening.

Shit.

I hammer down the thoughts and instincts that rear at her attention.

"Hoodie, light-colored hair, medium build. I wasn't close enough to get anything else."

I nod.

"If this isn't okay, I can leave. Maybe if I keep looking —" She rises.

"No, your first instinct was correct. You are safest here. Besides, Lewis could use some practice using his best social behavior." Denver looks at me, smirk smashed onto his face. She doesn't move to leave.

I am going to kill him for this. He knows exactly what he is doing, and how hard this is for me, being in the same space as Samantha. He is also acutely aware of what could happen if I can't control the persistent and over-whelming instincts the bond forces every minute she is close.

"Are you sure?" She is looking right at me still.

Her heart rate doubles.

If I didn't know better, I'd say the bond is mutual, that she is simply unaware of it or won't admit it. We are not exactly friendly toward each other. Her hand reaches for the pendant and hesitates before moving to grab the strap of her bag.

I suck in a quick breath. "It's fine. Stay out of my way."

Denver shakes his head at me and stands. "Come on, Samantha, I'll show you where you can put your things."

She follows him toward the hall to the left of the living room. She looks back, her face fallen, a glimmer of hurt lacing through her features. My gut twists. She turns back and follows Den down the hallway. I scrub both hands down my face.

Fuck.

An hour later, we sit around the old wooden dining table off the kitchen area. Denver and Samantha have cooked up a feast for three. Some kind of chicken that looks orange and well-seasoned, a green salad, a potato dish, and a pile of rare steaks sit on a plate by Den.

I'm glad they are having fun playing house together.

Sarcasm alights to envy, and I count through each breath that follows for the next few minutes. I am not jealous of my big brother. I am so sick of this damn bond. It would almost be easier to act on it; maybe then it would leave me alone for a few minutes. A good way to spend my last days, if we can't find an elemental witch who can break this insipid curse.

"Is your room comfortable enough?" I ask, my tone far from pleasant.

She stabs the chicken on her plate and pauses, staring at me. "It's fine, thank you."

Rigid politeness. Better than nothing. Better than her trying to talk to me. *Better for her.*

"You two are going to have to relax around each other if this is going to work," Denver interrupts the hard stares we have interlocked.

"If you say so." I bite the rare meat from my fork.

"Sorry, Denver." She blushes and glances at my brother before focusing on her food.

Blood thunders through my veins, burning like acid. I push my plate away and stand. I pluck my phone from the table and slide it into my back pocket. "I have work to do."

Denver curses under his breath as I make my way to the study.

We need to break this curse and find a way to eliminate the bond. Maybe an elemental can do both.

I have to try. Hurting an innocent person, even though she is technically a witch, is not an option. I'm not a fucking monster. Leaving my brother to fend for himself for the next however many centuries is also not an option. I need a solution.

And I need it now.

))) ● (((

Samantha stands on my front porch, the light of early Saturday morning hovering behind her like an aura. Her face is tight, her jaw clenched, her blonde hair mussed, her arms wrapped around her chest.

"You're leaving," she chokes out.

This shouldn't hurt as much as it does.

"Yes. I don't know when I'll be back."

"What if someone comes to the house?"

The question is like salt to a wound, and my mind is grasping as my heart flaps in my chest.

"I don't know. I—"

"We need to find someone to break the curse. Maybe a

few days, a week, tops," Denver answers for me and walks to the car.

"What happens if you can't find someone to break it?" she asks.

I resist the urge to tuck a stray curl dancing in the wind behind her ear.

"I'll see you," I whisper before spinning on my heel and stalking to the car. Denver sits in the passenger's seat, staring at me. I feel so helpless.

The last thing I want to do is leave her alone. But it's not like we can take her with us. Even without the bond, her out and about will only attract Anjelica's attention. Besides, she would never agree to missing classes, and I don't know how long this will take.

Every inch of me is numb. More than ever, I wish I could protect her from the Council, Anjelica. From me.

So much.

I fire up the Mustang. But this time, the familiar, relaxing feeling of driving doesn't come. Instead, every mile away from home, from Samantha, this overwhelming wrong inside me grows. My hands are tight around the wooden steering wheel.

"Lewis, this may just be an observation, but I doubt this bond is one-sided, brother. She's your mate."

I turn to face him. His face is flat, his mouth a thin line.

"I know she is, Den. And that's what I was afraid of."

"Why?"

"I don't want that for her. It's not fair. She deserves better."

"She deserves to know the truth. Not some half-assed story about Anjelica and the Council. *That* was underhanded, little brother."

I study the rows upon rows of trees flying past. Lies never serve, and in the end, I could lose her for it. But if she is safe and not mine, she is still safe.

My Mustang peels down the highway toward Salem, hands gripping the wheel tighter the farther from Castleton I get. The moment the weathered Castleton sign disappears from my review mirror, heaviness drops in my gut.

Denver has been quiet the whole way since his early revelation, scrolling through his google searches, one after the other. As if you can google 'where is the nearest elemental witch.'

It doesn't make any sense. Why is Anjelica hunting her? Samantha's magic is no asset to Anjelica. Why is the bond so strong between us? Maybe nature got it wrong. But, deep in my core, I can feel it. As if her existing is the only reason I do. That's what it's like. I've heard Denver describe it, and it's the same.

Usually, the bond is between two vampires, or sometimes a vampire and a witch. Strong witches can mate with us; the rest don't survive. I hope for Samantha's sake, if it comes to it, she is strong enough.

I push the thought from my head. Not happening. I will not allow it.

A gas station sits on the side of the highway, miles from anywhere. I pull in, startling Denver from his semi-conscious musings.

"You can't need gas yet?" he says, leaning over, eyes studying the dash.

"I don't. I need a break." I park and kill the engine. We haven't had anything to eat since last night, and it wasn't the nourishment we need. Having my nerves up has made my hunger worse. Denver reads my face and pushes his door open, joining me. The bell on the sagging glass-and-metal door chimes as we enter in one fluid motion.

"Can I help you boys find something?" An old man offers a smile, his flannel shirt and faded jeans stained with grease and dirt. Great, greasy old man. I was hoping for something a little younger.

Denver starts the dance, the one we always do when we divide, surround, and feed. I walk to where the old man stands behind his banged-up old wooden counter and rusted till.

"You need gas or something?" he says, a nervous laugh rounding out the last word, eyes darting between Denver's movements and me.

"Something like that," Denver says as he moves in behind the man silently.

The old man's eyes widen, hands gripping the bench. "Please, whatever it is you want, just take it and leave me be."

Denver tilts his head, as if examining the man's neck. A

snarl rips through his lips, and he latches his mouth around the terrified man's throat, eyes rolling back in his head. I hold the old man's gaze, willing him to calm. Taking his fear and filling his mind with his most treasured memories. It is the least I can do for him.

His eyes flutter shut, and he slumps against the counter. Denver releases, wiping crimson from his mouth. I jump the counter and move to the other side of the man, giving my brother the briefest of nods before sinking my teeth into the wrinkled neck. Warm, salted, metallic liquid drains from his skin, and I gulp down every last drop. Ecstasy threads through my body with every mouthful. Ecstasy and strength.

I release the man's pale neck as a sedan pulls into the pumps. A young redhead gets out and shoves the pump into the side of her car. She leans against her near immaculate sedan, studying her nails impatiently, ignoring her surroundings. Denver nods, and I clean my face with the back of my hand. We loosen our hold on the gas station attendant, and he slumps to the ground, breathing raspy. The bell chimes again. This time, before the door closes, our next meal is already entrapped.

Denver lays her on the backseat of her vehicle. She will be fine in a few hours; we didn't take that much. One of our rules since integrating back into the normal population is no killing. It's not that we aren't capable of it, but it raises too much suspicion. I am done moving towns every few months. It's no way to live.

Denver drives her car from the pump to the side of the road as my thoughts wander back to this morning. Samantha's face as she realized I was leaving. Every part of me was screaming to turn back around. I can't leave her now. If Anjelica thinks she has something to do with the curse, she isn't safe. The heaviness that has hung in my gut all day twists. I have to go back.

"You coming?" Denver calls from the car, arms folded on the top of his door, his dark hair whipping around his face.

I walk back and sit in the driver's seat, staring through the windshield. "I have to go back."

"No. You need to get to Salem and find an elemental witch."

"I can't leave her unprotected if Anjelica is hanging around, Den."

"Don't be ridiculous. We are going to Salem. You need to break this curse, brother."

"You. You go to Salem. Text when you get there. Again, if you find anyone. I have to do this."

"Lewis, Samantha is safe at the manor. She is smart enough to stay there until we get back. Forget about the bond for five minutes, please!"

My fists curl by my sides.

He crossed the line.

The look on my face reflects in his and he concedes.

It's not the bond, it's her. Alone. With a guy hanging around, tailing her only hours ago.

"Fine, you go to her. I'll go to Salem. You better hope

one of us is all it takes to find this elemental witch. We are running out of time." He walks to the driver's side. I extract myself from the seat and Den slides in, firing up the engine. The deep rumble lingers for a moment, and he gazes back at me in the rearview mirror. A second later, the rumble turns to thunder, and the Mustang flies down the highway, heading southeast.

I turn northwest and run.

Fast.

CHAPTER 14

SAMMIE

They say the enemy of my enemy is my friend. Lewis is far from my friend. He only tolerates me. Denver is nice enough. But despite everything I have learned and everything that has happened, I trust them. I know they can keep me safe. A temporary alliance is smart.

And surprisingly, I am at home in his house. The thought makes me pause, my hands on my open bag and clothes spread across the bed. I am comfortable with Lewis, but should I not be? Even with his almost hostile behavior toward me, something keeps drawing me to him. Something more than the physical, although that alone would be enough, if I'm honest.

Tossing every last item of clothing onto my bed, I groan. I forgot my underwear and PJs. Heat rushes my neck and face. I can't even comprehend the thought of going without underwear in this house. My gut flips.

I was so exhausted last night; I didn't get to unpacking and passed out on the bed in my jeans and shirt.

Maybe I could borrow a shirt? The sneaky thought worms its way into my brain. It's just a shirt. I'm sure he wouldn't mind?

I turn and walk from my room and down the hall.

I wander through the house, trying each door until I find another bedroom with a large king bed. Work boots sit under a chair by the door, with a flannel jacket draped over the back of it. Denver's room. I close the door and try the next one.

A clean and neat room, but no personal possessions. Spare room? I keep moving through the house. After minutes of walking around the sprawling home, I come across another hall and a set of doors. They seem to have a side of the house each. I try the first one. Bathroom. I try the next.

The second the door cracks open, his scent hits me. Lewis. I freeze in the hall. If I go in, he will know I was in there. My scent will linger on anything I touch. The thought of sleeping in jeans again or one of my own shirts that barely covers my ass propels me into his space.

The room is neat. I expected it. His bed is a king, the same as his brother's. His theme, grey and white. A stack of books sits on one bedside table, a lamp and more books on the other. That side must be his.

My heart rate kicks up. A wooden dresser sits on the wall to my left. It is old and handcrafted. A small silver bowl sits on top. There is nothing in it. Minimalist. Figures. I grip the two handles and slide the drawer open. Socks, boxer briefs, and a set of wooden boxes are nestled to one side. A set of three—small, medium, and large.

Guilt pangs at my chest for being in his space and opening drawers. I slam the drawer shut and pull open the next one. T-shirts and neatly folded jeans.

Bingo.

After plucking a light-blue shirt from the top, I close the drawer and turn back the way I came. A full-length mirror rests against the opposite wall. I hurry out of the room, closing the door behind me. Now to the bathroom Denver showed me last night.

After wandering through the house for half an hour, admiring the library toward the southern end of the building, the sunroom, and the oversized second living room with the most enormous TV I have ever seen, I reach the large bathroom.

The marble is so clean, it rivals the long wall of mirror above the double vanity. Everything is modern and immaculately clean. I dump the T-shirt on the vanity and close the door. A white claw-foot tub with silver feet sits in one corner. It's practically calling my name.

I pull my phone from my back pocket and place it on the vanity by the T-shirt. Excited for a long, hot bath, I pry my jeans from my hips, losing them to the floor. The button-down shirt goes next, hitting the marble. I run my hands through my curls, loosening them. I pad to the bath and turn the vintage-style chrome knobs. Water pours into the bath.

My phone pings.

I wander over and pick it up. Serena.

> You okay, girl? Did you find a place?

> Hey, I'm good. Found a place and it's safe. You okay?

> Yeah. Miss you lots, though. Hopefully this blows over soon and you can come home.

> I hope so too.

Not that I am in a hurry to do anything but take a long, steaming, amazing bath. I drop the phone back to the vanity and go back to the bath. It's almost half-full already. I look around for soap or something to wash with. In the shower, hanging in a chrome caddy is shampoo, conditioner, and something resembling lavender body wash.

I pull open the glass door to the shower and gather all three in my arms. I sit the hair products on the floor at one end of the bath and pour a generous amount of the lavender body wash into the running water. Fragrant lavender fills the room, mixing with the curling steam rising from the bath. Perfect.

I step into the bath. It's hot. Hissing as I lower myself

into the water, I lie back and prop my head on the end of the bath, turning the water off with my toes. It's absolutely delicious. I wave a hand over the waterline, and it sways.

Holding both hands over the bubbles, palms down, I curl my fingers inward. The water ripples toward me. Using the opposite motion, I send a wave away. I swirl one hand in an upward motion. A small bubble-filled funnel rises. I still my hand and it falls back down.

I close my eyes and sigh. I needed this. Vampires, shadow witches, the Council's demons, college workload, a social life . . . When did everything get so complicated? I let my muscles relax, moaning as my body unwinds from days of being wound up and ready to spin like a top.

I stay in the tub until it turns cold. With hunger eating at my stomach, I stand and grab a towel from the rack by the bath. Moments later, I am dry, and I pull on the T-shirt. Thankfully, it hangs mid-thigh. A much better decision than using one of my own shorter T-shirts.

Even with the brothers not home, it would still feel weird walking around their home with my naked ass for all to see. I should be here by myself for at least three days; that's the plan. The material is soft, and the scent of Lewis launches hundreds of butterflies from the deepest depths of my gut.

Trying to focus on my hunger, I make my way to the kitchen with my phone in hand. I beeline to the fridge. I rest my phone on the island in the center of the kitchen. The double-doored chrome beast is full. How can two people whose primary food source is blood need this much food? Did they put this here for me? I think back to last night's dinner. Maybe, maybe not.

I grab eggs and cheese and bell pepper, turn around, and set them on the counter before spinning around to hunt for more. Tomato, garlic, and a jar of caramelized onion come with me next. I close the fridge door with my foot and bundle my ingredients together before starting the search for a bowl and frying pan.

I find everything I need in the large top drawers of the kitchen island. I crack the eggs into the bowl and whisk them. I pull a large knife from the block to my right and cut the tomato and bell pepper. Popping a piece of tomato into my mouth, I grab the chopped ingredients and toss them into the bowl.

I add a teaspoon of the crushed garlic from the jar and season before giving it one last stir. The pan is a heavy copper-based monolith. I put it on the gas stovetop. My phone pings again.

"Your latest invoice . . . "

Ugh, fees are due. I hope my scholarship went through properly. My phone lights up again and Bluetooth brightens, showing a list of available devices.

House speakers CTN

Castleton?

I tap on the name, and my phone vibrates.

Success!

I tap the music app and scroll through my upbeat

playlists. I pick my favorite playlist and smile as Taylor's voice floods the house. I whoop and spin around the island, dancing to the vibe of "Gorgeous." I grab a wooden spoon from the utensils pot by the hot plate and sing along. "You're so gorgeous."

Cackling at myself, I drop the spoon back in the pot and move to light the stove. I hesitate, fingers shy of the knob. Fire. I can do fire. I turn the knob so the gas is released. I move the pan to the side. Pushing my shoulders back, I hold my hand in front of me, palms up.

The grounding feeling of warmth growing in my core steadies me. I concentrate on the flame I want to see. The pungent tang of gas increases. It's now or never. I open my eyes, curl my hands, and uncurl them toward the stove with a flick. Flames burst, and I wince. They die down, leaving a neat ring of blue flame.

Oh my god, I did it!

"Yes!" I dance on the spot for a moment before placing the pan over the flame. It stays on and the gas fumes subside.

I did it.

It's the most controlled use of fire I have ever been able to muster. The grin on my face goes from ear to ear. I bob with the music, pouring the egg into the pan. It hisses at me, and I poke a tongue at it. My stomach rumbles as I push the egg around the heat with the spatula, scrambling as I go.

The song changes.

"Don't Blame Me" thunders through the house.

The air turns electric.

I scrape the cooked eggs onto a plate and turn off the stove as I set the pan down. I dig into the hot eggs and shovel a forkful into my mouth. It's hot, but so good. I open the caramelized onion and spoon a generous dollop on top. The fragrance makes my mouth water. I stab a clump of egg onto my fork and swipe it through the onion. The flavor bursts in my mouth, and I moan, gripping the countertop with one hand.

Movement catches my eye from a few feet away. I drag my gaze from the plate. The fork falls from my hand and clatters to the floor.

Taylor keeps singing *about love making her me crazy*.

Lewis stands, rigid as always, staring with darkened eyes.

My mouth parts, and my breath stills. Heat floods my core, radiating to every inch of my body. I feel crimson cover my neck and face. I grab the T-shirt and pull it around myself.

Lewis tilts his head, his eyes darkening to almost black. Every curve I have is accentuated by the tighter fit. I drop the shirt and fold my arms across my heaving chest. A heartbeat later, he stands in my space. I raise my face to meet his gaze. My thoughts are a muddled, tangled mess.

Useless.

"That's my shirt," he rasps.

This close, I can see the blood bounding in his veins.

The tension in every single muscle. How much self-control does it take to be Lewis?

"Yes," I manage to whisper.

I step back.

He steps forward. I hold his gaze. He pushes a stray piece of hair from my face.

"If you wanted clothes, all you had to do was ask, Sunshine."

Sunshine?

"I—"

He presses a finger to my lips with a soft growl. Butterflies in my stomach turn to fire-breathing dragons. My chest heaves, and I let my arms fall to my side. He closes his eyes and lets his head fall back, dragging his finger over my bottom lip and letting it fall.

I wet my lips with my tongue and touch his jaw with a shaking hand. His eyes snap open and he grabs my wrist, lowering his head. His scorching gaze burns into mine.

"Don't." The word is pure gravel.

I suck a breath through a tiny moan. "Why not?"

He sets his jaw and growls. "Just"—he drops my wrist and steps back—"don't."

A second later, he is gone.

The front door slams.

I stand, fire coursing through my veins. My core is absolute liquid. If I had panties on, they would be soaked through.

Fuck.

I'm so screwed.

CHAPTER 15

LEWIS

I run through dark spaces in the rows of pines. The crescent moon hangs above the canopy. Feet hardly touching the ground, fire eats me from the inside out. That was the closest I have ever been to losing self-control. Samantha in my T-shirt, no underwear, dancing around. It was like watching the sun explode and loving every second it rips you apart as it turns into a black hole.

I catch the scent of a large animal. The musty, fur-filled, warm blood scent penetrates the burning desire commandeering my body. I take in lungful after lungful of the crisp forest air, letting every earthy aroma distract me from what I want. Samantha.

I don't want to bite her.

I don't want to feed on her.

I want her.

All of her.

Every fucking inch of her.

Fuck.

Fuck, fuck, fuck.

I slide to a halt, leaving a long path of debris worn into the ground. I slam a fist into the nearest tree. Sleeping birds scatter, squawking in disgust. The scent from moments ago is much stronger. I search the area. A black bear is making its way through the trees to the north of me. I stalk around it for a minute. Its heart pounds in its oversized chest. I pad over to where it eats. It startles and rises to its two back feet, towering over me. Good.

I step closer.

It swipes at me, and I snatch it up with one hand, crushing its bones. It howls, throwing its head back. I lunge, sinking my teeth into its thundering neck vein. Warm copper drenches the front of my shirt, turning white Armani to bleeding red. I suck the life from it in seconds.

The fire in my core remains. The only way to satiate it is currently walking around pantie-less in my house. I run both hands through my hair before dragging them down my face, not caring that I'm running the animal's blood through my hair and all down my face. I roar, the last of the wildlife fleeing around me. The sound echoes around the dark forest.

I make my way to a small stream trickling between the ridges and bend down. The turbulent water throws a distorted, tortured version of my face back at me. But that's how I feel.

Tortured.

Tormented.

Wanting someone so desperately, it physically hurts to be in her space without touching her. Without devouring her with my mouth, hands, and whatever part of me I can. Fire courses through my veins when she is close to me, and it is ten times worse than the scorching heat of hunger at the back of my throat. I fall back onto my seat and hang my head. These are dangerous thoughts. Ones that see her and me pay the highest price if we are caught.

Part of me thinks the risk would be worth the mating bond and all it means. But this isn't a one-sided affair. She has a choice. If her choice is not me, I will find a way to sever the bond. I will let her go. I won't let Samantha suffer. That would be the hardest thing for me to endure.

Sunshine shouldn't be smothered by storm clouds and snuffed out like it's not the most beautiful thing in existence. As if reminding me of my current situation, the moon appears from behind traveling clouds. Its beams pierce the rough waters, scattering light over the smooth round rocks on the stream's undulating, earthy bed.

I inhale, deep and slow. Vampire. Just short of the tree line on the other side of the stream.

Curious.

The hood over their head prevents me from seeing their face, but by the long, wavy locks of brunette hair and the hourglass shape . . . Female.

It isn't unusual to come across other vampires from time

to time. But this one is somehow familiar. She turns and disappears into the trees, and I let my gaze drop back to the water.

Perhaps I should let the curse play out. Then she will be safe. No bond to put her in the firing line of the Council. And whatever Anjelica wants with her will surely dry up after she has no reason to stay here, and I'm gone.

Resolved, I push up to my knees and lean over the stream, washing my hair and face clean of the half-dried blood. I wander back through the pines for a while before picking up the pace to get home.

The house is quiet. Dim light from inside spills onto the porch, and I open the front door. Closing it behind me, I walk to the kitchen. It's spotless, everything that had been spread over the counter earlier must have been cleaned and packed away. A lamp is on in the living room and a light is on in the hallway leading to my side of the house. My blue shirt is folded up, sitting on the counter.

My gut drops. Did she leave? I didn't check to see if her car was still here. My heart thunders in my chest. I snatch up the shirt, and her scent hits me. The heat in my core from earlier bursts to life. I track my way to her room and halt short of the door.

It's open.

She's asleep. Her heartbeats slow and steady, her breaths shallow. Golden curls are sprawled over the pillow. I let my gaze wander over her neck, her collarbone, the undershirt she must have found somewhere in lieu of my shirt.

I lock my jaw. The thought of her feeling hurt by our interaction claws at my gut. I step into her room. She stirs, as if aware of my presence even in her sleep.

"Samantha?" I choke out.

She rolls over and brushes hair from her face. In the dim light, the features of her face are so elegant. I move to the bedside and stare down at her as she lifts her eyes to meet mine.

"What is it?" Her voice is raw from sleep.

"I'm sorry if I upset you."

Her brows pull down as she pushes to sit up, folding her arms over her chest. "Why?"

"What do you mean, why?"

"Why are you sorry? That would imply you care."

My breath hitches. Of course, I care. That's the fucking problem.

"Why would I not care, Samantha?"

"You're not giving off warm and fuzzy vibes, Sullivan." She sighs and leans against the headboard. Her hands fall to her lap. The rounds of her chest rise and fall with every breath. The fire turns to lava in my center, and I move a step back.

She tilts her head as if to say 'see, my point exactly.'

"It's not that I don't care. I only have so much self-control. I don't won't to hurt you."

"So, you are an arrogant ass because you're trying to protect me?" She scoffs. "Does that work, Lewis? Do girls fall for that crap?"

"Girls?"

"Women, whatever, you know what I mean."

"Yes, I do, and I wouldn't know, Sunshine. I don't go around throwing out lines for whatever nefarious purpose you seem to have dreamed up in your head."

And we are back to square one.

Fuck.

This girl—this woman—is going to be the death of me.

I curb the urge to laugh out loud, acutely aware of the irony of the thought, and walk to the door, not looking back. "Get some sleep, Sunshine."

Her heart rate spikes. I have no control over the corners of my mouth pulling up into a gratuitous half smile as I walk to my room.

My room is smothered by her scent. It's fucking everywhere. In an instant, my body is tense. I pull the shirt from my back and toss it to the chair by the door. I slip into the en suite and loosen the buckle on my belt before unzipping my jeans and letting them crash to the marble floor. I turn the knobs and wait for steam to fill the room.

Stepping under the hot water, I feel every single drop blasting from the shower. The intense pressure of the water does little to curb the hardness that developed the minute I stepped into my room. I can't stop the visions of her in my shirt running on repeat through my mind. If I don't find release soon, I will lose it completely.

One hand on the tile above my head, I grip my hard length. Imagining lifting my shirt from her gorgeous curves and over her head, I close my eyes. Oblivion follows.

⟩⟩⟩●⟨⟨⟨

The smile plastered on her face is fake. Samantha passes me the rack of toast and the butter. She has been up for a while, by the looks of the feast piled on the dining table. Guilt pangs in my chest. After all the moments we have shared, this is how she responds when I hurt her. My heart cracks.

She busies herself with buttering toast before spreading jam over the top. Biting into it, she nods toward my food. I pick up a slice and bite into it, not taking my eyes from her and hoping my face isn't giving away my every thought.

"You don't like toast?" she asks.

I swallow the mouthful and place the slice on the plate. "I like the breakfast. I didn't get much sleep last night, that's all."

"Something bothering you?" Her eyes are laced with worry.

"Not your concern. Eat up. We are leaving in ten minutes."

"You go ahead. I don't have class 'til eleven."

"No. We go together; that's the whole point of you being here. To be safe."

"I am not going to get into trouble between this house and the university parking lot."

"I'm driving you, end of story."

"No! There is no end in sight, Lewis." She stands, knocking the table. The jug of juice she put out wobbles before settling. "I'm not some defenseless human you can boss around. I can look after myself." She looks to the floor; she doesn't believe her own words. Slowly, she lifts her gaze and sighs. "Besides, it's only twenty minutes from here to school, what could possibly happen?"

I tilt my head to one side and curb a growl, the frown on my face sees one grow over hers.

"I'm driving myself, Lewis. That's the end of this story!"

I throw my hands up in defeat. "Fine."

I can get home in two minutes and tail her as she drives to school.

She narrows her eyes. "Really?"

"Really. You're on your own, witch."

She pokes her tongue and screws up her face at me. I laugh so hard she stops frozen, her face slack and lips parted. That face was hilarious and gorgeous rolled into one elegant pout. It's the happiest sliver of a moment I have had for decades.

She shakes her head at me and stalks out.

After leaving alone and parking Den's truck at work, I ran home through the woods and backroads until I was hanging out in the secluded bushy forest short of my own house. I can imagine Denver's smug face if he saw me right now.

By 10:55 a.m., Samantha pulls into the parking lot, and I make my way to my lecture hall, waiting for her to file through the doors with the rest of her cohort. She trails behind the rest of the class. I wander toward the door and greet students as they enter. Their confused responses remind me this is not my normal behavior.

Samantha steps into the room and stops as she looks me up and down. Her face pinches, and she tries to suppress a smile, but it wins, lighting up her face. She reaches toward my head, and I flinch, waiting for the heat in my core to scorch through my skin.

It flickers and quietens as she closes the space between us. Her hand brushes my hair. She lowers it in front of my face. Between her fingers is a small twig adorned with green pine needles.

"All by myself, hey?" She grabs my hand and turns it palm up, dropping the twig onto it. My heart is flinging against my chest so hard, I'm sure the entire room can hear it.

"Better safe than strung up by Anjelica or some demented demon." I curse under my breath as she walks away. She turns back before walking up the steps to her usual spot in the center row. Her face has transformed to stone. I have officially pissed off Samantha Williams. After her peace offering of breakfast this morning, I would feel guilty, if it wasn't for the fact her staying alive is far more important than her feelings today.

I start the lecture with a warning about the upcoming midterm for this class before diving into the content on the slides. Students sit, shifting in their seats occasionally as we cover the intriguing topics of first year archaeology linguistics. I catch Samantha's gaze, and she forces a satirical smile before dropping her gaze to her notepad. Back to our tense peace truce, it is.

The air in the room plummets. Students look around for the draft, hugging their arms around themselves. The hairs on the back of my neck rise. Only one thing is preceded by a frigid drop in temperature—a shadow witch spell.

Fuck.

I connect with Samantha's focus. Her eyes are wide, stunned. She sits frozen in place on her seat. Through the muddle of beating hearts, I try to home in on hers. It's fast. Too fast.

She knows what's happening. Tendrils of dark fog drift into the room from the seam where the floor meets the wall, before it begins to also spill down the walls.

"Everybody out!" I yell.

Students fly from their seats, screaming about fire and smoke. Samantha sits, unable to move, fear lacing her eyes. I usher out the cohort, pushing stragglers through the door.

I rush to the center row and lay a hand on her face. She whimpers and tries to speak.

"Shhh." I press a finger to her lips.

The gut-churning feeling of helplessness rages through my body. I grab her under the arms, lifting her from her seat. She screams in pain, and I lower her back down.

"It's no use, Lewis. You can't shift her."

Anjelica.

Fuck.

I spin back at her words. A second later, I have the shadow witch pinned to the front wall of the lecture hall with one hand. "Let her go." The words roll out of my throat with a low rumble.

Anjelica tries for a strangled laugh, and I hoist her up the wall further. It's too easy. She curls her hands and the blood in my veins turns to barbed wire. Pain rips through every limb. I sink to my knees in front of her. She lands on her feet and smooths out her clothes, a smirk on her face.

Another whimper leaves Samantha's lips.

I growl, curling my hands into fists, and lunge at Anjelica. Pain lances through my blood, flesh, and bone. But the force of my fist to her chest penetrates whatever magical defenses she has around herself.

Crack.

Her face falls in shock. Even the best shadow witches are no match for us when a mate is provoked to protect their bonded. I will rip her limbs from her fucking body if she doesn't let Samantha go. "Let her go. Now, Anjelica!"

"Fine," she pants through short breaths, "she can go. But you stay."

She straightens, recovering too quickly. "Ugh, you vampires are so dramatic with your bonds, so ridiculous."

Shut the fuck up, witch. The last thing I need is this demented bitch spilling something I'm not ready for Samantha to hear.

I step back and jump over the chairs to where Samantha sits. I grab her under the arms. This time, she is limp and pliable. Once I have her up from the seat, I scoop her up and take her to the door.

"Lewis," she rasps.

"It's fine. I'll be out in a moment." I force a small smile and nod.

"Okay?" Her brows pinch, and she grips my shirt. I swallow past the lump in my throat and try to ignore the flames licking at my insides with her against my chest. Her scent surrounding me. Her skin on mine.

I put her down and steady her with both hands. She steps out of my hold and wraps her arms around herself, eyes scanning her surroundings. Smart girl.

I storm inside, ready to take on Anjelica or face my fate. I stop. The room seems empty.

"Does she know?"

I spin, following the voice. She sits in the furthest chair at the top of the tiered seats. Checking her fucking nails as she dangles the top half of her body over the back of the chair in front of her, one leg crossed over the other twisted to one side.

"Know what?" I growl, knowing perfectly well what she is asking. How the hell did she find out?

"Does the witch know she's your mate?"

"What do you want, Anjelica?" I grind out. Tingling starts in my fingers, and my gut flips. Jesus Christ, could this get any worse?

"Oh, just one more thing."

A scream penetrates the wooden doors.

Samantha.

Apparently, it can.

Her gaze flicks to toward the sounds. "And I have already acquired it. Honestly, Lewis, you make life so easy for me. It's so darling of you. Such a lovely lecture hall you have here, but I don't need to hang around." She vanishes from the chair and appears three rows in front of me. Standing with her hands outstretched, she twists her hands in a swirling motion. The wire from before hardens in my blood, contorting my body. Pain filters through me, and I gasp for breath, hunching over in agony before my knees hit the floor.

I fight my way back to my feet. The door opens and closes. Anjelica's hold on me eases. Samantha's friend Serena stands in the doorway. Her face is wrong. Instead of shock, she looks annoyed. They know each other. And well, by the way Serena shakes her head at Anjelica. The old witch curses at Serena and waves her off. She doesn't move.

Another scream.

Serena flinches.

I use the distraction to fly through the door and outside. Struggle sounds from the parking lot. I'm there in an instant. Three shadow scouts are manhandling Samantha into a van.

"Get off me!" she screams, kicking them. Every human stares, stunned. No, frozen. Anjelica has frozen them, immobilizing each one, so no one can help. They won't even remember what they saw. I take out the closest witch, tearing his head from his shoulders, before the others back off. I stalk into their space and grab their necks with two one-handed grips. Squeezing until their necks snap, I let them crash to the ground. I turn back to Samantha.

Fire dances in her palms, but her face is rigid with fear still.

"Samantha?" I hold both hands in front of me.

Her focus snaps, and she meets my gaze.

"We need to leave, right now," I say, lowering my hands. She nods and steps away from the van. Her hands ball to fists and the flames snuff to smoke. I grab her hand—it's still cool to the touch—and lead her to the truck. I open the door, and she slides into the passenger's seat without a word. I drop into the driver's seat and fire up the engine.

A moment later, we are flying down the asphalt. She gazes out the window. Her chest rises and falls with shudders. Saltiness fills the car. We can't stop until we are safely on our property. I push the old girl faster and wind up the one-way road faster than she ever has before. I park and kill the engine.

"Sam?"

She turns her head to face me. Tears streak down her face. Her hands tremble in her lap.

"Are you still in pain?"

She shakes her head.

I get out of the truck and come around to open her door. I offer a hand, and she slips hers into it. She rises on wobbly legs but forces herself to stand tall.

"We should get inside." I lead her behind me, her hand wrapped in mine still.

She gazes at the porch, looking at nothing. I lead her up the steps and open the door. She stops short of the threshold.

I turn back.

She swallows. "Thank you." Her words are barely a whisper.

I pull her into a hug, and she lays her palms on my chest, resting her cheek between them, her head under my chin. For the first time in weeks, the fire plaguing me in my core settles with her touch.

Like some sort of ironic joke on any male whose mating bond has snapped, the constant fire only ebbs when a female comes willingly, ensuring males behave. Something to do with the right type of endorphins. Denver's area of expertise, not mine.

I fold her in my arms and drop my face into her hair, breathing her in.

God, I could get used to this.

CHAPTER 16

SAMMIE

Lewis is the storm and the fury all rolled into one. It only took a split second for him to kill three shadow witches. And the only thing I felt was grateful. Not scared or stunned—well, maybe a little stunned at the raw power he has when he needs it. I sit on the couch, nursing a mug of tea. He paces the living room floor, talking fast to Denver. I'm pretty sure there will be a worn path in the marble by the time he is done fussing.

Things have quickly gone from an inconvenience to dire. The power Anjelica had over me was nothing I have felt before. And what's worse, I had absolutely no defense against her. None. She could have easily stolen the air from my lungs, stopped my heart, or twisted my neck.

I could feel what she was capable of, and I could also feel she wanted me alive. For some reason, she needs me. Or wants me where she can control me. That's all I could garner from the bond she had to make with me to hold my useless ass on the chair. While she tampered with me like a spoiled brat with a new toy.

"Fine, I'll make the arrangements. You keep looking."

Lewis taps the screen on his phone and shoves it into his back pocket. A second later, he is standing in front of me. I stare mesmerized into the amber liquid of the warm tea, too ashamed to meet his gaze.

"Samantha?"

I close my eyes and hope if I wait long enough, he will leave and retreat to the study, like every other time he has since I came here.

"Look at me, Samantha." His voice is gravel.

Tears burn behind my eyes, and I swallow past the lump in my throat. God, I am pathetic. Now I'm going to cry? When did I get so emotional? I keep my head down, and he steps back.

"I need you to pack your things. We leave in ten minutes."

I nod.

He leaves, heading toward his room. I push up from the sofa and pad to my room. Setting the tea on the dresser, I grab my bag and start shoving my clothes and things into it. How did things get so bad, so quickly? Grandma had told me stories about how shadow witches can interfere and ruin people's lives. I always thought they were just stories.

What about my studies? I cannot afford to miss class for however long. Why can't we stay here? At least then I could attend class virtually. If we end up somewhere with no internet, I will fall behind. I toss the piece of clothing in my hand onto the bag and storm from the room, stalking my way across the house and through the hall to Lewis's room.

His door is open. I walk in and prop my hands on my hips. "I can't leave."

He turns from his packing and moves into my space. I lift my head and let my gaze incinerate his.

"You don't have a choice, Sunshine."

"Stop calling me that."

"No."

"I can't afford to miss class. Unless you can guarantee me good internet service to attend class virtually, I'm not leaving."

He huffs a laugh and returns to his packing. "I don't know whether to be impressed or annoyed."

"I don't care what you feel; I'm not jeopardizing my studies for this."

His hands are still on his bag, and he growls, low and soft. "I am trying to keep you alive."

"Why? What's it to you if a shadow witch is hunting me, Lewis?"

He turns, slow, too slow. I step back, folding my arms across my chest, face screwing into concern.

I inhale.

He stands taller.

I exhale.

He is in my space, his face so close to mine, I can feel

his breath, smell him, see his blood pumping through the veins in his now tight neck. His dark brown eyes study mine for a heartbeat. "How is it that you cannot comprehend this?"

"Maybe it's because you only give me half the information," I say, dropping my hands to my sides. My breaths shorten as my gaze leaves his eyes, and I study his face—his jaw, his lips, his throat as his Adam's apple bobs.

"What else do you need to know, Samantha?" he grinds out, leaning a little closer.

God, I so want to touch him.

My heart flings against my chest, and I swallow as I raise my eyes to meet his. Fire laces his, along with something far stronger. Desire.

Holy shit.

My breath stops.

"I—" I press a hand to his chest, and he closes his eyes. The thought that I would willingly go anywhere with this man slips past my rational mind. "Where are we going?"

"Anywhere you want, Sunshine." Every syllable is raw. His body is wound tight, every muscle taut. I let my hand slide down his chest a little.

His breath stops.

"Lewis?"

"Mhmmm."

"Why do you call me Sunshine?"

He opens his eyes and meets my gaze, sucking in a breath. "One day I'll tell you." A small smile blooms on his face. He looks so happy. His eyes soften and he wraps a hand around mine, still on his body. I look down to where his skin touches mine. The front of his jeans bulges from his body responding to my touch.

Fuck.

I mean, Hail Mary, or whatever it is good girls are supposed to say instead of thinking about what I would find if he let my hand wander.

"Fine." I remove my hand from his and move out of his space. The heat that's been pooling in my center since I laid my hand on his body is almost too much to bear. "I'll be ready in five." I turn and head back to my room.

His door shuts behind me, followed by a soft thud, like his head met the wood, followed by a low groan. I chuckle.

At least it's not just me.

·)᛫)᛫)᛫●᛫(᛫(᛫(·

L ewis sits in Denver's truck, engine idling with a low rumble. Much like its current driver. I smile to myself. I throw my bag into the back before opening the passenger door and sliding into the seat.

"So, we can go anywhere I want?"

"If anywhere you want is an isolated cabin in the heart of the Alaskan wilderness, sure." He throws me a serious look.

I roll my eyes at him and groan. Great. Just great. How the hell am I supposed to study off-grid? "Are you serious?"

"Deadly," he says, shifting the stick and letting the truck roll forward. I know exactly how deadly Lewis can be. If he thinks we need to leave to be safe despite his unnatural ninja abilities, I guess we're leaving.

I flick Serena a text telling her I'm going away for a few days. I hate lying to her, but I don't want her involved in this. I stare out the window. Rows of pines fly past as we travel north toward Alaska. I shake my head at the thought.

"If you're worried about your studies, don't be. I can help you catch up or fix any papers you flunk on."

"What? I am not cheating my way through a degree."

"You would rather fail?"

"You know what I mean. How long will we be away? I need all the information you can give me. And"—I square my shoulders to face him—"any you have previously left out."

He glances at me, returning his focus to the road and his grip on the wheel tightens.

"Anjelica is after you and me. Me because of the curse. You because—" His pulse hammers in his neck. "You because she may assume you would be helping me."

"How could I help you?"

"Elemental witches can break the curse."

"What? You think I can break it?"

"No. I don't think you can."

"Thanks," I say flatly.

He looks at me, brows lowered. "Only an experienced or very powerful elemental witch can break it. Even then, it's dangerous. The magic used to bind the hex can be fatal for a witch not strong enough. I have seen it with my own eyes." The last three words drift off as if he struggles to say them out loud.

"Oh." I return to looking out the window. I grab my pendant and roll it through my fingers. How powerful would be powerful enough to cure his curse?

"What if she dies?" I say, surprising myself and startling Lewis.

"Who dies?"

"Anjelica. What if she dies? Are you released from it then?"

"Maybe, I don't know. No one seems to. Don't worry about it. Keeping you safe is more important." His eyes don't leave the road.

So, Lewis knows what I am. Why didn't he insist I try to help him when we first met? Can vampires have a conscience? Kindness? Does he have a soul? I lay my head back and let the hum of the engine lull me to sleep.

·)·)·)·●·(·(·(·(·

Four days later, we roll down a narrow driveway toward a log cabin. Rustic would be an understatement. It's white everywhere. Snow covers everything. I shiver in my seat, rubbing my hands up and down my arms. Even with three layers ending with my warmest coat, I am still cold.

Every breath creates a cloud in front of my face. Lewis parks and kills the engine. I crack the truck door open and step onto the glittering white ground. The tall pines surrounding the cabin in every direction are adorned with piles of snow, their branches weighed down under the icy mounds.

"Get yourself inside before you freeze to death," Lewis says, walking around the back and grabbing up the bags. I pad up the three steps to the porch and grab the knob on the front door. It's unlocked and opens. Huddling in my coat, I walk inside to find a small wooden kitchen and a large hearth with a sofa in front of it. A throw blanket that looks deliciously warm hangs over the back of the sofa.

Three doors are dispersed along the wall to my right. I try the first one. Toilet. Next door, a large shower and vanity sit. It's clean and light. Third door is a bedroom. A queen bed with a small dresser and two bedside tables are the only furniture in the room that reaches to the back of the cabin. The back wall has a large window looking out to the forest and a large bare space between the trees. On the opposite wall to the bed is another hearth, a little smaller than the one in the living room.

Two bags thump to the ground by the door behind me. I turn back. Lewis is leaning on the doorframe, brows lowered.

"There's only one bed," I say softly.

"I'll take the sofa." His mouth moves to a thin line. His arms wrap around his chest, hands snug under his arms.

"Okay." I walk to where the bags lie at his feet and pick mine up. I huff a laugh, and he smiles a little, studying me before taking his to the dresser. I feel the crimson heat crawl up my neck.

Shit.

Playing house with that face is going to be the end of me.

Three drawers make up the piece. He opens the second one and starts unpacking his things into it. When he's done, he stores his bag in the small closet by the door to the en suite. He moves back to the door and places both hands on the frame above him. His sweater lifts, exposing the sculpted lines of his stomach and the outline of muscles making a V that disappears behind his belt and jeans.

"You take the top drawer. I'll light the fires."

I offer back a smile. He studies my face for a moment before he releases his hold on the doorframe and walks into the living room.

Goddess save me.

After a minute, I remember what I was doing and dump my bag onto the bed and start packing my clothes into the top drawer. The front door opens and shuts. A moment later, Lewis appears with an armful of snow-dusted split logs. His forearms flex with the movement as he lowers them into the wood storage box.

With all my things unpacked and laptop set up on the kitchen table, I try to create a hotspot from my phone. It barks back at me. No service. Crap.

"You can get some service in town. We have to go in for food tomorrow. There is enough in the pantry for tonight," Lewis says as he stacks the wood into the hearth in a triangle fashion. A few moments later, the fire is blazing. I could have helped with that.

He wanders to the kitchen and opens a cupboard. I tap on my phone and hold it above my head, desperate for even one bar of service.

"It's no use, Sunshine." He hands me a glass of red wine.

I eye the glass and its contents for a moment before plucking it from his fingers. They brush against mine, and the warmth of them makes me crave more of his heat. I take a long sip of the wine and swallow. It burns all the way down, and I cough. He sips his wine before making his way to the sofa.

I follow and sit on the opposite end, not trusting my body not to go hunting for his warmth again. He stares into the fire, quiet. I pull the blanket around my shoulders and take another sip. Relishing the heat it brings. My shivers subside, and I tuck my feet under myself and lean back onto the sofa. Maybe this won't be so bad, after all.

Stuck in a snow-covered cabin with wine and a gorgeous guy. Most girls I know would die for this. The thought is followed immediately by the realization that the reason I am here is to stay alive. Dying is a very real possibility for me.

I let my gaze wander to Lewis and study him, every inch of him. His sleeves are pushed up, forearm working as he takes another sip. The overwhelming desire to straddle his lap, grab his face with both hands, and plant my mouth on his is burning me up from the inside. Heat pools in my stomach, low. My breath hitches and my heart paces up a storm. He turns and stares at me, eyes darkening, blackness filling up almost every part of his pupils. His jaw tenses.

I raise a hand and glide my knuckles over the tensed part of his face. He flinches, stands, and places his glass on the small side table. He's so fast; I don't even see him leave. The open door bangs against the wall. Frigid air rushes in, filling the room, chilling the space where he sat and the part of my heart that had finally opened to him.

The part I had been fighting to keep shut for weeks.

CHAPTER 17

LEWIS

After an awkward trip into town to grab supplies, I stir the pot, blending together the tomato sauce, garlic, and herbs for my favorite pasta dish, pomodoro. Samantha hasn't spoken more than a few words to me since we were on the sofa yesterday afternoon, keeping to herself shut away in the bedroom.

The small chunk of parmesan I found at the convenience store sits on the wooden chopping board. I stare at the aged cheese and compare it to the fresh, young Roma tomatoes. The cheese is reminiscent of me, hard and sharp. The tomatoes, relenting under my touch and easily bruised, are Samantha.

At least, that is how it feels. For some reason, every time she tries to get close to me, I screw it up. I can't even manage indifference without damaging her feelings. How the hell am I supposed to contain this bond around her in a confined space without Denver as a buffer? If we make it out of this fiasco with Anjelica and the Council, I have no doubt her resentment toward me will turn to an eternal hatred.

If the risks were not as great, if being different species didn't carry dire consequences for this bond, I would—

"Dinner ready?"

I drag my focus from the violently bubbling sauce to Samantha's face. Stone, that's what it resembles. I deserve no less.

"Almost. Grab some bowls?"

"Fine."

She pads around the counter and pulls out two bowls, sitting them by the stove. I try to offer her a smile, but she turns away.

Killing the gas and snuffing the flame, I drain the spaghetti and dish out generous portions into both bowls. Samantha uncorks a bottle of red wine and hunts for glasses.

"Next cupboard to your left," I offer.

She opens the door without looking at me before placing two glasses on the bench and pouring two drinks. She putters around, setting the table and carrying over the drinks as I plate up the meal. The moment of domestic bliss makes me ache for it to be real. I set a bowl at each place and wait for her to sit. She stares at me for a moment, gaze laced with annoyance, and pulls out her chair and sits. I follow her actions and pick up my fork, twirling the steaming spaghetti around my fork.

Watching as she takes her first bite, I study her face, hoping for some kind of clue as to how far down the I-hate-Lewis scale she has slid. She closes her eyes after slurping up a strand of spaghetti. A small moan rumbles in her throat. I suppress a smile and continue eating.

"Okay, so we are on the same page, I would like for us to be at least civil to each other while we are here," she says softly.

Her words catch me off guard. I tilt my head, lowering my brows. Civilized?

She digs her fork into the spaghetti and turns it. "You know, it's a small space. If you don't want me in yours, I understand. I'll keep out of your way. Pay me the same courtesy."

"Samantha, what are you—"

"I'm sorry about last night. I obviously got my wires crossed about this whole thing. If we could forget it, that would be great."

I clear my throat, swallowing past the lump that rapidly materialized. She is all but confessing her attraction to me. At least physically, anyway. The amount of pheromones she was giving off last night was enough to send any male into a frenzy, let alone one with an unrequited bond. My heart thunders in my chest.

Focus, Lewis.

This changes nothing.

The situation is still the same. The Council still punishes interspecies bonds. Anjelica would still use her up and spit her up to torture me if she realizes we have acted on the bond. She would revel in it. I cannot let that happen. I school myself to indifference.

"Whatever you say, Sunshine."

She winces and shifts her gaze back to her bowl. I twirl my pasta around the fork and eat to stop my mouth from running off with everything I want to tell her. Every stupid thought I have had about her. The very kind that would put her in even more danger. Or worse.

I finish the meal and take my wine to the sofa. Samantha retreats to her room. I open the book I brought on ancient mythos, species, and their history and settle into the sofa. From behind the closed door to the room, Samantha paces, her heart rate climbing.

Her breaths quicken. The footsteps slow and the bed makes a low squeak. I put the book down and stand, placing the wine glass on the side table. A second later, I am by her door, hesitating. Do I knock? Sit back down? Go in? I run both hands through my hair.

A sniff is followed by a whimper. The tang of salt penetrates under the bedroom door. She's crying.

Fuck.

I am the world's biggest asshole. I open the door without knocking and move to where she sits on the bed, her head in her hands. The fire in the hearth is almost out, the bed made but rumpled. I stop inches from her space. The only thing I cannot bear is her hurting. She can be indifferent to me, annoyed, sassy, and resentful; I don't care. But hurt and upset I will not stand for.

"Sunshine?"

"Go away, Lewis."

"No."

"Why not? This whole thing is a disaster. I can't even leave the cabin. You barely tolerate me. I have no connection to the real world up here. I feel like I am suffocating. There's all this space," she says, waving her arms toward the window, to the clearing outside made by the frozen lake now covered with thick snow, "and I can't even be outside." She drags her hands down her face, letting them fall into her lap.

Her face is twisted with pain and frustration. I swallow, hands hanging by my sides. "Maybe we could go for a walk later? I have some papers I need to finish, but maybe in a couple of hours?"

She looks up, her eyes red from crying and her cheeks wet. "Whatever," she utters, shaking her head.

"I know this is not ideal, but it is only temporary."

"'Til when? Do you even know?"

Until the next moon. If I'm out of the picture, she is safe. "It will all be over by the next moon." I turn to walk out. She grabs my hand. I stop, still facing the door.

"You mean when the curse ends?"

I turn back slowly, gaze dropping to where her hand is

tight around mine. "Yes. Then you can go back to your life. And this will all be over, Samantha."

"What? No." Her face twists again and my heart aches like it is caught in a vice. I move into her space and brush my hand across her cheek. "I'm sorry."

She raises her face, her big blue eyes meeting mine. "Don't be sorry; fight. How can you just let her win?"

My hand on her face wavers as my breathing shallows. It's not that simple. And if I am gone, she is safe. "I'm not going to make a choice that puts you in further danger. I have caused you enough grief."

She stands, and I am forced back a step.

"Don't use me as your excuse to bow out." Her words are fierce, matching the fire in her eyes, the curl of her fingers to fists.

"I have had a long life. I won't jeopardize yours."

She thumps the heel of her hand into my chest, and I falter backward. Her breaths are sharp and quick. Her heart races. Fire in my center bursts to life. She moves closer, and I step back until my back hits the wall by the door. She keeps walking, closing the space between us, and studies my face, her gaze hovering over my mouth, then down my throat. "Fight, or I will do it for you."

"Taking on Anjelica is suicide," I breathe.

She flings her hand downward. Flames burst over her skin, and she throws the ball of flame into the dying embers. It roars back to life.

"Tell me about the bond."

Her question startles me. And I inhale, taking in her scent. So close to me. She is too close. The heat in my center waxes bigger. I force my hands to stay by my sides. "What about it?"

"You only get one. Have you had yours?"

I was not expecting that. "Yes, I mean no—"

Her eyes drill into mine. "Has your bond snapped, Lewis?"

"Yes, but—" I lean my head against the wall and inhale. "It's not reciprocated."

"Oh," she says, and her face falls.

"I have no intention of acting on it. She is free to do as she pleases."

"Another vampire, then?"

I slam my mouth shut, not trusting the words lodged in my throat.

"It's fine." She presses a hand onto my chest and steps back, the movement too slow, as if moving away from me is as hard for her as it is for me. "You don't have to tell me. It's none of my business."

I stand, stunned.

She makes her way back to the bed and picks up her phone. Her body settles, breaths slowing, heart slowing, body relaxing. Mine, on the other hand, is strung out like a marionette on new strings. I walk out the door, closing it behind me.

I grab the stack of papers on the kitchen counter and sit

on the sofa. I pick up the wine and scan the front of the first essay. I could mark them on the computer, but old-school methods will be forever lodged in my brain. I mark with a red pen, then with tracked changes in the digital version before uploading to the student portal for release at a later date.

Samantha walks around the kitchen before grabbing her coat from the brass hooks on the wall. Bundling up, she heads for the door.

"Don't go past the tree line," I say, trying to catch her gaze. She ignores me and stalks out the door. She walks across the porch and down the few steps. Her boots crunch the fresh snow, and I count the paces as she moves from the cabin. The woods start around thirty paces.

Twelve paces.

Crunch, crunch, crunch.

I run the pen over the first sentence in the paragraph, not seeing the words or taking in their meaning.

Eighteen paces.

I start again. The tip of the red pen smears the first word.

Twenty-two.

A tug starts in my chest. I track the pen across the first line, willing concentration to show itself.

Twenty-seven.

Second sentence. The words muddle into nothingness, melding into a black line of odd shapes.

Thirty-two.

Crunch, crack, snap. Crunch.

Sliding the papers from my lap onto the sofa, I drop the pen on top.

Thirty-nine.

I stand, realizing the steps are coming from the wrong side of the cabin.

The lake. She is walking toward the lake.

Crack. Crack. Crunch.

I fly out the door and around the back of the cabin. She is stalking her way across the snow, hands shoved tight in her coat pockets. I slide to a halt at the edge of the frozen river. "Stop!"

She spins and pulls a face at me.

"Samantha, stop where you are!"

"You don't get to tell me what to do, Lewis. For god's sake, you won't even help yourself! Don't you dare get off lecturing me!" She spins back and walks on, her pace faster, harder with her newfound mood.

"STOP! Sam, please, stop!"

The ice cracks. She turns, her terrified eyes finding mine. A whimper leaves her chest, and she disappears into the water.

Fuck!

No, no, no, no.

Hell's fury, fuck!

The water is turbulent under rocking, frozen plates. Its

muffled roar fills my ears. I leap from thickest point to thickest point, calculating her direction and speed. I can hear her heart, rapid under the plate of ice. I speed up to get ahead of her. Sliding to a halt, I slam a hand into the ice.

White shards explode around me, leaving a massive hole. She is panicking, arms flailing through the frigid water. She reaches the hole, and I grab her, ripping her from the water and into my hold. Her lips are blue, her chest still. Each heartbeat that flops in her chest is too far apart.

FUCK!

I fly into the cabin and lay her by the fire, tearing the waterlogged coat from her trembling body. I press both palms onto her chest. Over and over. Water spills from her lips.

Jesus Christ.

Her heartbeat quickens, and she convulses under my hands. I roll her over and slam a hand onto her back. Water gushes from her mouth as she coughs, gasping for air.

I rub her back as she struggles to find steady breath. Her eyes open, searching aimlessly in panic. I lay a hand on her cheek, and she turns toward me.

"Hey, you're okay. You're okay."

Ragged whimpers tumble from her throat. I sit her up and pull her into my hold. That was too fucking close. She sobs into my chest. Her fingers grip my sweater.

"Lewis." Her teeth chatter violently around my name.

"I'm here, Sunshine."

Her chin wobbles. Tears spill from her eyes, streaking down her cold white cheeks. Her head drops to my chest and her breaths shatter, each carrying a soft moan.

I need to get her warm.

Right now.

CHAPTER 18

SAMMIE

Lewis scoops my shaking body off the floor and carries me to the bathroom. I use everything I have left to stay standing on wobbling legs as he turns the knob and steaming water tumbles from the faucet. Steam fills the bathroom. His face is stone. I can't tell if he is mad or upset. I shake, leaning against the vanity.

He turns back and gestures for me to take off my top. I try, but my fingers are too stiff to grip anything. He stares at me for a moment before grabbing the hem of my shirt. I lift my arms tentatively, like a stickup in an old western, my gaze not leaving his.

He peels the freezing material from my gooseflesh-covered body, letting it hit the tile. His warm fingers brush my belly and hips as he unzips and tugs my jeans down. They stick over my hips, and he moves closer, forcing them over my curves.

I step from the heavy, ice-clad denim and stand on shaky legs. He makes quick work of my bra, and I slide my arms out, not taking my gaze from his face. I try to use my fingers. The movement burns, and I gasp. His eyes flick back up to mine, pupils fully dilated.

Heat pools low in my stomach, and, as ridiculous as it feels, I am glad for the warmth. My heart rate kicks up as he peels down my panties and lets them fall into the pile of half-frozen wet clothes. He wraps his arms around my shaking body and picks me up, walking us both into the hot water, him still fully clothed.

The water burns my skin. I grip his arms, moaning through a cry. His hold tightens. I lower my feet to the ground, breathing through the sting from every single burning drop of water. He hums into my hair. I let myself melt into his warmth, eliminating any remaining space between us. After an age, my fingers stop burning, my heart rate steadies, and I drag in a long, deep breath.

As if reading my mind, Lewis releases me and leaves the bathroom. I lean on the wall of the shower and slide to the floor, staring at the door he went through. Every cell in my body is missing his. Every thought damaged by seeing him walk away. His bond has snapped with someone else. And that burns more than any frozen water ever could.

Sobs crash up my throat. I lay on the shower floor and curl up, letting my tears flow down the drain with the steaming water. When the water starts to come in cooler waves, I push up from the tile to my feet. My eyes are sore from crying. I'm still stiff despite spending this long in the hot shower.

A knock on the door startles me. A hand appears with my PJs. I turn off the water and grab a towel, wrapping it around myself. I take the clothes from his hand. He retracts it and closes the door. I dress and walk to the bedroom, not wanting to see his face. Not wanting him to see mine.

I crawl into bed. The fire in my room is stoked and burning high. Three extra blankets are laid over my bed. I start shivering again, my teeth chattering almost as bad as before. I close my eyes and pull the blankets around myself tight.

My jaw aches from the chattering. Footsteps stop in the doorway. I open my eyes. Lewis stands there, watching me chatter myself to pieces for a moment. He walks to the bed and studies my face. Pulling his sweater and shirt from his back, he tosses them to the floor and walks around the bed, climbing in on the other side.

A second later, his arms wrap around me, one under me, one over my tucked-up legs and butt. He tugs me into his chest and holds me tight. His warmth is delicious. He sinks his face into my neck. I slide my hand over his on my legs.

"Thank you," I whisper.

"Any time, Sunshine."

I wriggle backward, chasing more warmth. Hardness presses into my bum, and he groans. My breath hitches. He has a mate.

I try to pry myself from his grip. "You don't have to do

this if it's uncomfortable." But his hold doesn't relent. He chuckles into my hair, and I stiffen. "I thought vampires were supposed to hate us witches?"

"Mhmmm."

I settle back into his hold, running over every interaction we have had since we met. Searching for some kind of evidence to either back up what I feel or tear it down. After half an hour, I turn in his arms and make space between us.

"I'm okay now, you don't have to do this."

He studies my face, his gaze wandering across my throat, the bounding heartbeat in my veins. Angst washes over his face. He tucks a piece of hair behind my ear and forces a smile. I slip a hand around his before he can take it away.

"I thought vampires were supposed to hate us." I am repeating myself, but I am desperate to hear something from him. Anything.

I search his face, waiting.

"They are. I don't, at least not all of them. Not anymore." The small smile fades. He removes his hand and removes himself from the bed.

"Lewis?"

He turns back, bare-chested, blood bounding through the veins in his neck like wildfire.

"Thank you, not just for now."

"You're welcome, Sunshine."

"Sammie," I breathe.

"Sammie," he says, his lips tugging into a smile, adoration filling his eyes. A soft smile blooms over my face, and I snuggle into the pillow, pulling the blanket around myself tighter. Minutes later, sleep smothers my exhausted body and I let it drag me under.

)))·◐·(((

T he moon is high in the sky when I wake from the less-than-pleasant recurring dream. The mist, Lewis on the cliff with Anjelica contorting his body every which way, lacing his face, his eyes, with pain. I shuffle into the kitchen for a glass of water.

The fire in the living room hearth is down to embers. I fill a glass with tap water and chug the entire thing. Lewis is asleep on the couch, papers spread on his chest, his red pen fallen to the floor. His laptop is open, the screen saver cycling through a twisting neon loop. How old-school is this guy?

I pad toward the sofa. His chest rises and falls softly, his arm hanging over the side of the sofa. I move to the hearth and grab two logs from the wood box and place them over the embers. Sparks fly upward with the weight of the logs. I pluck another two from the box and rest them on top of the first two. As the bottom ones burn down, the top two should fall into the fire, lasting longer than a single layer.

Lewis mumbles in his sleep and rolls onto his side. His hair flops over his face. Butterflies take flight low in my stomach. I suck in a long, low breath to temper the response I have simply being next to him.

I inch closer and lift the papers from his chest and place them on the side table. Closing the laptop, I put it down on top of the papers. The blanket is draped over the sofa still. I pull it down and lay it over his body, spreading it over his chest, legs, and feet.

I take off his shoes and replace the blanket. He inhales, releasing a sigh. He moves on the sofa in his sleep. The moonlight pouring through the window is enough to see his face change from relaxed to a small smile.

"Good night, Sammie."

The butterflies in my stomach melt to warmth.

"Night, Lewis."

I make my way back to bed and snuggle in. Something has shifted. Like after the ice and the river, the tension which had us at each other's throats was washed away with the current. Like we both let go of the ball we had been tossing back and forth between us.

For the first time since I met Lewis, I'm scared for him. Devastated he would give up, to protect me. Burning in my chest floods my body. Tears prickle behind my eyes and I let the moisture soak the pillow. It might be the selflessness of the man in the next room, or the stress of the dramatic events of today, but I just want to cry. I want this feeling out of me.

I want him to live.

I want him.

Period.

·)᠈᠈·●·(·(·(·

Lewis's hands are at ten and two. Nerd. He reaffirms his grip on the wheel. "You can get service in about three miles." His eyes are on the road, mine are on him.

"You will burn a hole in my face if you don't stop staring, Sunshine." He laughs.

My stomach flips. Goddess above, I love that sound.

A lump grows in my throat. "If you only get one bond and yours has snapped, why didn't you claim it? Especially with the curse . . ."

His gaze flicks from the road to me. His jaw clenches. All humor has drained from his face.

"Why would you waste it when you have limited time left?"

He pulls the car over, planting his foot on the brake. I brace my hands on the dash. He shifts the stick to park and is out of the car faster than I can see.

What did I say?

I open the door and get out of the car. I hold my phone up. One bar! I open my messages. Three messages ping. They're from Mom, Serena, and Jackson. Yes! Bless the Goddess, I have missed this.

I read all three messages. All the same, wanting to know how I am doing on my 'getaway.' Ugh. I hate lying to my family. But it is so much easier than telling them a deranged shadow witch is hunting me.

I pull my coat around myself and hold it tight. Shoving my phone into the side pocket, I wander off the side of the road, following Lewis's footprints in the snow. A few minutes later, I find him. He is leaning against a tree, his back to me, hands in his hair. His shoulders rise and fall quickly.

I walk up behind him and rest my hand on his forearm. "Hey."

He drops his hands to his sides and turns to face me. His eyes are filled with devastation.

"I'm sorry for bringing it up." I rub my thumb over his jaw, fingers cupping his face. He closes his eyes and leans into my hand.

God, right now, in this moment, I would give anything for his bond to be with me.

But I know how rare it is for a vampire and a witch to bond. And from everything I have researched, and he has told me, a bond between a vampire and another species doesn't always end well for the person of the other species.

"I should have told you this the week we met, but I . . . " he starts.

"You what? Lewis, what is going on?"

"Back in the lecture hall at the start of term, I felt—"

His phone rings. He startles and pulls the phone from his pocket. Staring at it for a moment, he taps to answer.

"Den."

He turns and wanders further into the forest.

"Okay, yep, we will head back now."

He hangs up and walks back fast, grabbing my hand and dragging me behind him. I wince in his rough hold.

"Lewis, please answer at least one of my questions."

He trudges through the snow, pulling me behind him. I pull my hand free and plant my feet in the snow, crossing my arms over my chest, brows down, mouth a thin line.

He spins back. "What are you doing? We need to get back, now!"

"I am not leaving this spot until you tell me something. Tell me what's going on with you. Tell me what Denver said. Tell me what you were supposed to tell me the week we met." Blood thunders in my veins, almost drowning out every word.

He stalks into my space and growls. "Not now, not here. We have to get back, Samantha."

I feel like a little kid in trouble. I shake my head. "No way. Talk or I am not going anywhere with you."

"Now is not the time, Sunshine," he snarls.

"Make it the time, Lewis."

I meet his fire with my own. And his chest heaves, inches from mine. "We are not safe here."

"What did Denver say?"

"There are six scouts tracking our way. The only place they can't get to us is in the cabin. It's warded against uninvited guests. Now, move!"

"Fine!" I drop my hands, shoving his shoulder with mine

as I march past him. He grunts at the contact and follows close on my heels. I drop into the car and slam the door.

He shuts his door and fires up the engine, spinning the car back around in one quick motion before he opens up the engine, the rumble echoing through the snow-covered forest flanking the road we fly down.

Twenty minutes later, we pull up in front of the cabin. The front door is open. Snow is tracked up the stairs and around the porch.

"What about the ward?" I ask.

"They must have found a way around it. Stay here." He points to the seat I'm sitting in. "I mean it, Sammie."

I roll my eyes at him and grab my pendant, turning it between my fingers. He disappears into the house.

CHAPTER 19

LEWIS

I follow the footprints into the kitchen. Nothing is out of place, but their scent is everywhere. Two scents, actually. That's better than six. Following the stench of witch, I walk into Sammie's room. Her things are tossed around the room, draped over the bed. Clothes, underwear, books. What were they looking for?

The hairs on the back of my neck rise. I spin back. Something hard connects with my face. Pain splinters through my cheek and down my jaw. I drop to my knees, pressing a hand to my burning face. A woman steps in front of me, a man flanking her side. Her short red hair touches her shoulders. Her green eyes are narrowed and locked on me. She folds her arms over her chest. "Where's the pendant?"

They came all this way for Sammie's pendant?

"Do I look like I wear necklaces, witch?" I grind out

through my damaged jaw. The man by her side moves behind me. I go to rise, and she holds both hands over my head. Heaviness holds me on my knees. The weight crushes me into the floor. I hunch under the weight of her spell with a groan.

"Again, blood sucker, where is the pendant?"

I shake my head, my body almost seized up. Fire courses through my veins. If they so much as lay a finger on Sammie, I will rip them apart limb by limb. Slowly.

Her hands descend, and the weight crushes the air from my lungs. I gasp for breath, hands falling to the floor in an effort to hold myself up.

"Let him go," Sammie rasps.

Fuck.

No. God dammit.

Which part of *stay in the car* didn't she get? If we get out of this, I will—

Scorching burn floods my skin, and I twist, struggling to get out from under its hold. A low rumble spills from my throat.

Sammie's eyes widen as she swallows and moves closer to the three of us. I try to hold a hand up, to get her to back off. The redheaded witch turns on the spot, her hands still steady, suspended above me. She scans Sammie up and down. The pendant sits over her chest, only partly concealed by her coat.

"Why do you vampires always have to lie? Life would be so much easier if you told the truth," she coos, nodding to her companion. He moves in behind me, getting closer for better leverage. Rough palms press against the sides of my head.

I find Sammie's gaze.

The hold on my head tightens. I brace my shoulders, trying to pluck my fingers from the floor. The witch's hovering hands rise a few inches, allowing for movement. Space to snap my neck.

"I'm sorry, Sunshine," I choke.

"No. No, no, no, no," she breathes.

Her beautiful face, even contorted, is stunning. Sammie closes her eyes, letting her arms fall to her sides. I hold my breath. Her breathing turns rapid. In the next heartbeat, every inch of air is sucked from the room.

Wind hollers around the small cabin, homing in on the two intruders. The redheaded witch loses her focus on me and turns to face Sammie. I growl, free from her hold, and spin, rising to my feet. I shove my fist into the guy's chest and pluck out his beating heart. His eyes widen and he falls to the floor. A scream from the redhead sees me turn back.

Sammie has her suspended from the floor in a flurry of wind. The frantic witch turns in the wind's turbulent grip, eyes wide and devastated as life leaves the eyes of her companion. She screams, thrashing against the continuous funnel of wind.

Sammie's eyes are homed in on her prey. Her face is absolute stone. She holds her brethren up with one hand.

The other she flings open by her hip and flames burst from her skin.

She tosses the fire into the funnel, and it explodes throughout every inch of the twister. The smell of burning flesh and hair permeates the cabin. The screams eventually die out, and Sammie drops both hands in front of her.

The wind and fire disappear like they were sucked out by a vacuum. The body crashes to the floor and ash scatters around the cabin. Tears are flowing down Sammie's cheeks as she shifts her gaze to the burned body.

I take a step toward Sammie. Her body begins to shake. She slumps to the floor and loses her stomach. Wiping her face, she plants her face in her hands. I drop to my knees and crawl to where she sits. Her stunned gaze lifts to find mine. I rest both hands on her face. She lets her forehead fall onto mine. Heat waxes in my center.

Lifting my face from hers, I lift her chin with a finger until her gaze finds mine. I force a wobbly smile. She gasps, recoiling, her face twisting with pain. She scrambles backward and hits the wall behind her. Her face is a mix of pain and surprise. Her hand curls to a fist and she rubs it over her chest. Sobs leave her lips, and she gasps for breath. I inch closer, holding out a hand. She flinches back.

I would know that face anywhere. A hand rubbing an ache in the chest.

Her bond just snapped.

Fucking hell, Sunshine.

Her chin wobbles. "What's happening to me?"

"Your bond snapped."

"I don't understand."

"Your bond has snapped." I move closer, desperate to comfort her, but not closing the space between us.

"How can that happen? With who? Your bond has already . . ."

"I said my bond had snapped. But it was unrequited."

She shakes her head, brows lowering. A moment later, she raises her head, mouth agape, eyes wide. "Lewis, I'm a witch. You're a vampire."

"Thanks for the update, Sunshine," I chuckle.

She moans and closes her eyes. Her heart rate accelerates. Her hands cover her face. "Did you know this whole time? No—" She looks up. "Of course, you did! Oh my god!" She plants her head in her hands and groans.

I move into her space and pry her hands from her face, wrapping my hands around hers. "You don't have to act on a bond. Not if you don't want to." Every word burns like fire. Like shoving wire through my veins. But I will honor her choice. Always.

She stares at me for a moment and rises on shaky legs. She wraps her coat around herself and wanders out the door, down the steps, and into the woods. I hang my head. Ash covers everything. The burning lingers in the air.

Jesus Christ.

What a fucking mess.

S ammie hands me a plate of food. Her cooking skills outshine mine, and I enjoy every mouthful. She eats in silence. I rise and find a bottle of wine, pouring two glasses. After cleaning the mess while she was wandering outside, I came to the conclusion that she is well equipped to protect herself, at least against a small number of witches. If she was severely outnumbered, it would be different.

"What happens when I'm old and you're still this?" she says, waving a hand up and down toward me as I hand her a glass.

She is seriously considering this.

"I would spend the next five or six decades with you, if you want me." For a three-hundred-year-old vampire who has defeated death and various other impossible, terrifying events and people, I am anxious. This bond will be the only one I get. She is the only one I have ever wanted. Ever been drawn to inexplicably.

"Can you turn me?"

I recoil at the words. I could never take that from her, what makes her so alive. I wouldn't.

"No," I growl, and she glances at me. She mulls over the word, swirling the red wine in her glass. I sit on my end of the sofa and try to focus on anything but her. I take a mouthful.

"What is a joining?" she asks.

I choke on the mouthful of wine, forcing it down my throat.

"Consummation, the same for humans."

"Oh," she says. Her face flushes, and she drags her gaze to the fire.

"You don't have to do anything you don't want to, Sunshine."

"How would the Council find out?"

"Your scent would be on me, mine on you. Other species are usually quick to pick up on it."

"And you can't disguise it at all?"

"Maybe. But not easily, and probably not all the time. It doesn't matter; you are under no obligation to me, Sammie." I face her this time, and she puts her glass on the floor and stands. She disappears into her room for a moment before returning. In her PJs, she pulls on some socks and grabs a blanket. She lies on the sofa and lays her head on my lap. I chuckle at her, and she smiles.

"It matters to me, Lewis."

Her heart is thundering in her chest. Her hand finds my free one and she laces her fingers through mine. Her blue eyes scan the ceiling, narrowing. "I thought they were going to kill you."

I stare into my wine. They were. I can't trust my own words at this point, so I force a sad smile.

"That was the worst thing I have ever felt in my entire life," she breathes.

I turn my head. She is looking up at me, silver lining her eyes. I put the glass down and run my fingers over her forehead and down her cheek. She closes her eyes and leans into my hand.

Fire intensifies in my core, hardness growing under where her head lies. She moves her head, frowning before her mouth parts with a little gasp. I hold her gaze, and a small smile peeks one side of her mouth, like she is trying not to let me see.

"Sammie." My voice is gravel, her name thick in my throat.

She kisses my palm and places my hand on her neck. Her blood thunders in her veins. She sits up then stands, making her way between my legs. I look up at her.

Blonde curls fall around her shoulders and over her chest rising through deep cycles. I close my eyes. The pheromones she is giving off are intoxicating. I pull my mind back to every hurt look on her face, every time she loathed me, trying to rein in some sort of control over my body responding to hers.

She moves out of my space. I am so hard it's painful. I don't know if I would be able to control myself if she touched me. I replay the look of annoyance she gave me in the lecture hall the first time we met. God, I think that's making it worse. The roar of blood through my veins drowns out every other sound.

Her weight settles over my lap, and I snap open my eyes. She is straddling my lap, hand flat on my chest. My lungs currently commandeered by shallow inhales. She runs a hand through my hair and slides it down to the back of my neck.

"Is this okay?" she utters.

I shake my head. Her brows lower.

"I won't be able to stop, Sunshine," I rasp.

"Then don't."

Fuck.

Her face is so close. She dots kisses on my cheeks. Forehead, nose, eyebrows, the shell of my ear. I strain against my pants, painfully. I grip her hips, and she moans, so low and sweet my chest all but explodes. Her lips track kisses down my neck. Her hands work the buttons of her PJ top, and I release a low growl.

No. I have to move. I have to make space between us.

"Sam—"

Her top hits the floor. I grip her hips tighter, anchoring my hands so they don't wander to her chest.

Fuck.

"We can do this, Lewis."

I shake my head violently. She leans back, face crumpling with hurt and confusion.

I gesture for her to stand. She does, wrapping her arms over her chest.

God, this is the last thing I want. The look of hurt on her face.

"Sunshine, I will hurt you. If we do this, I can't guarantee I will be able to control myself."

"You won't hurt me, Lewis."

"You don't know what you're talking about. The joining between vampires is rough. Really rough. Between a vampire and a witch . . ." I stare at the fire, as if what I need to say dances between the flames. "They, the witches, don't always survive."

She steps toward me.

"But Denver and Zahli. They were both vampires?"

"Zahli was a human, actually. But that was different; Den had a witch physically bind him, partially."

"What does that mean?"

"He was only half as strong. For the first few times at least, it was necessary. Otherwise, he would have broken her."

"Oh."

I step into her space. Her eyes are dilated, her breathing still too fast, her heart racing like galloping horses in a lightning storm. I trace a thumb over her lips. "You have no idea how badly I need you, Sunshine. But I'm not going to risk breaking you. Ever."

"Okay," she whispers.

"You need to be in one piece to get that degree of yours," I say and kiss her forehead. Her gaze tracks me as I walk away. I step into the bathroom and close the door behind me. Sammie wanders into her bedroom and crawls into bed. I hear the blankets rustle, her breathing, her sigh.

A glint of possibility sparks in my chest.

But I won't turn her.

I would rather have the chance to see her happy and growing old than sentence her to this life.

CHAPTER 20

SAMMIE

This is absolute bullshit. How dare other people dictate our lives. This is 2024, for fuck's sake. It's not Salem in the 1700s. The Council can go and take a flying leap off a short pier for all I care. Lewis gets one bond. In three hundred years, he has *one*. One chance at happiness. Over my dead body is he losing that. I throw the blankets off and stalk from my room to the living room.

He isn't here.

The shower is running. My gut flips. I pad to the bathroom door and rest my hand on the doorknob. Letting my head hit the door, I force breath into my lungs. I have never needed someone as much as him. Ever. Bond or no bond. Even before today, he was my choice. I turn the knob and open the door. He looks out from under the falling water and stills. I walk in and leave the door open.

"Sammie, no."

I unbutton my shirt and let it fall. I walk toward the shower, pushing my pants over my hips. My heart flings in my chest, breath short and choppy. His toned body tenses. And he closes his eyes, washing out the shampoo from his hair in a hurry. Wiping the hair from his eyes and the water from his face, he steps partially out of the water. I open the glass door and step into the water. He steps back into the stream, dark eyes watching every move, his arms tense by his side.

God, he is stunning. I drag my gaze from his face, down his throat to where his Adam's apple bobs, down his rapidly heaving chest, over his hard stomach, tracking down the V between his hips to his hard length.

Holy shit.

His leg muscles are tensed. Like he is using every fiber of his being to stay rooted to the spot.

"I will break you, Sunshine." His voice is almost inaudible.

I lift my gaze to meet his and press a finger over his lips. "No, you won't. I won't let you."

I run my finger down his neck and between the ridges of his chest and move into his space, covering his mouth with mine before pushing back.

"Do you have any idea how much I need you?" I whisper over his mouth.

"That's the bond talking," he utters.

"No, it's not," I say, letting my hands wander to his hips. I trace circles around his stomach and dip them lower now and then. He growls into my neck. Stepping around me, he slams a hand onto the shower wall, caging me under his frame. He kisses his way down my neck and over my collar-bones. My body is on fire. Like it's going to burn me alive if he isn't inside me.

His hand leaves my hip and tracks to my center. His fingers find my apex before brushing over my wet core. My body shakes and he presses his hardness into my belly. His lips find my breasts, tongue flicking over a nipple before sucking it, releasing it with a pop. He leans back and finds my gaze.

"You sure you want to do this, Sammie?"

"Yes."

He slips a finger into my core, and I buck against the wall. His mouth finds mine. "Tell me to stop, Sunshine."

"No."

"Samantha. Tell me to stop."

"Never. Don't you dare."

He crushes me against the shower wall. I gasp, but I was ready for this. I dig deep, chasing the wind from earlier, and hold him back with one hand. Far enough he can't hurt me, close enough he can love me. His face lights up with surprise when he realizes I am holding him back. A smile washes over his hooded features. "Good girl."

I close my eyes and let him closer. He drops to his knees and grips my hips. Water flows down over his head, through his hair, and down his face. He lifts me up and holds me against the wall before moving my legs over his shoulders.

He buries his head into my center, his finger brushing over the bundle of nerves throbbing for him.

One broad stroke of his tongue and my body turns limp, my legs shaking with every hot stroke. The water gushes over us both, and I run my hands through his hair. Closing my eyes, I arch my back from the wall and moan.

Lewis slides two fingers into my center, and I tighten around him. He growls, and the vibrations send me over the edge. He holds me until the last wave of oblivion subsides before standing and pressing a kiss to my forehead. He turns and opens the shower door. I grab his hand.

"Where are you going?"

"To make you dinner."

"What about you?"

"I'm not worried about me, Sammie." He steps from the shower and closes the door. "Besides, I just watched the most beautiful thing I have ever seen. I'm satiated." His body betrays his words. He is hard, and huge, his veins flushed to the surface over every muscle.

Liar.

I move under the water. His gaze tracks me as I move my hands over my breast, before letting a hand slide to my still throbbing wet heat.

He clenches his jaw, eyes feral.

I close mine and sink a finger into my wet heat, hoping it will torture him enough to come back into the shower.

The whip of the wind of something fast makes me open my eyes.

The door is shut.

Lewis is gone.

>))>•☾•❂•☾•((<

Something savory baking drags me from my pouting in the bedroom and into the kitchen. If it wasn't for the rumbling in my stomach, I would wait him out. Lewis is dressed and puttering around the kitchen, chopping ingredients for what looks like a green salad. I spy the baking dish on the counter sitting on the heatproof mat. Lasagna. My favorite.

"Hungry?" he asks.

I slide onto the stool at the counter as he scrapes the chopped peppers and tomatoes into the salad bowl, forearms flexing. My voice is low and breathy. "Starving."

He stops and looks at me. I bite my lip and pull in deep breaths, trying to stamp out the heat pooling in my core. And failing.

Lewis clears his throat, pushing his sleeves up past his elbows, and nods to the side cupboard. "Wine?"

"Sure," I say, sliding from the seat. I make my way around the kitchen and grab a bottle of red. I slip between him and the counter. "This okay?"

He slams his palms either side of me and lowers his head, nuzzling my neck. "You are not making this easy for me, Sunshine."

I twist back a little and put the bottle down. "Good."

As I turn back, his mouth finds mine. My spine curves around the edge of the counter as he presses into me, hard. I shove my hands into his hair. The kiss is deep, and I open my mouth wider, letting him in. His tongue finds mine.

I run my hands down to the hem of his sweater and slip them under the soft woven fabric, finding his hard stomach. I walk my fingers up his stomach and over his chest. He pulls back and rips his shirt and sweater from his back and tosses them to the floor.

"Hold me back, Sunshine."

"Uh-huh."

I close my eyes and dig into the well of power low in my center. I gather the force and let it funnel between us as he rushes me. He is almost too strong to hold back. He bites his way softly down my throat and over my chest. Teeth find my nipples through my PJs.

"Lewis."

"Sammie." My name is a low growl.

One hand moves to my hip, the other sliding behind my head and through my hair. With every ragged breath from my lips, I inch toward his face. I push on his chest, and he pulls back. My eyes alternate from his gaze to his lips.

Blood thunders in my veins as he lowers his mouth to my neck. He runs kisses up my throat. I release a low moan. His grip on my hip tightens, and I close my eyes. At this point, if he fed on me, it would be a welcome release.

He won't.

He's Lewis.

Self-control personified.

"Lewis," I choke out, wanting to see his face.

"Mhmmm," he rumbles against my neck.

"Lewis, please." The words are nothing more than breath.

He raises his head. His eyes are dilated, almost fully black, thirst and desire competing their way across his gorgeous face. He picks me up, and I wrap my legs around his waist. We make it to the sofa before he drops me and covers my mouth with his.

Warmth flickers across my palms. I push back, moving up the sofa, and Lewis trails kisses down my throat again. I pull in a sharp breath, glancing at my hands, now behind him. I clamp them shut and the small flames disintegrate to wisps of smoke.

I can't burn him.

Fuck.

I concentrate on holding him back with wind. Ragged breaths cycle from my chest. I need to change this up before I lose my concentration again and hurt him. I tap his chest with a hand, and he stills, moving from my space, eyes wide. "Did I hurt you?"

"No," I rasp. "I just—" Heat floods my neck and face.

"What is it?"

I move from the sofa and kneel on the floor. "Can I show you?"

He nods, shifting on the sofa. He studies my face, trying to figure out what I need to show him right now. I huff out a nervous laugh, and he sinks into the sofa further. I lift his hands from his lap and start working on the buckle of his pants. His eyes lower to my hands.

"Sunshine, you don't have to."

"Believe me, Lewis, I want to."

He growls, low and heady, as I make quick work of his pants. His hard length springs from its confinement and I grip it with one hand. With a moan, he lays his head back on the sofa. I lick the tip, and he tenses, his breaths quickening.

He grabs my shoulder and shoves a hand through my hair. I smile around the head of him and lower myself as much as possible. He is freaking perfect. Sliding my mouth back up, I suck and release with a pop.

"Sammie?"

"Yes?"

"If," he pants.

I move back down his length, tongue swirling around the base of his head.

"I," he rasps.

Pulling back up, I grip him tight with my hand, skating my teeth over the top of his tip.

"Move," he moans.

I take the full length of him in my mouth.

"Hold me," he utters, hands falling from my hair and shoulder to grip the sofa.

"Mhmmm." The sound vibrates through him; I feel it in my hand.

"Hold me back," he grinds out.

He moves. In an instant, I am knocked to the floor. His hands grab my shoulders, picking me up and my back slams into the wall beside the hearth. His eyes are completely black.

Hold me back.

He was trying to tell me he lost control. Pushed into the wooden cabin wall, my shoulders bark with pain. Tears burn behind my eyes. His hand moves from my shoulder to my neck, crushing it. My breath stops.

I pull at his wrist. He is built like stone. His eyes are vacant, blackened by whatever has him entranced. His teeth descend.

Shit!

I pull at the center of my power. I buck against the wall, out of air. The wall of wind I had made before is nowhere to be found. I fling my palm open and let the fire go. "I'm sorry," I choke.

Flames lick his sweater. He rears back, mouth open, canines sharp and deadly.

"Lewis, stop," I rasp.

His sweater smolders, and flames creep up his torso. I throw another round of fire. Sobs slam into the crushed part of my throat. His fingers curl harder into my neck. Fire isn't working. I raise a hand and curl my finger toward us, hoping like hell water follows.

Nothing.

I try again. The sink rattles and the pipework groans.

A heartbeat later, water is pouring over a stunned Lewis. I cough and gasp, sucking in as much air as I can gather. His face turns from stunned to devastated in a second.

I slide down the wall and close my eyes, breathing in deep cycles.

I hear his zipper work before he hits his knees on the floor in front of me. His warm hands shake, brushing over the angry burning area of my throat.

"God, Sunshine, I am so sorry."

I open my eyes. "It's okay, Lew."

Tears line his. He pulls me into his hold and his chest shudders. I pull back in his hold. Tears cascade down his cheeks and over the sharp shape of his jaw. Every breath he takes is pained and short. "God, I'm sorry, Sammie."

"I'm fine; you took me by surprise, that's all. Next time I'll be ready."

He flinches and drops his arms. "There won't be a next time."

"Lewis, no. Please, it's fine. I'm fine."

His gaze drops to my neck. "I could have snapped your neck, Samantha."

"We'll take it slower next time."

"I said *no*, Sunshine." He stands and disappears out the front door.

I bury my face into my hands and sob. For the first time in my life, I feel like I have lost something so precious. Something I would do anything to get back. I can bear facing the Council or being banned from magic. I can even stick it out in isolation on the run from Anjelica.

But I can't bear to see Lewis hurting. I can't bear to see him not have what he needs, all in order to keep me safe. I won't stand for him going without the one thing he has waited hundreds of years for because he thinks I am too fragile.

He can't hurt me if he turns me first.

CHAPTER 21

LEWIS

"Bite me," she snaps.

"No."

"Why not?"

"Why?"

"Turn me, then you can have at it. *We* can have at it. Your bond isn't wasted. And I get to keep you."

I drop the plate I am washing back into the water and turn to face her. "You're forgetting about the curse." I squeeze the water from the rag. "Not happening."

"Why not? It *literally* solves every problem we have. Well, except for the curse. But we can find the cure after."

"Samantha, becoming a vampire is not the answer to your problems."

"Says you, the three-hundred-year-old vampire who is basically indestructible."

"As you will remember, I was absolutely destructible a few days ago when those witches were here."

"You know what I mean. You would give up on your bond so easily?"

"Who said I was giving up?" I lean on the counter and toss the wash rag into the water.

"You said we couldn't try anymore. Doesn't that mean the bond won't be consummated?"

I did say that. I wander to where she sits on the countertop, stopping between her legs. I take her hands and rest my head on her stomach. She has no idea how much I want this to work. But it can't. And with only two weeks left to find a cure, besides.

I'm pretty sure the curse is going to take me out before we get the chance to do this properly. As if reading my thoughts, she slides a hand under my chin and lifts my head until I'm looking into her eyes.

"I don't give up so easily, Lewis. When it comes to you, I don't want to."

I force a smile and take one of her hands, pressing it to my lips.

"Turning takes longer than we have. To do it safely, for everyone. There is an adjustment period of a few months for the transition."

"Oh." Her face falls, and she slumps, brows pulled down.

"Why don't we focus on something useful, like your magic?"

Her brows furrow further. I chuckle, and she sighs.

"I don't know. It only seems to work properly when it involves you."

"Well, what if I help you train?"

"How? You don't have magic."

I roll my eyes at her and try and fail to flatten the smile growing over my face. "Use me to fuel your powers. I am more than happy to be your guinea pig, Sunshine."

She groans and slips from the stool. "Fine. But outside —I don't won't to burn any more of your property." She waves to the scorched floor that will definitely need refinishing.

"We can go into town later and find something sweet and settle in for a long reading session after dinner, if you want?" I offer.

Sammie rounds the kitchen island and presses her chest into mine. Her fingers run through my hair. I fight to keep the burning in my core to a minimum.

She pushes up on her tiptoes, leaning in so her mouth is by my ear. "I want."

In a heartbeat, she has left my space. Her absence creates a dull ache in my chest. I follow her to the door, and she plucks our coats from the hooks by the door. I take mine from her outstretched hand, letting our fingers brush. The small bit of contact is enough to send the blood thundering through my veins.

She pulls on her coat, tying it up around her waist before lifting her cream beanie from the lower hook and pulling it onto her head. Her blonde curls skirt her shoulders, the beanie bringing out the blue in her eyes. I stare, well aware of my ogling.

"What?" she breathes.

"You are stunning, Sunshine."

Her face reddens. She clears her throat and walks out the door. I have never been so desperate to have fireballs tossed my way. I follow her out the door, closing it behind me. Sammie bends down and scoops up a handful of snow, rolling it in her hands. She flings it my way, and I move fast to dodge the snowball and come to a stop in her space.

Her breath hitches.

I bend my head down, covering her mouth with mine. I bite her lower lip before releasing her. "Is that the best you've got, Sunshine?"

Her gaze narrows and a smirk pulls up on her pretty mouth. She holds her hands in front of her chest and twists her wrists until her palms are facing up, fingers curled but spread. The air around me turns to a tunnel, twisting around me. My coat flings upward, hair flying every direction. I try to hold a hand up to shield my face, but the current of her wind is too strong.

Holy shit, Sunshine. Someone has been practicing.

She curls her fingers toward her and flings them in my direction. I try to plant my feet into the snow, but it is no use. My ass hits the icy powder a heartbeat later. A little winded, but in awe of what else she can do, I jump to my feet.

Sammie stands, hands by her sides, chewing her bottom lip. "Sorry."

"Never be sorry for being incredible, Sammie."

She scoops more snow and tosses it my way. I block it with a hand. It bursts with the contact, snow sprinkling to the ground at my feet.

"This time, water." I nod toward the broken patch on the ice-plated river.

She walks toward the river's edge, still mostly hidden under the snowfall, and scans the length of the frozen river by the cabin.

"What do you want me to do with it?"

"Well, don't drown me this time." I try to force a laugh, and her face turns apologetic. "Sammie, I—"

She holds up a hand. "Please don't apologize. We both know what we have gotten ourselves into. If I was scared of you, Lewis, I wouldn't be here."

I straighten. I didn't expect her to say that. I was anticipating her to insist I control myself after the last time we connected. She's not afraid of me; instead, she feels bad for hurting me. Stunning inside and out, this girl.

"Okay, in that case. Can you make one of those water funnels and send it down stream?"

"Breaking the ice or on top?"

"On top would be easiest, I think."

She stares at me and shakes her head for a second before sucking in a breath. She turns toward the river and closes her eyes, chanting under her breath.

Water flows.
Water stows.
Flee your restraints.
Feel your pull and head north.
Go now, go quick, go forth.

She raises her hands, this time palms facing each other. The water continues to flow undisturbed under the ice, the turbulent wash still audibly the same.

Sammie repeats the incantation and widens her stance. Her cheeks and nose have pinked from being in the frigid air. Her fingers are pale and shaking. She is too cold. Her chest heaves, and she moves her palms a little closer, tilting her head, like she can feel the water. The ice cracks in the center of the river, splitting for a few feet toward the north. Water flows through the long crack, spinning on an invisible axis as it churns higher and higher.

Her eyes are still closed. She presses her palms together and laces her fingers. The funnel roars above the river before sinking a little lower. She lets her hands go, pushing her palms away from her. The base of the funnel busts through the ice, splintering it as it travels north. I'm in awe as the girl beside me manipulates one of Mother Nature's masterpieces. Her entire body trembles, her jaw is set, her breathing quick.

She opens her eyes, scanning the distance between us and the funnel, and slams her hands together. The water falls over the ice.

She collapses into the snow.

Fuck.

I have her off the snow and into my arms before her next heartbeat thumps. Her face is pale, save the bluish tinge to her lips.

"You need another hot shower, Sunshine."

"Only if you're having one, too," she rasps, a small, cheeky smile blooming over her sweet face. I kiss her forehead and carry her inside. She lets her head lean on my chest. I dip my head, breathing her in as we travel up the steps and inside. My body wakes up to hers, the fire not so bad as she runs her hand behind my neck. For a second, I feel like we could do this without me hurting her. God knows how much I want to right now.

Her hands fold together behind my neck, and she pulls my mouth to hers. She tastes amazing. She is amazing.

Incredible.

She is my mate.

She is right.

This is worth fighting for.

She pulls back and studies my face. "What are you thinking about? Your heart rate doubled."

I look down. Her hand is pressed over my heart. I didn't even feel her take it from my neck.

"You," I rasp, and the breath in my lungs disappears.

Her eyes darken, dilating the blue hues in them to deep ocean cerulean. Her hands frame my face, so soft. I carry her to the bedroom. She is busy running kisses down my neck and stops when I come to a halt at the foot of the bed.

"Are you sure?" My breaths turn ragged.

She looks up. "Very."

Holding her up with one hand, I slip her boots off. She moves out of my hold and kneels on the bed. Her hands are still trembling.

"Are you still cold?"

"A little."

I pick her up, and she wraps her legs around my waist. Walking backward toward the door, I claim her mouth with mine.

We hit the door to the bathroom, my back against the cool wood. I shiver at the contact.

"Are you cold?" She leans back, both hands on my face as she searches my gaze.

"A little. Nothing a hot shower won't fix."

She turns in my grip and flings a hand downward. Fire flickers over her palm and she tosses it into the hearth by the bed. The small fire, struggling to breathe, roars to life.

"How am I going to get your clothes off if you're cold?" she asks, wide-eyed and innocent.

I chuckle and sink my face into her neck, nipping and biting my way toward her collarbone.

She moans, hand sliding through my hair. "Lewis," she breathes.

"Mhmmm?"

"Take my clothes off, please."

I laugh against her neck. Her hands fumble behind me, searching for the doorknob. I move sideways and she finds it, turning it and shoving the door open as I spin and walk her into the bathroom, depositing her on the vanity. She tugs my coat off and slides my sweater and T-shirt up my chest. I raise my arms, letting her undress me. The clothes hit the floor, and she stills, her eyes wandering over my shoulders.

"Your turn, Sunshine."

Sammie holds her arms away from her body, and I slip off her coat. I slide her sweater up over her head and arms. Her shirt does a lousy job of concealing her underwear. My blood turns to acid in my veins as her breasts rise and fall rapidly. I feel the burn flood my body. Darkness creeps into my vision from the periphery.

Her hands grab my face. "Lewis, no, stay here."

I groan and drop my head onto her shoulder, breathing through the overwhelming fire feeding my instinct to claim the bond, to taste the copper of her blood.

"Sammie, I don't want to hurt you."

She lifts my face to connect our gazes. "I won't let you hurt me. But you have to stay here, with me. Please. I want to feel all of you."

I smash my mouth over hers. Wind, her invisible force, holds me where I am—no closer, no further. She opens, and I claim her with my tongue. Tasting everything. Hands working her thin shirt up her body.

She moans. The material between my hands rips, and

she breathes a desperate laugh. I release the clasp on her bra, and she wiggles free. The movement sends embers through my chest. I growl, lowering my lips to her nipples, hands gripping her hips tight. She whimpers.

I startle, backing off. Heat licks the back of my throat.

Her face is strung out with desperation. "Don't you dare stop."

I breathe through methodical breaths until the burn in my throat settles.

She tugs me closer between her legs. Her finger trails down my jaw, throat, over my chest, and dips behind the button of my jeans. My mouth parts, breath so shallow it stings.

"I love that face," she whispers and pulls me into her space until her mouth is on mine. She kisses my lips then tracks kisses and nips down my neck, hovering over the bounding vein. I slam my hands onto the vanity. Small pieces of stone chip from the impact, falling to the floor. Grip hellishly tight, I brace myself against her assault of sweet kisses and wandering hands. My throat is thick.

"Sunshine."

"Yes, Lewis?" Her voice is high and sweet. What I wouldn't do to claim her, over and over. No woman has ever taken me to the breaking point before. Her scent. Her touch. Her words. Her fire. Her kindness. Her loyalty.

I still.

This is more than only a mating bond. I growl and grab her up from the vanity. She giggles, her blonde curls bouncing over her shoulders and caressing her breasts. My chest all but explodes.

Fuck.

I let her find her feet before ripping her jeans from her. She huffs a laugh, hands running through my hair. Her breasts bounce with each movement from her body being uncovered. I stand up and step back after the last piece of clothing leaves her skin.

"God, you are gorgeous, Samantha." My voice is gravel.

She stands, arms hanging by her sides, breaths shallow and quick. She swallows. A sound like a groan mixed with a sigh leaves her lips. She closes the space between us and makes short work of my pants. I hoist her onto my hips. She wraps her legs around my waist.

All humor has left the both of us. I walk into the shower and turn on the hot water. Steam fills the small bathroom quietly, and I turn on the cold faucet. I wander into the hot stream, and Sammie hisses when the heat hits her skin. I groan into her neck, biting the space around her thundering vein.

Heat prickles at the back of my throat. I growl and slam her into the shower wall. She wedges wind between us, but it wavers. She is too far gone to concentrate. I can't hurt her.

I won't hurt her.

I release my hold on her and step back.

She opens her eyes, stunned by my absence. "What's wrong?"

"I need a minute."

She steps into the water. It cascades over her face, shoulders, and breasts. "You could just watch?"

She slides a hand between her legs. The discomfort at the back of my throat is dulled by the heat pooling in my spine, low. I grab her wrist and remove her hand. I claim her mouth and brush my knuckles over her throbbing clit. She whimpers in my mouth.

My body burns with thirst again. I tilt my head to the ceiling, closing my eyes. Her mouth finds my neck, hand wrapping around my painfully hard cock. With the first pump of her hand, I growl, lowering my gaze to hers. Her hand finds my jaw.

"You're okay. Stay with me, Lew."

"Sammie, I need you now."

"You have me."

I pick her up and shove past the shower door, through the bathroom, and across to the bed. I drop her on the bed, and she smiles, wriggling back, opening her legs for me.

"Come here," she rasps.

"I am not letting our first joining be missionary, Sunshine."

She laughs and squeezes a breast with her hand, propped up with one elbow, half sitting up. "Whatever you want, Lewis."

I drop to the bed on my knees and crawl to her. I move over her, covering her body with mine. I let my hand wander to her wetness, and she bites her bottom lip.

Sinking two fingers into her wet heat, I rub her clit with my thumb. She arches off the bed, sweet moans tumbling from her pretty mouth. She tightens around my fingers. The growl tumbling from my throat startles her.

Her eyes widen.

"Wait," she breathes.

Fire rips through every inch of my body.

My canines descend.

"Lewis," she gasps.

I sink into the soft flesh of her neck faster than she can stop me. The copper warmth of her bounding blood is divine.

She tenses under me. Her body shakes, and her whimpers turn to moans, her mouth open, head back, eyes closed. She bucks around my fingers. I lean back and study her as she comes. God, she is beautiful.

Blood trickles down her neck and over her breast, over her peaks. Planting kisses across her chest, I suck every drop of blood from her skin, hovering over her nipples, letting my teeth graze the sensitive tips.

She settles, her face wrecked with pleasure. I wipe my mouth with the back of my hand and rest on my heels, heart pounding in my chest, terrified I crossed the line.

CHAPTER 22

SAMMIE

L ewis looks devastated as he moves to the opposite side of the bed, putting space between us.

No, no. Please. This is what I wanted.

I scramble across the bed, grabbing his face with both my hands. "Hey." I run a thumb over his lips. My finger comes back reddened with my own blood.

"I—" His gaze drops to my neck. A small trickle of warmth still moves down my skin. I move my hair away from my neck and tilt my head to expose the bite.

"If you need it, take it."

His dark eyes find mine. "No."

The word is no more than a breath.

"Please, I won't break. You won't hurt me, I promise."

"How do you know that?" He flings his focus back to mine.

"Because you value my life over yours. You have since the day we met."

He looks surprised. Surprised I noticed? Or surprised it's the truth?

"Listen to me. The only thing that could kill me right now would be you not wanting me. That's it. You not wanting me the way I want you would *actually* kill me." I push off the bed and straddle his lap, knees digging into the soft mattress either side of him. His eyes follow me as I get closer, moving into the right place.

"You have done so much for me. I want to make you happy, Lewis."

"And you think this will make me happy?"

I line his hardness up with my center.

"I know this makes you happy," I whisper and sink onto his lap. He groans, hands snapping onto my hips.

"God, Sunshine. You are fucking perfect." His head falls back, eyes closing, his entire body tensing. He is big and hard, and the stretch takes my breath away. I gasp.

With my hands on his face, I pull him back down to me and cover his mouth with mine, forcing it open and claiming his mouth with my tongue. His fingers dig into my hips.

He leans back, opening his eyes. Concern twists his gorgeous face. "Too much?"

"Lewis," I whimper. My mouth waters; it's too much and not enough. The tension builds in my core, heat balling low in my belly, sensitizing every inch of me again. I arch my back, and his teeth find my nipples. A breathy moan spills from my chest. Lewis thrusts upward, hard. I tighten around him. I try to think of anything else, praying I don't explode around him too soon.

I rise from his lap, slowly. His fingers dig painfully into my skin. I push a wall of air against him, not sure if I can hold it in place like this. He pulls his head back. His eyes are completely black. A growl leaves his throat.

I channel everything I have into the wall of wind keeping us apart. His grip on my hips tightens further. I cry out.

"Lew—"

His crushing grip loosens for a moment before returning with more force. I can't leave. I can't get off his lap. I try to pry his fingers from my hips. Nothing. I grab his face and press my forehead to his.

"Lewis, you're hurting me," I sob.

His hands leave my hips, grabbing me under the arms. He pulls me off him, lifting me from the bed and slamming me into the wall. The joining—only the strongest of witches have survived this.

Holy shit.

His hand wraps around my throat. His body crushes mine into the wall. I dig deep for my only defense. I want this. I want him. There is no way his instincts will be the end of me. That would be the end of *him*.

I push both palms into his chest and channel the harshest wind I can muster. He buffers against it before we settle into a rhythm. His darkened gaze greys and he settles. I slide one hand from his chest and cup his jaw, which is set in stone. He flinches.

"Sammie," he chokes. The feral haze that had his features trapped disintegrates.

"Still here," I whisper.

His chest heaves; his face falls. I slam my mouth over his, and he closes the space between us. He sobs into my mouth, and I pull him into my arms.

"I'm sorry, Sunshine."

"I'm not."

He pulls away, eyes scanning every inch of me, as if trying to see the damage he caused. His gaze lingers on my bruised hips for a moment. Ten fingertip-shaped purple contusions are littered over my reddened skin. He stares at them, wide-eyed, before tracking his way over my chest, arms, neck, and face.

"We don't have to—"

"Yes, we do." I caress his horrified face with my thumb, cupping his jaw. Letting my hand slip, I drag it over his chest, and rest my palm over his heart until it settles. He sinks his head into my hair and pulls me into him. I dot kisses over his chest, working my way up to his neck and then finding his mouth with mine.

He kisses me back with the fury of a man who has waited over three hundred years for this. I open my mouth, and he claims it. His hands sweep under my ass, lifting me onto his hips. My back presses into the wall again as Lewis brushes his knuckles over my apex.

"Please, Lew," I breathe.

"Sammie," he rasps.

"Mhmmm?"

"You have no idea how much I have needed you since the day we met."

"I have some idea."

He leans back and catches my gaze, tilting his head.

"I wasn't exactly indifferent to you, either." A cheeky smile grows over my face, and I bite my bottom lip.

"I was more than interested, Sunshine," he growls.

"Oh?"

"The day in the lecture hall when you thought I was having an episode." He nips kisses up my neck.

"I remember," I say, moaning the words.

"My bond snapped"—he lifts his head and presses his forehead to mine—"with you."

I flatten against the wall, mouth agape, eyes wide, sliding down the wall a little way.

"Why didn't you tell me?"

"I wanted it to be your choice."

"It is my choice. You *are* my choice."

He smashes his mouth over mine and hoists me higher up the wall. He breaks away, his megawatt smile lighting up his face and eyes. "Now *that* makes me happy, Sunshine."

"Good to know." I laugh, and he lowers his mouth to my breasts, rolling the peaks through his teeth.

A breathy, high-pitched moan cascades from my lips. He growls, sending vibrations through my chest.

His hand trails down my stomach, his finger gliding over my apex before sinking into my wet heat.

"Sunshine, you're driving me insane."

I buck my hips off the wall as he rubs the sensitive bud, swirling his fingers inside me. Absolutely desperate for him inside me, for his heat, the stretch, the fire in my core he brings, I lift his head and kiss his mouth, hard.

"Please," I breathe, breaking away from the kiss.

"You don't have to beg, Sammie. You can have anything you want."

Every single too-shallow breath burns. "I want you."

"You have me."

He nudges my entrance, my only warning before he thrusts into me, hard.

The stretch and heat are delicious.

Whimpers turn to moans.

He nips my neck, one hand tweaking my peaks and crushing each breast. This man is my own heaven. His body starts to shake, his touch roughening.

"Sammie," he growls into my neck.

"Still here," I moan.

He pulls his head up. His eyes are black again, his canines descended. I throw the wall of wind between us. Lewis struggles to fight off the instinct driving him. I can't even imagine how hard it is for him.

His movements grow harder, rougher. I spiral higher and

higher with each one, heat coiling in my center until my body explodes into a million tiny glittering pieces. I turn my head to the side. Each breath carries a moan, every thrust splintering me and sealing me back together. God, he really is my heaven.

I turn my head back. Lewis's gaze is feral again. His lip is curled up, his fire-laced eyes focused on my throat. I sweep the volume of curls from my neck with one hand and tilt my head, holding his gaze.

"It's okay, take what you need."

He grunts, glancing at my face.

"No," he growls. "I don't want to hurt you."

"You won't."

His gaze turns desperate.

"Lewis."

He shakes his head violently.

"It's okay," I say softly.

He takes up his rhythm again, and his head lolls forward. "God, Sunshine."

With every thrust, I spiral again. His mouth finds my chest, nipping the flesh of my breast, sucking each peak.

"Lewis." His name is a plea.

"Come for me, Sunshine."

I still and grab his face with my hands. "We go together."

He shakes his head again. I rest my hands on his chest. "Why?"

"I won't have any control if that happens."

"I do." I slide my hand from his chest and raise a palm, letting flames burst from my skin and dance over my hand. Watching the flames flicker, his mouth pulls into a smile at one side. Seeing him smile will never get old. He drags his focus from my palm to my face. "Fire didn't work last time, remember?"

"Then I'll drench you again if you get out of hand."

"Fine." He winks at me and dips his head to my chest again. "Nice knowing you, Sunshine."

His tongue flicks over my peaks.

Oh god.

He thrusts upward without restraint.

Oh, my fucking, god.

His low growl brings me back to the moment. Breathless, every inch of me buzzing from the intense pleasure I'm riding, I drag my focus to his face. Gorgeous is an understatement. His dark brown eyes penetrate mine.

He slams a hand above my head and picks up the pace. I spiral for a third time and explode around him, tightening hard and fast, matching him.

Lewis roars. His canines descend, quickly. I shove the wall up and send it around my body, cushioning me from the hard cabin walls. His hips slam into mine. He grabs my hair and pulls my head to the side, sinking his teeth into my neck. I gasp and whimper as the skin burns with the punctures.

He stiffens, but drinks.

Good man.

I slacken against the wall, shield still up. He swallows mouthful after mouthful. My head lightens and I tap his shoulder.

"Lew."

He doesn't respond. My eyes feel heavy. I raise a hand toward the bathroom, pulling water toward us. The pipework rattles again. I wait for the water to slam into us.

Nothing.

Shit.

I try again, digging deeper.

Pipework squeals and a gush of water flies toward us. It hits us, soaking our hair, running down our faces, necks, and chests.

Lewis doesn't respond.

Pinpoints of light creep into my vision. Too much. He is taking too much.

"Stop, Lewis, please stop." I trace a hand over his neck.

Mine burns.

"Lewis."

My head lolls to the side and his snaps up. My blood coats his mouth and teeth and runs down his throat.

"Fuck, Sammie. Fuck! No."

His hands grab my face, and we slide to the ground in a heap.

Darkness swallows me whole.

Trembling fingers sweep across my forehead and run through my hair, over and over. Daylight penetrates my eyelids, and I open them. Blinded, I raise a hand to shield my eyes. Everything is too bright. Something thuds onto my chest. I look down. The ruffled blond hair of Lewis rests on my chest. He grips my hand with one hand and the bed with the other.

I pull in a long breath. Everything feels normal. Except for the sledgehammer lodged in my brain. Ouch. I swallow. My throat is so dry, my tongue almost gets stuck to the roof of my mouth.

"Hey," I rasp.

Lewis pushes up from the bed. Redness lines his brown eyes, grey bags hovering below. He brushes his knuckles across my jaw. "Hey, Sunshine."

I sit up and he backs up, making room. "What happened?"

He closes his eyes and shudders through a breath. "I lost it."

"That's not how I remember it. In fact, I think we found it. Three times." I push up a cheeky smile, desperate for him to not hate himself right now.

He shakes his head. "No, Sammie. It's not funny."

"Says you." I pick at the blanket over my lap. "Will that happen every time?"

"The first time is the hardest." His face is stone. I hope he means there will be a next time.

"Are you hungry?"

"How long was I asleep?"

He runs a hand through his hair and grips the back of his neck before meeting my gaze. "A day and a half."

"Holy shit," I say, regretting my words with the next breath. "It's fine. I practically begged you to bite me. I was not an unwilling participant."

He stares at me for a moment before standing and walking to the kitchen. I stare out the window, watching rays of sunlight dazzle their way through the trees of the piney Alaskan forest, piercing the air and through even the slightest gap between the trees and undergrowth. It is perfectly natural. It's what happens.

It's the natural world. Just as the cheetah drains the life from its prey's eyes. The way we turn to dust when dead and buried, to feed the natural world above us from the depths of the warm earth's embrace. That's the way it is supposed to be. If it happens easily, without interference, it is what is supposed to happen. It's Mother Nature working her magic.

Like a mating bond between a three-hundred-year-old vampire male and a witch. Our connection was fabricated; it existed long before I was born. The thoughts snap from my mind, as if a teacher had slammed a book shut. A premonition or a warning? Grandmother used to get snippets of information or visions. Maybe it was that. If so, this bond we have been given is a gift. Not an abomination. How could anything this beautiful be wrong?

How can Lewis and me be wrong? Unconventional, maybe; but wrong?

Never.

He has lived three hundred years trying to be the good guy in a world of monsters. Who takes care of him? Who defends Lewis?

I straighten in bed; the revelation hits me like lightning.

I do.

I crawl out of bed and pad to the kitchen. I'm in my PJs, socks on, pants tucked in. I laugh at the sight. Lewis is whisking eggs in a glass bowl. He sprinkles in herbs and twists the pepper grinder twice over the bowl. I jump up and sit on the counter, regretting it as my brain slams against my skull. He looks at me, a soft smile on his face. But it doesn't reach his eyes. Those are still laced with guilt and sadness.

I rest a hand on his, and he stops whisking.

"Come here," I whisper.

He slides sideways, and I trap him between my legs, pulling him in close.

His head falls to my chest, and he releases a strangled moan. "I'm sorry."

"Hey, look at me."

He doesn't move. I lift his head with my hands and kiss his mouth.

"You are not the bad guy, you hear me?"

"Sammie, I—"

"Uh-uh. Nope. You waited three hundred years for this. I am not letting you lose it. Ever."

He huffs through a strangled laugh, and it turns to a sob. His brows lower, and he composes himself.

"What if I can't stop next time?"

"I think we got through the toughest part."

"We should be, but"—he glides his thumb over my lips —"are you sure you want this?"

I study his face. His brown eyes sink into my soul. His hands grip my heart, holding it, wrenching tight and caressing it at the same time. I try to imagine what it would feel like to live without this. An ache bursts in my chest and my throat closes over. His eyes narrow, pain gripping his features.

I shake my head.

He goes to step back, and I grab him, holding him where he stands. Swallowing back the sobs clawing their way up my throat, I blink, and tears burn down my cheeks. "I can't live without this."

His face softens.

"I can't live without us, Lewis."

He moves into my space, running a hand behind my neck. His mouth hovers near mine. "Nor can I, Sunshine."

His phone vibrates on the bench beside us.

Denver.

God, I hope he found the cure for the curse.

Please, let him have found it.

CHAPTER 23

SAMMIE

After a week of driving, we pull into the driveway in front of Lewis's house. Tired and stiff, I climb from the car and stretch my back. The air here is warm and moist compared to the dry, frigid forest surrounding the cabin we spent almost two weeks in.

Two weeks.

Pressure builds in my chest, closing up my throat. It is only a matter of days before the full moon. I follow Lewis inside to where Denver waits on the sofa, whiskey in hand, one glass poured and waiting on the side table. He plucks it from the side table and throws down the amber liquid. Denver stands and puts his drink down, pulling his brother into a hug. He stiffens and releases him. I move to stand beside Lewis as Denver's gaze alternates between us.

"Good to see you in one piece, Samantha," Denver says, stepping into my space and hugging me.

"You can call me Sammie, Denver."

His scent is overwhelming, and I suppress the urge to recoil from his grip. He sighs and removes his hold. Gaze tracking to his brother, he shakes his head. Lewis laces his fingers through mine, eyes burning into his brother's. Denver's eyes widen before scanning me up and down. He is looking for damage. He has realized what we did. We acted on the bond. We made it through the joining. I made it.

"Lewis." He runs a hand through his hair. "Saman—Sammie, give us a minute, will you?"

I lean into Lewis, and he says, "Go ahead, Denver."

He hesitates. "Fuck, Lew. She has your scent all over her!"

I step forward. "I think you mean Lewis and Sammie. It's not *his* fault; I was there too, Denver."

"Den," Lewis starts.

Denver holds a hand up and walks toward the hearth. I turn back to my mate. His brows are pulled down, his mouth a thin line. My gut flips. What if he regrets everything that happened in the cabin now that we are home? I fumble my pendant with shaking fingers. Lewis releases my hand and stalks to where Denver is leaning on the mantel with one arm, a fresh glass of whiskey in his other hand.

"Did you find someone to break the curse?" Lewis asks.

"No." Denver drags his stare from the fire to his brother's face. "Not one witch was willing to go up against Anjelica. And there is something you need to see . . ." He holds his phone up for Lewis to see.

"Jesus Christ, Den. When did you find that?"

"Yesterday. Remember her?" Denver's voice is soft, broken.

Lewis runs his hands down his face and slides them behind his neck before walking to the sofa and sinking onto it. He leans forward, resting his elbows on his knees. His blond hair hangs around his face.

What did he see on the phone? Remember who?

No. This is not happening. How does Anjelica have the market on all things magical? Why is everyone scared of her? Even these boys, who have abilities far greater than any other species on the planet, are running from her.

"Why not?" I ask.

Both brothers snap their focus to me.

"Why not what?" Denver says.

"Why is everyone afraid of her?"

"Sammie," Lewis utters.

"No! She can't possibly be indestructible."

"No one has been close enough to do damage to Anjelica. She is the cruelest witch to ever have practiced. Many have wanted her dead, but those who try don't last long enough to inflict any significant damage to her."

"What is her power?"

"She wields most strains of magic. But her strongest is mind control and dark magic, shadow magic."

Oh.

Deflated, I pad to the sofa and sit by Lewis. He throws me a small, forced smile and bumps my shoulder with his.

Denver turns from the hearth. "If we split you up, hopefully she won't come after Sammie before the next full moon."

"No! Not an option. Lewis has a handful of days left. There's no way he is going through this alone."

"He won't be alone, Sammie; he will have me."

Air lodges behind the stone that rose to my throat with my last heartbeat. I push from the sofa and stand between the brothers on shaky legs. "Please, I want to stay here until the full moon."

Lewis's face is wrecked, his gaze fixed to the floor, hands clasped in front of his face.

Denver shakes his head. "It's not safe for you here, Sammie."

"I don't care! I am not leaving him!"

"That's the bond talking," Denver says softly.

I storm into his space. "Fuck the stupid bond! I am not leaving him to die alone." My words have turned to a growl, tears burning behind my eyes. My shaking hands ball to fists by my sides.

"Denver, take her home to her family," Lewis says, his voice a low rasp.

"No! I am not leaving."

"Losing my brother is horrific enough, Sammie. Him losing his mate because Anjelica finds out and feels like torturing him in his last days . . . " Denver crosses his arms over his chest, but his jaw feathers.

Zahli.

Everything he has watched his brother go through—the good, the beautiful, and the tragic—must be dragging back up every single moment he had with her and their bond. I swallow and look at Lewis. If me being gone will prevent Anjelica from using me to hurt him, I'll go.

But I fucking hate it.

I move to stand in front of Lewis. He looks up, his brown eyes dark with pain and loss already. I cup his face and bend to rest my forehead on his. "Hey."

"Sunshine, please do this for me."

I nod, trying to strangle back the sob growing in my throat. "Okay."

"I'll get some cover for you. You can't travel with Lewis's scent all over you. Someone is bound to pick up on it and tattle to the bitch."

Denver walks off, tapping his phone before speaking to someone. Lewis stands and folds me into his chest. I sob into his sweater, and he sinks his face into my hair. I breathe him in and grip his arms tight, fingers pressing into the soft fabric of his sweater. God, what I wouldn't do to go back to the cabin. Even if was only for the last days he has left.

Fifteen minutes later, a knock rattles the door, and Denver gets up to answer it. I lay on the sofa, head in Lewis's lap while he strokes my hair, staring at nothing. I wish I could help. I wish I was able to save him. So far, all I can manage is manipulating elements. My spell work is not good. Not like Serena's.

"Come in, Axel." He steps back from the door, allowing

in a built guy, the same height as himself, with dark hair, a wide face, and broad shoulders. The man steps inside and nods to Lewis. Lewis flinches, and I push off his lap to sit up on the sofa.

"What's going on?" I ask.

Denver leads Axel into the living room.

"Lewis." Axel nods. His gaze darts between the brothers.

"Axel." Lewis tenses and stands, pulling me up beside him, tucking me into his side.

Axel rubs a hand behind his neck and glances at me before turning to Denver. "You sure this is okay?"

"At this point, man, we don't have another choice."

"Ahhh, okay. Lew, I'm on your side. Right, bro?" Axel says.

Lewis all but growls at him. "Fine," he grinds out.

Denver gestures for me to step forward.

"What happens now?" I ask.

"Axel is going to hold you for a minute or two. To cover Lewis's scent. He will have to bite you once to make sure his scent is stronger than lover boy's." Denver winks. He is trying to lighten the mood. Lewis is all but strung out. His eyes have darkened, hands fisted by his side.

"Get on with it, Axel."

I back up and Lewis stands in front of me. I don't want another male to touch me. Bile rises in my throat.

"Lew," Denver says, stretching out a hand to his brother, "she will be a sitting duck if we don't do this."

Lewis snarls, his breaths ragged and short.

I swallow and step around him. The last thing he needs is to be put through more torture by Anjelica because of me. I step into Axel's space and meet his gaze. "Go ahead."

Axel glances at Lewis and then to Denver before pulling me into his hold, running his hands over my back. I tamper the shudder twisting through my center. He turns me so I am facing Lewis and wraps his arms around me, hands tracing over my belly.

My breath stops. Lewis falters on the spot, and Axel freezes. Denver is behind his brother in an instant, arms wrapped around him in an iron grip a second later. Axel runs a hand over my chest and a whimper leaves my throat. Denver struggles as Lewis bucks in his hold.

"Sorry, darlin'," Axel says, sweeping my curls from my neck, his hands shaking.

I close my eyes and let the tears burn down my cheeks. The sting from his bite steals the last of my breath.

Lewis roars.

Denver is yelling at him to calm down.

"You want her to die? Because that's what will happen if Anjelica finds your scent all over her!"

I open my eyes.

Lewis stares at me. Tears cut over his jaw; his hands are gripping his brother's arms, his eyes devastated and dark. His canines are down. He trembles in Denver's grip.

Axel pulls his mouth from my neck. A sweep of dizziness claims me, and I steady myself on his arm.

"All done. Sorry, lovely." He dips his head and nods to Denver and flees the house so fast he is nothing more than a blur.

Lewis looks ready to kill him.

I step toward Lewis, and Denver holds up a hand. "You can't touch him, Sammie. Unless you want to go through it all over again?"

What?

I sob where I stand.

No, please, no.

I can't even say goodbye.

My heart cracks in two.

Lewis stands, stunned.

"I'll grab your things. Make your way straight to my truck. Don't touch the Mustang."

My ears ring. His words are muffled but I manage to nod. Denver releases Lewis and runs for his keys and jacket. I step toward Lewis and stop a few feet short. Not where I want to be at all.

Tilting my head to the side and forcing a smile, I suck in a breath. "I'll see you soon." I raise a hand, but don't touch him.

He stares at my hand before returning his gaze to my face. I turn back and fold my arms around myself. My entire body is numb. Every step away from him is wrong.

"Sunshine," Lewis rasps.

I stop, looking back.

"I'll see you soon," he whispers, but the words wobble. I

don't think even he believes it. I nod and wander through the front door. Denver waits in the truck, running on a rough idle, watching me teeter down the steps and to his truck. He leans over, pushing the door open for me, and I climb in. My belongings sit in the tray. I pull the door closed with shaking hands. The lump in my throat makes each shallow breath difficult.

"Ready?" he asks. His words are soft. Brows pulled down, he glances to the porch. I follow his focus. Lewis stands, arms hanging by his sides, jaw clenched, eyes pained.

I turn to face Denver. "If I do this, can you promise me you will figure out a way to keep him safe?"

His face falls. "Sam—"

I suck in a breath, swallowing a sob, and slam my eyes shut.

"For what it is worth, I am glad my brother found his mate and had happiness, despite its brevity."

I choke through a sob as he slides the truck into gear and gravel crunches under the tires.

We drive for an hour before I work up the mettle to say what I think. How can they submit to this witch? Two weeks of happiness out of three hundred years of life is nowhere near fair. Anger courses through my body, reddening my neck, sending a quake through my hands.

"How can you just sit back and watch him die?" I snap.

Denver's gaze doesn't leave the road. "We have been trying to crack this for centuries, Sammie. It's not like we haven't tried."

"Someone must be able to fix this, to beat her. Giving up shouldn't be your only option. *Our* only option."

He turns and studies my face; a sad smile pulls over his lips. "It's more complicated than just letting her win." He returns his focus to the road.

"Then explain it to me, please."

He glances at me and slows, pulling the truck over before pushing the stick into park. "You want to know why Lewis is letting this play out?"

"Yes, why doesn't he fight?"

"Normally, my brother would scour the earth to oppose Anjelica. And he has, most of his life, until weeks ago."

"What are you talking about?"

"I am talking about you, Samantha. Things were different when it was only him. Then he met you. His mate."

"If anything, that should make him more determined. Or am I not worth it because I'm a witch?"

He huffs a strained laugh.

"What? How can you find any part of this funny, Denver?"

His face turns to stone. "Trust me, girl, I don't. Not a single bit. Lewis is the only family I have. But he made a choice to protect you even it means he—"

"Means he what?!"

He stares through the windscreen, jaw tight.

Every word Lewis said to me over the past few weeks flies through my head. The Council. Interspecies relationships being banned. The punishments for acting on a mating bond between species. If he dies, they can't prove our bond. Or it is no longer a concern. No . . .

"Denver, no . . ."

"It's his choice, Sammie."

"Like hell it is. It takes two to make a bond. The burden belongs to both of us." My voice is rough, angry, and broken.

"Let's get you home." He shifts the truck into gear and pulls back onto the road.

They never intended to give me a choice.

Another thirty minutes later, we pull into the driveway of my family home. Denver's gaze wanders as he takes in the large colonial-style home. I fling the door open and jump out, pulling at my bag with rage and hurt fueling my thoughts. How dare he make such a huge decision without me? It's not only him who this affects.

I wanted this bond, just as much as he did. It's my burden as much as his. He might think he is keeping me safe; he couldn't be more wrong. Losing my mate wouldn't be hard, it would be devastating.

Losing Lewis would be devastating.

My bag snags on the tub of the truck. My arms hang over the side, and I drop my head onto them, burn prickling behind my eyes.

Denver reaches over beside me and plucks the bag up. He stands, holding it out for me. I push off the vehicle and force a smile. Taking my bag from his hands, I hesitate, wondering if I should beg him to keep trying.

"I'll see you, Sammie," he mutters and rounds the truck. He backs down the driveway and shoves the vehicle into drive. For a moment, the truck is still and he stares at me as if thoughts are running through his head. Finally, he pulls out from the curb and rolls down the road.

I lug my bags up the steps and onto the porch. It is so good to be home. But the ache in my chest since I moved from Lewis's side earlier pulls tighter, reminding me why I am home. I push through the front door and call out for Mom.

"Kitchen," her voice comes before quick footsteps. She appears from the door to the kitchen. "Sammie! What are you doing here, baby? Is everything okay?"

"Hey, Momma," I choke.

She has her hands around me, pulling me into a tight hug before my next breath. "What is it, sweetheart?"

I sob into her shoulder, letting my heart shatter. She pushes back, holding me at arm's length, studying my face. Hers pulls into a frown. "What has you this upset? You can tell me, baby."

I shake my head. Mom and I have never had secrets. But we don't share every single aspect of our lives, either.

"Is it school? Is it too difficult?" She tilts her head.

I shake my head.

"Is Serena okay? You two are okay?"

I nod.

She sucks in a breath. "A boy?"

I have had boyfriends before. I am no stranger to the opposite sex, but somehow the word boyfriend feels wrong, too insignificant for Lewis. When I don't respond, she steers me by the shoulders to the living room, depositing me on the sofa. She sits beside me, rubbing my hands. I want to ask her so many things. About magic-related things. Species related. About her and Dad.

"Was Daddy your mate?" I choke out.

She startles, like the word mate is akin to something from a horror movie that produces jump scares on the regular. Her eyes widen before she composes herself and schools her face. "What's brought this on?"

"Answer the question, Momma." My voice is pained and my hands shake.

She shuffles closer to me and takes my hands again. "Your father and I are mates. But . . . " She hesitates, staring out the window toward the road for a moment before turning back. "It wasn't what most people imagine a mating bond to be. We couldn't stand each other. We came from *very* different families. Different covens. Before most of them disbanded, at least."

"But you two are inseparable?"

She chuckles. "We are *now*. Why do you ask?" Her brows draw down again and her head tilts.

"My mating bond snapped," I say, the words almost a whisper.

"At college? With another witch?"

How could I tell her the truth? She would be beside herself if she knew I was bonded with a vampire, one who was three hundred years old, on death row, and we consummated our bond. "Yep, he is in one of my classes." Not a total lie. Lewis is definitely part of my classes.

"That's wonderful! Which coven is he from? Is he in one?"

"No coven. Only him and his brother." I force a smile.

God, I hate myself right now.

"A mating bond is a wonderful thing. But you take things at your pace. Don't let him force you to act on it. Did he force you? Is that why you were upset? That can take as long as it needs. Months, years, whatever it takes."

How about three weeks? And Lewis never forced me to do anything. If anyone was a bad influence, it was me. Her face turns expectant.

"He didn't force me, not at all. I should unpack; I'll be here for midterm break." I stand, my skin crawling at the web of deception I am spinning. Not trusting myself not to say too much, I grab my bags from the hallway and take the stairs two at a time.

"Come back down for supper later, honey," Mom calls, moving back into the kitchen.

I walk into my room and shut the door behind me with a foot. I drop the bag and lean back on the door. My thoughts turn to Lewis. The ache in my chest intensifies. I drop to my knees and shove my head into my hands. Sobs cascade, one after the other. I grip my shirt and slump to the floor. I never should have left him. I can't breathe without Lewis. The crushing realization he will be gone forever in a matter of days steals the last of my ragged breath.

I lie on my side in the center of my bedroom, every muscle tensing until they cramp. We only had moments of happiness, a few measly weeks. Only a handful of nights together. The sweetest thing I have ever had, to be only allowed a glimpse before it was ripped from my hands.

With a swell of wind, I propel my pillow toward me, catching it with both hands. I hug it to my heaving chest and bury my face into it, letting out a scream that destroys my heart and buries my soul in the depths of anger.

And there is only one way to retrieve it.

One person who can bring it back.

Lewis.

CHAPTER 24

SAMMIE

The musty scent of papers and ancient tomes fills the dim space of the basement. With a full belly from supper, and my heart somewhat bandaged by hugs and words of encouragement from Mom and Dad at the dinner table, I hunt.

Hunt for the answer. Hunt for a spell. A weapon. Anything I can use to defend Lewis. He may think giving up will save me. He's *wrong*. Giving up will do irreversible damage. I will not live with half my soul. Without my mate. The Council and Anjelica will have to get the hell over it.

Another brown leather book, another mass of useless pages. I toss it onto the pile and pick up another from the box of Grandma's things. A bluish leather book, smaller than the last few. I flip through the pages. Spells for binding, banishment, and such.

I scan each page, turning the yellowed paper gently.

Nothing about curses or how to break them. I groan, dropping the book with the rest. A knock rattles on the hollow wall by the basement door.

"Come in?" I say quizzically. Like Mom needs to knock in her own house. I look up from the pile of books and other miscellaneous items. It's not Mom.

Serena stands in the doorway, a meek smile on her face. She waves and mouths, *Hey*.

"Hi," I say, standing as I brush off the dust from the books.

"You look like hell, Sammie."

I huff a laugh. "Thanks."

She picks her way through the piles and pulls me into a hug. "How was your trip?"

I move out of her hold and stumble over the mess. I try to find more words to spin into lies but my mouth is thick and useless.

"Sammie," she utters.

"It was fine." I drop my gaze to the floor.

"Really? Then why are you home and digging around in the basement, surrounded by your grandma's things?"

"What are you doing here, if you thought I was on my trip?"

I haven't told her I was back. We didn't tell anyone our travel plans.

"Your mom called. She was worried about you and some boy?" Her face turns to mocking disbelief.

"I'm fine. You wasted a trip."

"Samantha Jane Williams, you are far from fine. I have known you for over a decade. Do not even *try* to lie to me."

"Whatever. I was overwhelmed, okay? I spun Mom the story about the boy so she wouldn't be disappointed in me, that's all."

She stares at me flatly and folds her arms over her chest.

I can't do this anymore. I slump to the floor and sit amongst the books. She loosens her stance and sits on the cool floor between the strewn items. "Okay, Sammie, spill it, girl. What the hell is going on?"

I tell her.

Everything.

Her face goes from surprised to shocked to horrified. And I skim over the bonding part, the part where Lewis and I joined, hoping not to gross her out.

"Sammie, no," she chokes.

Heat floods my neck and cheeks. "No?"

She is shaking her head furiously. "You can't be bonded to Lewis. He is a vampire. Witches and vampires do not mix. And they certainly do not mate." Her hands wring in her lap. My hand lifts to my pendant, fingers twirling it around. Her gaze drops to my hand, and she snaps a hand over mine, stilling the movement.

"Don't." The word is soft, but her face has hardened.

"I don't care what the Council says. If it wasn't supposed to happen, it wouldn't have."

"Sammie this is bad—like colossal bad." She swallows.

"Why are you here? To hand me over to the Council?"

"What? No! I'm—" She rolls her eyes to the ceiling and closes them. "There are far worse consequences to being with Lewis than what the Council can dish out."

"What are you talking about?"

"There is a witch who has been hunting him and haunting him and his brother for centuries." Her gaze finds mine.

My breath stops. How does she know this?

Is it some cautionary tale amongst shadow witches? Someone told her from her old coven? I don't understand.

"Sammie, the woman chasing Lewis, the one with the grudge who holds the curse is—"

"You're friends with her?"

"Not exactly." Her face turns pained.

"What, Serena?"

"The shadow witch, the one who no one will challenge. She's my mother."

I stand and stagger backward, putting space between me and her. Bile crawls up my throat. Heat floods every part of me. What does she mean, her mother?

I've known Mrs. Stewart for years, and she is definitely not Anjelica. As if reading my thoughts, Serena gestures for me to sit back down. By the look on her face, there is more, and I am not going to like it.

With trembling legs and quick breath, I settle onto the cool floor. Palms flat, I soak up the cool, trying to ease the heat flooding my body.

"How can that woman be your mother?" I rasp.

"Mrs. Stewart is the woman Anjelica put me with so I could integrate into *your* world. I was supposed to keep an eye on you."

"Keep an eye on me? What for?" I stare at her in utter disbelief. The girl who has been my best friend for years is a liar. Worse, she is the daughter of the cruelest shadow witch to have ever lived.

"To make sure you didn't come into your full powers." Her head tilts back. "I'm sorry, Sammie."

"What do you mean?"

"My mother has been obsessed with torturing that vampire ever since he failed to kill our coven leader centuries ago. The only witches able to break his curse are elementals—powerful ones." She shifts on her seat. "Like you."

My heart thunders in my chest. My powers are not fully controllable. Anything significant takes incredible concentration, unless . . . Unless I am defending someone. I manipulated two elements with ease when those witches had him ready to break in the cabin.

Or the time with the frozen river, I was with him, and it felt controlled, although still difficult. But I managed a water funnel, through ice. It is as if my happiness, my connectedness to Lewis is the key to my magic. Before being around him, making the water rise in the sink was an effort, let alone a funnel from under solid ice.

"You think I can break his curse?" I rasp.

"You could, but—"

"But what, Serena?"

"I bound your magic." Her face twists with regret and pain. My fingers automatically reach for the pendant, but I curl them into a fist and drop it into my lap. She did what?

"How? I mean, I'm not bound. I have been using it for the past few weeks."

Her eyes grow wide. "What? How? That's not possible, unless . . ."

"Unless what? Please tell me!"

"Your powers surpassed mine. Your powers will still be dulled but must be growing." Her mouth doesn't close, her brows drawing down.

I stare at my hands. My gift blossomed when I was with Lewis. The key to everything in my life. And now he is days away from not existing. Days from being taken away from me. I won't only lose my mate. I'll lose the source of my happiness and my power.

"How do I break the curse?" I hiss.

"You can't, Sammie. Please don't tell me you are going to risk your life for a vampire."

I stand, fists whitening by my sides. "He is not 'a vampire,' he is Lewis. He is my mate," I grind out.

Serena scrambles to her feet and stumbles over the piles of books to where I stand, shaking. She grabs my arms with both hands, shaking her head. "No, girl, no. It can't be him; he is another species."

I sigh, feeling tired of every part of this tangled mess.

"Interspecies bonds are rare, not impossible. Lewis is my mate, Serena."

She drops her hands, mouth agape. "I'm so sorry."

"Tell me how to break the curse, please. You owe me that much."

She doesn't respond for a moment. Her eyes wander over the books scattered around us. "There is a spell. Your grandmother knew it."

"How do you know that?"

Not trusting any assumption about her at this point, I need to hear it from her.

"Sam, I need to tell you something. But it's going to hurt. It also may change the way you see Lewis."

Anger rises in my veins, dressed as heat and dancing on every nerve that hasn't already been shot through. "What is it?"

"The last witch who tried to help Lewis, around eight years ago, she—" The words lodge in her throat.

I know where she is going with this. She doesn't think I can do it.

"She died trying to break Lewis's curse. Please, you can't try. I—we can't lose you." Serena sits beside me and wraps an arm around my shoulders.

Nothing about this is Lewis's fault. Refusing to be a murderer had him turned and hunted for over three centuries. There isn't a bad bone in that man's body. I have threaded mine with his deep enough to know.

Composing myself, I lift my head to meet her gaze. The

eyes of my best friend stare back at me. But now, they are so much more. They may be the key to saving Lewis.

"Unbind me, Serena."

"Okay." Her voice is weak and fragile. "Sammie, I am sorry. You have no idea."

I study her face. Through the years that we have been best friends, never has she let me down. Not even for the small things. More guilt-driven actions? I don't think so. So, what is it? Why would she agree to do her mother's bidding?

"Why?"

"Why did I bind you?" She looks confused. "To keep her away from you."

"Why do you help Anjelica? Apart from her being your mother—which, by the way, was the jump scare of 2024."

Her gaze drops to her hands, wringing in her lap. Silver lines her eyes in a heartbeat.

Shit.

I brace myself for the next slam to the heart.

"She said she would kill my mate, Theo. And it's no hollow threat." Her voice is a whisper.

"Oh god, babe." My heart thunders against my ribs. That utter bitch.

Anjelica is the epitome of the scorned woman. She doesn't only make males' lives hell; she tortures anyone who is happy.

"Where is he, Rena?"

She lifts her gaze and meets mine. "You wouldn't believe me if I told you, girl."

I shuffle toward her and pick up her hand in mine. "Try me."

After everything I have seen and been through over the past month, I doubt anything could shock me at this point.

"He is asleep." She studies my reaction.

I stay still for a moment before tilting my head. "Asleep?"

"He's in a sleeping spell. I did it when I was eighteen, like over two centuries ago. And I kind of stuffed it up. Now, to get him out of the spell, I need Anjelica. At least I think we do . . . Plus, I can't risk waking him and her finding him until I have completed the task she assigned to me."

"What was your task? Keep tabs on me?"

"That was part of it."

"What is the other part?" The second the words leave my mouth, I regret them. I don't think I want to know.

"Keep you from Lewis, so she can finish what she started."

"Oh." The word leaves on a stalled breath. None returns.

I drop her hand and raise mine toward the pendant. Her hand clasps over mine, like it has before.

"Why do you do that?" I ask.

She stiffens. "It's not simply a pendant."

"Okay . . . ?"

She lifts hers from her chest. It matches mine. Every detail is identical.

"What do they do?"

"It is my connection to you." She forces a sad smile.

"Like a tracking device?" I huff.

She nods.

"Is that it?"

She shakes her head. I open my mouth and close it again. At this point, I don't think I want to know how many more ways she has betrayed me.

"When you need me, it senses your distress and I can find you, like at the party. But it also can be turned." She moves the inner circle of the pendant bordering the gem. "If you spin it, like you always seem to want to do, it will take you to another place."

My mouth gapes. Transport?

"Actually, it moves through time, not just space." She stops the pendant from moving.

"Why did you give it to me if it is so particular?"

"I didn't have another way to track you. Besides, you don't know the spell to activate the travel part of it."

"Have you used it? To travel?"

She nods. "I use it every weekend."

"What? You use it to get to your shifts?" My face scrunches with disbelief.

"No, not to work. To Theo."

"What? How?" I hold a hand up before she can speak. "I mean where?"

"Actually, you mean *when*."

I gasp.

"Theo is hidden in 1892, in a part of France where no Englishwoman would travel to amongst the war, with a family on a remote farm. They swore to protect him in exchange for help."

"Rena, we can't kill her, not until she undoes every last evil thing she has done. Including Lewis!"

"I will die before I let her hurt Theo, Sammie. He is my mate. Our bond was consummated centuries ago." As if she didn't mean to say so much, her face turns stunned, and she studies my reaction.

"How old are you, Serena?"

She huffs a strangled laugh. "Not much younger than Anjelica. I'm her biological daughter."

"So, you are like two hundred and eighty?" I laugh, trying to compose myself, but this entire thing is too much. I fold in half, gripping my side, hysterical cackles spilling from my lips. Serena starts laughing, too. We laugh until tears streak both our cheeks. What else can we do? Anjelica is determined to break us both, and the people we love.

"So, you're not angry with me, Sammie?" Her hysterics fade, and the tears of laughter turn to those of sadness as she tries and fails to hold back sobs. I can't even imagine living for centuries with the person I love used as a bargaining chip.

She has had to live for centuries without him. It's heart-breaking. And for that alone, I want Anjelica dead. Ripped to shreds, preferably. Ashes on the ground. Heat flickers through my palms.

"This is what we are going to do, Rena. First, unbind me. Second, let's find the spell. Third, we free Theo. Then, we will kill the bitch before she can hurt another person. We will fix this. I promise."

She nods, still sobbing. I pull her into my hold. "We can do this. Her days are numbered."

After a moment of consolation, Serena stands and gestures for me to rise. I do as instructed and straighten my clothes. She closes her eyes and raises both hands toward me.

"*Elements one, elements all. No more will you be bound. Let your true nature be felt. I call on fire. I call on earth. I call on water. I call on air. May your bindings be released, your will free. You are no longer bound to thee.*"

Burning floods through my body, stealing my breath. Fire dances over my palms before it flickers out. Something snaps in my chest, similar to my bond with Lewis, but this time it consumes my body, mind, and soul. I feel light, like for years I have been living in a haze, or some sort of invisible confines. I wonder, without restraint, how powerful could my elements be? I conjured that water funnel—it was hard, but I did it. Would it be simple for me? The beginnings of my power now?

"Do you feel anything?" Serena asks.

"I feel lighter, freer."

She smiles at me. "Good, now we might actually stand a chance."

"And so do Theo and Lewis." I step into her space and hug her tight.

"Thank you." Her voice wobbles. I push her back a little, so she is at arm's length.

"What are friends for, babe?"

She scrunches her nose at me and winks. I roll my eyes at her.

There we are.

CHAPTER 25

LEWIS

The roar leaving my chest barely registers as I toss the side table at the wall above the hearth. If it all burned to the ground, I wouldn't care. I don't care. Everything I wanted left in my brother's truck hours ago.

The image of the last witch who tried to help me sits on Den's phone, and that was the final straw. The second I recognized who she was . . . I will not let Sammie get hurt. Her family has lost enough. The moments we had together feel fleeting. Like the heartbeat of a small bird trapped in the snare of its predator's teeth. My heart has been shredded into a million pieces.

I just want to die.

Where the fuck is Anjelica when you need her?

The bond between Sammie and me was so much more

than a mating bond. She is my soul. They say vampires have no souls; with her, I was complete. Heart, mind, and finally a soul. One that shone like the sun and loved hard. She made me human again. I would give anything to get that back.

Anything.

But I know it won't happen now. It can't. Her life is not worth mine.

Ever.

So, in two nights' time, I will let Anjelica find me. I will stand under the brilliant, devastating moon and accept my fate.

If only to save hers.

I guess in the grand scheme of things, I should be happy I had her at all. I should be happy I had her for a handful of days. I knew weeks after meeting her that one lifetime with Sunshine couldn't come close to enough for me.

The way she looked at me when I told her to leave. *That's* what broke my heart. That look, the one that told me she couldn't breathe without me. How many decades does a vampire need to wait to find that? Thirty-six-plus decades, apparently.

I would wait another thousand to fold her into my chest again. To touch her face. To see the look on her face when she falls over the edge the way she did during our joining. I would live every day in hell to give her one more day of that.

Pure happiness, my Sunshine.

Growling through a moan, I pluck the drinks cart from beside the sofa and toss it with reckless abandon toward stone and mantle. It bounces, metal hitting the stone, and crashes to the marble floor, glass shattering in a glittering explosion. Amber liquid quickly floods through the chaos of wasted furniture. I heave through burning breaths, arms hanging by my side.

The door opens and slams behind me.

Denver.

His footsteps are slow. He stays silent, stopping by my side.

"I'm sorry, Lew," he rasps.

I suck back a sob and stare at the flames inching toward the whiskey on the marble. It catches, and flames whip across the spilled spirit over the floor.

"What have I done?" I choke.

"If you wanted her to stand a chance around Anjelica, you shouldn't have touched her."

"You think I don't know that? You think I didn't try to stay away from her?! She's pure fucking sunlight, like oxygen. I can't breathe without her."

His face is gripped in devastation's harsh clutch. Everything about this situation must be dragging back every morsel of agony he felt losing Zahli. I stare at the broken living room at my feet.

"Not to mention the Council. Fuck, brother! This situation turned into one hell of a mess, brother." Denver turns to find my gaze. We both know he is not talking about the strewn chaos at our feet.

"If it's any consolation, you did the right thing, sending her away."

I pull my gaze from his, back to the burning whiskey. I drop to my knees and let my head fall into my hands. It feels anything but right, being where Sammie is not. I thunder through a roar, slumping to the floor.

A hand lands on my shoulder. "Hey."

"Kill me now, Den. Please."

He squats in front of me. "Look at me, Lewis."

I don't.

"Lewis Matthias Sullivan, fucking look at me."

I drag my head up to his eyeline.

"Please, Den."

He shakes his head furiously. "Not happening. Not until we have exhausted every last option."

A moment later, he is pulling me off the floor. I stand on trembling legs, numbness creeping through my entire body like molasses on a fall morning, agonizingly slow. The grip of it passing my skin burns.

Grief cuts through his face. I almost forgot Denver is losing a brother—the only family he has left. I have been so fixated on losing Sammie, I was lost in my own pain. I suck back the sob threatening to pull me under and stagger to my feet. He rises and stands in front of me. His lumberjack coat still sports a light sprinkling of snow.

I clear my throat. "Let's go for a run. I could use something to sink my teeth into right now."

Denver goes for a laugh, but it chokes out. He nods and follows me to the front door. A heartbeat later, we fly through the forest. Too fast for the human eye to detect, not fast enough to outrun my fate.

Or the damage I have done.

·))) · 🌑 · (((·

I shouldn't be here. Just for coming, God or whoever pulls the strings should have struck me down. But there is no part of me that could stay away. At least seeing her eases things, if only a little. Regret, agony, desire, and sadness pull me in every direction as Sammie unknowingly walks toward me through the stacks of the Burlington town library.

Even when dealing with all this, she is the devoted student. Why did I ever give her a hard time in class? I regret it, like so many other things. The time I wasted trying to ignore the bond makes the top of my list. I'm a fucking idiot.

She is talking to someone, but her phone isn't in her hand. She exits the row and the shadow witch, Serena, appears from the next row over.

Oh.

Sammie stills, scanning the room, as if she knows I'm here but can't see me. A smile pulls up on my lips, dragging my heart rate up with it. I duck my head, hoping the hoodie I'm wearing is enough to conceal me from her. The last thing I want to do is cause her more pain.

Out of sight, out of mind. I hope it is for her. If she is feeling even a fraction of the devastation I am, I will hate myself for the rest of my days. The rest of the day ought to do it. I scoff a laugh at my own stupid humor and flip the page of the magazine on the table in front of me.

Her heart is beating steadily, as is her friend's. Thankfully, they haven't noticed me. If Denver knew where I was, he would snap my neck himself. I keep my head down. Simply being in the same space as her has my senses keening for her. Her footsteps move closer. I flip the page. My wristband and watch poke out from my sleeve.

"Fuck." Her voice is so soft, it wobbles.

Books slam onto the table across from me. I still, not wanting to look up. Wanting it to be her. Hoping she is still walking toward the door.

"Lewis." My name is a strangled breath on her lips.

"I'll leave you two be," Serena says.

Sammie swallows. I can feel her from here, across the ancient, hardwood table. Her heart is racing a million miles an hour. She whimpers. Salt penetrates the air around me. Oh god, I am the world's greatest ass. Truly.

I close my eyes before brushing the hoodie from my tousled hair. The second her tortured gaze meets mine, fire splits my chest. I stand, stumbling backward, and knock over the chair.

She stands fixated on me; shock washes out her face. Tears flow freely down her face. She places a trembling hand over her mouth. Every inch of me burns to hold her, to take away the hurt now consuming her face.

"Sammie," I choke out.

She huffs through a sob.

"I wanted to see you before—"

She drops her hand and sobs.

Before tonight. I wanted to see her before tonight. It was selfish, and in this very moment, I hate myself for it. I hate myself for the pain in her beautiful blue eyes.

"Lew," she rasps, holding out a hand, her head tilting to the side. Her curls fall around her shoulders. What I wouldn't give to run my hands through them one last time.

"Can we talk outside?" I ask.

She nods.

I can't even carry her books. That would leave my scent on her things. Fuck this. If there is an afterlife, Anjelica is going to pay, dearly. Sammie picks up her books, hugging them to her chest, and composes herself enough to check out the bundle at the front desk. I follow a few feet behind, making sure not to get too close.

I push through the front doors of the library and traipse down the old stone steps after her. Daylight floods my vision after being under the artificial light for over an hour stalking the only woman I have ever loved. But it is dull compared to my Sunshine. She steps to the side and leans against a stone half wall, dropping the heavy bag now stuffed with what looks like reference books onto the ledge.

"Are you by yourself?" Sammie asks.

"Denver would never forgive me for coming here. It was selfish, I—" The stone rapidly materializing in my throat steals the rest of my words.

Sammie wraps her arms around herself and cycles through a handful of deep breaths. "Let me try."

"What?"

"Please, Lewis, let me try to break the curse."

Every muscle in my body tenses. Not even if hell froze over would I allow her to risk her life for mine.

"No." The word is gruff, and she flinches.

"I can do it. At least I think I can. Serena—"

"No. The answer is a resounding no, Sunshine."

Her chin wobbles. My last few moments with her, and I am making her upset. Fuck. World's biggest loser, right here.

"I'm sorry, Sunshine. God, I am an ass. But the answer is still no. I would never accept your life for mine. Not happening. It's not your burden to carry."

"You are not a burden, Lewis." She moves closer. Every part of me burns to hold her. "You are my mate. And I want to fight for you. Please, can I try?"

I study her face. How did I get so lucky, so late? I step back and she all but crumples back onto the stone behind her.

"Promise me one thing, Sunshine."

She refuses to meet my gaze, letting hers fall to the ground, shaking her head as if it will change my mind about keeping her safe. After a handful of heartbeats, she looks from the ground to me. "Whatever it is, it's yours."

I am losing the most perfect person in the world. *Dammit, Sammie.*

"Promise me you will stay away from Anjelica. Stay away. Stay alive. Please, Sammie."

Her arms fold over her chest and she straightens, her chin trembling and tears welling at the bottom of her eyes.

"I promise to stay alive, Lewis."

"Sunshine," I growl.

She tilts her chin up, eyes burning into mine.

Good, hate me. Stay alive.

"I promise to stay away," she almost snarls through her teeth.

If it wasn't her life on the line, that sound from her pretty face would almost be humorous. But she's not laughing, and nor am I.

"Goodbye, Sunshine."

God, I want to hold her. Every inch of me vibrates with the need to fold her into my arms and take away the ache in her chest currently etching sadness over her face.

I turn on my heel and wander toward the parking lot. The Mustang blends in with the other cars, parked in the far back.

I walk away. Every step heavy and too far.

Fire burns in my core. I want to scream. I want to trash every single car in this stupid lot.

"Bye, Lewis," she whispers, sucking in a long, shaky breath.

I don't turn back.

One foot after the other.

She slides down the wall and collapses onto the ground, sobs heaving from her chest.

Footsteps, quick and light.

Muffled words. Whimpers.

Serena must have found her.

"Shhhh, babe. It's going to be okay."

"It's never going to be okay again, Rena," she chokes and screams into her hands.

Her heart flings against her ribs, blood gushing through her veins. I make it to my car and try to tune out every single noise she makes. I fire up the Mustang and fly backward before shoving it into gear. I peel out of the parking lot at a ridiculous speed, not letting myself look at the steps to the library. My already shattered heart would stop its half-assed attempt at beating altogether if I did.

After a mile, I pull over, letting the car idle. I fling the door open and fall onto my knees in the dirt by the side of the road. Screams turn to roars. I grab my hair, forehead hitting the dirt and murky snow. Never before has anything come close to breaking me. Three centuries, and not so much as a scratch from this bloodthirsty life.

One happy blue-eyed blonde waltzes in, breathing life

into my stagnant existence, and I am devastated. As if Denver and I haven't lost enough, watching our family die around us. Losing every friend and having to move more times than I care to remember.

If Anjelica wants to end me, she has a fight on her hands.

I will not go easy.

CHAPTER 26

SAMMIE

"There has to be something here, Serena. We cannot let her win."

"We will find it; keep going. We have six hours before the full moon is at its apex."

"Six hours doesn't feel like enough to find everything and prepare for the spell."

I hunt through each tome Grandma left behind. If she had the spell the other witch used fifteen years ago, it has to be here. Rena tosses another book onto the not-helpful pile and plucks another from the oversized packing box. My back aches, my neck is sore, and my stomach twists with hunger, but I am not stopping.

Pushing down the feelings, I flip open another leather tome. More spells—at least I'm on the right track. I run my finger down what seems like the millionth page. The top of my index finger is numb from repeated use, but I don't stop. I won't stop.

"Anything in that one?" Serena asks.

"Spells, maybe," I mumble and turn the page.

More spells for healing.

I turn the page.

Another banishment, this time for unwanted spirits.

Next page.

My breath stops.

The word 'Cursebreaker' heads the yellowed leaf in elegant handwriting.

Grandma's handwriting.

My breath stops. I grab Serena's arm and shake her, not trusting my eyes to wander in case the spell disappears from my sight.

"Rena, I found it."

"Shit, good on you!" She shuffles closer on her bottom, leaning into my side. We read it in tandem. The words feel oddly intoxicating as we chant each line together.

> *I call on the power of earth.*
> *I call on the power of wind.*
> *I call on the power of water.*
> *I call on the power of fire.*
> *I beseech you to this bidding,*
> *Unbind what was bound.*
> *Free this soul from curse.*

Bring forth pure light.
May the cursed be free, be found.

The ingredients call for an item belonging to the pure soul connected to the curse, the blood of the wielder of the curse, a bunch of common herbs, and a silver dagger.

"It says you need to dip the dagger into the blood of the curse wielder or sink it into their flesh." Serena stills and rests her hand on the book. "Sammie, if we kill her, she can't undo the spell on Theo. We can't kill her."

Her voice is almost panicked. I shut the book with a crack and turn to face her, taking her face in my hands. "We will stab the bitch where it hurts but doesn't kill, then free Lewis, and force her to remove the enchantment on Theo. Then, do you think we could bind her? Would the both of us be strong enough to do it?"

"I—" She shakes her head, as if combing through the steps I suggested. "Maybe we would be. But, after we save Lewis, we have to leave her bound, like until we have the chance to get to Theo, and then put her down."

"Oh, we will be."

A small, sad smile blooms on her face.

"How are we going to get her blood?" I ask.

"Leave it to me. I can use the time spinner to do that. You grab the rest and meet me in the forest behind Lewis and Denver's in five and a half hours."

"Why there?"

"That's where she will be; I can guarantee it."

"How do you know where they live?" I ask. The second the words leave my mouth, I feel stupid for asking. Of course she knows where they live; she has been tracking Lewis for centuries. A fact I will never be able to wrap my head around—my best friend is hundreds of years old.

I tidy the stacks of books back into the packing boxes and jump into Serena's car. She throws me a wry smile before accelerating down the street, heading off the highway. It's good to go back to Castleton, even with everything that may or may not happen tonight. I promised Lewis I would stay away from Anjelica. This is one promise I am happy to break. He can be angry with me later, when he's still alive.

I'll take his fury over his absence any day.

"When I first moved in with Mrs. Stewart, I never intended to be your friend." Serena catches my gaze, hands tight around the steering wheel.

"What changed?"

She stares at the blacktop for an age before replying. "The day you burnt Jackson, I realized how innocent you were in all this. You barely had a handle on your powers, let alone the ability to interfere with my mother's sick revenge plans." Her eyes are dark, fire lacing her dark brown irises.

"Oh. Why did you bind me, then?"

"Insurance. If you were completely useless, you weren't a threat, and she would leave you alone."

"Thank you, I think."

"You're welcome, bestie."

336

The fact she is literally ancient makes the use of *bestie* sound ridiculous. I try to contain my amusement, but a snort slips past the hand I slap over my mouth. Serena's laugh is hearty and warm.

I am glad she is here.

I am honored to call her my friend.

Serena stands beside me on the porch. I knock.

Nothing.

She steps forward, fist rattling the door with impatient hammering. "Denver?"

Interesting.

Footsteps move toward the front door, and we step back. It opens quickly. Denver's dour face greets us. God, please don't let us be too late.

"Sammie, you shouldn't have come."

I step inside, brushing his shoulder with mine. He hangs his head. Serena doesn't follow me. I scan the living room for Lewis. No one else is here.

"So, there was no one who would help you, I take it?" Serena says. Her words are firm, but not unkind.

"Nobody will go against Anjelica, no."

Serena scoffs. Her footsteps travel over the threshold and the door closes. "We may be able to help you, Denver. But I need you to promise me something."

I turn back to face them both.

"How can you two help?" He scans both our faces.

"Sammie"—she gestures to me—"can help, actually."

"No, Lewis has already ruled that option out. She isn't strong enough. Besides, he won't risk her life for his. That decision has already been made."

"Fortunately for my mate, he doesn't get to decide for me. Now or ever," I growl. Angry at Lewis for pushing me away. Angry at this whole situation.

"He won't let you, Sammie. He just won't. He has always done the right thing by others; he isn't about to change now, *especially* with you. You are his oxygen. His words, not mine." Denver's face is pained, as if he is reliving the last moments of his time with Zahli.

My heart squeezes in my chest. I am his oxygen.

And he is mine.

I step into Denver's space and grip his upper arms with my hands. They look small around his lumberjack frame, but the sadness in his eyes drives me forward.

"Listen to me, Sullivan. This ridiculous tirade of hers ends now. It's my choice. Not yours, or Lewis's. Nor Serena's. Mine. If I die trying, Lewis will follow me into the next life or whatever it is that happens to us supernaturals. I am absolutely sure. But I will not let him do this alone. Or at all, if I can prevent it. This isn't anyone else's choice. It is *mine*. The last gift I can give him. Don't you dare try to take this away from us."

Denver's eyes burn and his Adam's apple bobs. "I'll stay out of your way," he finally says.

"Good boy." Serena slaps him on the back and waltzes back to the window. Pulling the curtain back, she peers out before disappearing down the hall to the right.

"Where is he, Den?" I ask.

He closes his eyes, arms hanging by his side as his chest heaves. "Out by the lake."

"Thank you," I whisper.

He pulls me into a fierce hug.

"Thank you for loving him, Sammie," he chokes into my hair.

"The privilege is all mine," I say, trying not to let the words get stuck around the stone lodged in my throat.

Serena clears her throat. "Sammie, the moon is almost at its peak."

"Right. I'll see you in a while, Den."

He stares at me, mouth moving but no sounds coming out.

I force a smile and walk through the house to the back door. Serena pops out from the hallway a heartbeat later. She obviously knows where she is going. She has either done excellent surveillance on this house or has been here before. Maybe when the brothers were not home?

We head to the double glass doors leading to the backyard. I push through, and Serena follows a step behind. The moon's piercing rays bounce off the mostly calm water of the lake. I walk across the grass and snow. The chill in the air curls around me. Our footsteps crunch on the snow.

Lewis stands with his back to me at the water's edge. Waiting.

A gloved hand grabs my arm. Serena holds me in place for a moment before pulling me behind the shrubs to our left. She gestures with her other hand to the other side of the lake. A figure stands, dark robe billowing around them. The contrast on the white snow makes them an easy target.

"Let's see what she does first," Serena whispers, almost inaudibly.

I return my gaze to the two figures. Lewis doesn't move. A heartbeat later, the robed figure stands a few feet from where he is rooted in the snow. He turns to face them. My heart thunders blood through my veins, drowning out any other sounds.

Heat laces every inch of me. I pull from deep in my core, readying myself if the robed figure makes a move. With a smooth motion, the robe is pushed back and thick, wavy dark hair flies from its confines, tousled by the frigid winds.

Anjelica.

Now that I know the connection to Serena, it is so obvious they are mother and daughter. How did I not see this before? The moon inches closer to its peak. Lewis's time is fast running out. From what he told me, unless the curse is broken before the moon peaks, he shatters into millions of pieces of stone. He would be obliterated.

Irretrievable.

I shove my hand into my pocket and pull out the paper

with the spell and the herbs I found. Serena makes a start on drawing a pentagram in the snow. Its lines illuminate silver under the moon's sharp light. It's breathtaking. But I don't have time to awe over a basic shape in the snow right now. The clock is ticking. The wind changes, and Anjelica's voice drifts toward us.

"Did you actually think the baby witch could help you, Lewis?"

"Leave Samantha out of this. She has nothing to do with any of it," he snarls.

"Touchy subject. One you will be free of in a matter of minutes."

"Go ahead, Anjelica. Do your worst. I am not afraid of you or of dying."

"Shame. Oh well, at least you can leave your mate behind for your brother. After all, it's your fault he lost his in the first place." She waggles a finger like she is chastising a small child.

A low growl hums from Lewis.

A cackling laugh cracks through the frozen air. God, I hate this bitch with every fiber of my being. She is the epitome of evil. She is actually getting off on torturing him in the last moments of his life.

I unfold the paper and step into the center of the star. Serena does the same. We join hands, and she pulls a silver dagger from the depths of her fleecy coat, before fishing a small vial of blood from her jeans pocket.

"How did you get that?"

"Time travel has its uses." She winks at me.

"We need to start."

I start the incantation and Serena matches my reverence with her own.

I call on the power of earth.

Sprinkling salt over the silver-lined pentagram, we chant the line again.

I call on the power of air.

I light a match under a bundle of sage, praying the wind stays in our favor, blowing toward us.

I call on the power of water.

I pull a small bottle from my back pocket and toss water around us. Snow melts under its weight where it lands.

I call on the power of fire.

I hold out a palm and focus on the flames I want to birth. Embers turn to a spinning ball of fire in my hand.

I beseech you to this bidding,

Serena pours the blood over the dagger, the crimson liquid dripping onto the snow.

Unbind what was bound.

I train every thought onto Lewis.

Free this soul from curse.

Plucking the last item Serena procured as she traveled through the house, I take the leather band he wears every day from her palm. He had most likely taken it off to leave for Denver. I drop it at our feet.

Bring forth pure light.

Serena plunges the dagger into the snow, piercing the leather band, pinning it to the frozen earth.

May the cursed be free, be found.

We stand tall, reciting the enchantment line for line six times. On the last line, the sixth time round, I hold both hands in the air, pulling all four elements into me. It burns like nothing else, and I whimper.

Serena gasps.

My body trembles, and I force myself to stay upright with every searing breath.

"Sammie," she chokes.

A white light, like looking into the hottest flame, bursts from my hands. Blistering heat ravishes my skin. A horrendous crack splits the air, thunder and lightning flooding the area surrounding the lake.

I drop to my knees.

Serena's terrified face stares back at me.

I slump to the ground, smudging the pentagram.

Darkness swallows me whole.

I stand, frozen. Terror has ensnared my body. White, blinding light pours from Sammie's hands. Serena staggers back a few paces. The look of horror on her face echoes mine. Oh god. *Sunshine, what have you done?* I groan through a locked jaw.

Cackles bubble beside me.

The loudest crack slaps through the air. Warmth washes over me. The brightest white flare lights up our surroundings.

Anjelica hisses a curse.

I shift my gaze back to her.

Something tightens around me. The fear that had me rooted to the spot moments earlier has been replaced.

Anjelica's hands are outstretched. She is holding me here by her own ministrations. I track my gaze back to Sammie. She slumps to the snowy ground and collapses, snow puffing up around her as she hits the ground. Snowflakes settle on her face and hair as the color drains from her face.

Fuck. No!

She fucking promised to stay away.

Where the hell is Denver?

Serena drops to her knees and scrambles to where Sammie lies, her chest rising in shallow, irregular bouts. I roar through my teeth at Anjelica. The second she loosens this hold, she is a dead woman. The sluggish beating of Sammie's heart echoes through my head. Through my heart and soul.

"Sammie, wake up! Come on, babe." Serena's words are strangled and desperate.

"I should have known," Anjelica mutters. "Useless girl."

Who is she talking about?

Sammie doesn't move under Serena's rousing touch. Serena pushes to her feet and stalks toward the shadow witch. She throws her hands up, face twisted with hate, tears streaking down her face. Darkness seeps from her palms before shooting through the air toward the older witch. Anjelica releases a hand from my holding pattern and blocks each dark swirling ribbon of attack, one after the other.

"You are a despicable person!" Serena screams, picking up the pace, both hands wielding the dark ribbons at an alarming rate. Anjelica drops her other hand on me and returns fire. Her attack is like nothing I have witnessed before.

She wields lightning like a plaything. It arcs through the air, crackling and hissing like a savage serpent. Serena dodges each one. The shadow witch anticipates Anjelica's plays. How long have they known each other?

Sammie moves, but I don't dare move to where she lies, not trusting lightning not to follow and find its mark in her instead of me. Instead, I lower in a crouch. Like a predator lining up its prey. A low growl is the only warning she gets as I leap toward her.

Too late, the witch drags her focus from Serena to the side attack. My canines descend. The burn in my throat is extraordinary. I sink my teeth into her neck. She staggers sideways. Scrambling in the snow, she bats me away before throwing searing, bone-piercing lightning into me, one hand after the other. I pull on her blood. I don't even want to swallow the filthy stuff.

Hard hands grip my shoulders.

Denver.

What the hell?

I release my hold on her and spin back. He stands, shaking his head. "You can't kill her, brother."

"Why not?" I roar.

"She has other wrongs to undo. There are others." His gaze flicks to Serena.

These two know each other.

"Please, Lewis, I can bind her. But I need her alive. Please." Serena's eyes beseech mine.

I struggle in my brother's hold, Anjelica's blood staining my face, neck, and sweater. The older witch stands on shaky legs. Her face is pale.

"Fine. But then she is put down."

"Solid plan," Denver says.

I push past the two traitors and stagger to where Sammie lies in the snow. Her hands are burned, her face pale. Her breathing is ragged and far too shallow.

"Sammie, can you hear me?"

She doesn't respond. I wrap her face in my hands, sliding one behind her neck. "Sunshine?"

Her breathing stalls.

No.

Please, Sunshine. No!

Footsteps fall in behind me. Serena whimpers, and Denver pulls her into his side. They definitely know each other.

"Can't you wake her up with your blood?" she asks.

I can't risk her dying with my blood in her system and turning. I shake my head. Denver frowns, his brow lowering.

"You may not have a choice, little brother."

"I will not make that choice for her!"

Shuffling in the snow sees all three of us turn.

Too late.

The flash of a silver arc spirals through the air above us

and penetrates. Serena and Denver collapse into the snow. An evil smirk slides over Anjelica's face. "Oh, don't worry, they're not dead, only knocked out."

She staggers toward where I kneel in the snow by Sammie. "You and your little witch, however, won't be so lucky."

She raises both hands. Silver threads snake through the sky, rising high before plummeting toward us. Sammie jerks, coughing and gasping for breath. I turn back to find her face. Her eyes widen and she throws a hand up. Anjelica's silver threads burst into tiny sparkling pieces like confetti. She tracks their source with her gaze, pushing off the ground to sit up.

"Why can't you just stay down, you *interfering* little witch!" Anjelica screams.

Serena murmurs and rolls over, pushing to her feet with trembling limbs. Sammie shifts her gaze to her friend.

Anjelica strikes.

Two shards of silver fly into Sammie's chest, disintegrating into nothing as they penetrate their mark. Serena screams. "No!"

Sammie falls back into the snow, her golden curls lying on the soft white around her.

Denver sits up, dazed, eyes scanning everyone before landing on Sammie. Serena lets her hand wind through the air, muttering an enchantment. Anjelica goes for Serena and Denver grabs her, holding her out of the way. Anjelica stiffens before screaming at the younger witch. "How could you do this to your own mother!"

What the hell?

"You were always a flake!" Her insults don't find their mark as the young shadow witch works through the spell; eyes closed.

After a moment, she lowers her hands and opens her eyes.

"There, no more torturing innocent people. You are bound until I say so, *Mother*." The last words she forces through gritted teeth.

She drops to my side and takes my hand. I look at Sammie. Her chest has stilled.

She's gone.

I can't hear her heartbeat.

She slipped away while we were all focused on Anjelica.

No. Oh god, Sunshine.

What have I done?

Sobs choke out with every painful breath. I drop my forehead to her chest and grip her coat.

"Lewis," Serena says so softly.

I don't respond.

Sammie is gone.

It is all my fault.

"Lewis, take my hand." Her words are louder now.

"Brother, do as she says."

I rise and fall back on my heels. I run my hands through

my hair, ugly groans spilling from my chest. Serena's eyes are lined with silver, and she takes my hand in hers.

"What are you doing?"

"*We* are getting her back. Do you trust me?"

I stare at her, trying to quell the sobs wracking from my aching chest. If Sammie trusts her, so do I.

After a handful of heartbeats, I nod.

"Good."

She turns her pendant through her fingers with her free hand, muttering something that sounds like another enchantment. Everything blurs.

Sammie disappears.

Everything disappears into darkness for a heartbeat.

I am standing on the damp earth beyond the tree line of the forest flanking our home and the lake. Serena is standing beside me, her hand still holding mine tight.

"What the hell?"

"Shhhh. Wait."

I track my gaze back to the lake. I hardly believe my eyes. The four of us are standing there. The two girls in the pentagram. Me by the water's edge with Anjelica.

How in the world is this possible?

Methodically, the girls work through their spell. How did I not hear them? I scan the area. The leaves of the shrubs concealing them stand as high as a full-grown hedge, but the wind blows toward them. They were upwind. The frigid squall carried away the sound of her voice, along with the scent of my mate I would recognize anywhere. Smart girl.

My chest aches. Her cleverness just got her killed.

"If you want to save her, either way, you needed to intervene before she started dying, Lewis." Serena's voice startles me, reminding me I am not here alone. *We are going to get her back*. The words chant through my head.

We have to. Sammie cannot die for me. It's fucking unacceptable. "What do I have to do?"

"You have to intervene when I say."

"How do you know when she starts dying? Can you feel it or something?"

"I can edge my way into weakened minds. And when she was dying, I slipped into hers."

"So, you can pinpoint it for me?"

"Yes. Pay attention, you only get a matter of seconds between healing and dying as far as your blood goes."

I nod and fix my gaze on Sammie as she collapses to the snow-covered ground all over again. It hurts just as much as watching her fall the first time. With a clenched jaw and fisted hands by my side, I see her face slacken. The grey wisps of smoke leave her burned hands. The rest plays out as it did mere moments ago.

"You were talking to Denver and me when her mind slipped, and I could feel her body and see her thoughts." Serena turns to me, silver lining her eyes. My breath stops as I scan her face. Chin wobbling, she sucks in a breath.

"You were the last thing she thought of." A sob tumbles

from her lips. "You can't let her die, Lewis. She is far too loved to leave us all now. The heartache to follow would be inconceivable."

This I know.

I would take her place in a heartbeat.

Sammie refuses to let me.

She is the most selfless person I have ever met.

"Tell me when to give her my blood, to heal her so she doesn't die."

We turn back.

Serena grabs my arm after Sammie protects me for a second time.

"Now. Right after she falls the second time, you have like six seconds before she realizes she is dying."

"Take me back. Now!" I growl.

She forces a sad smile and grabs my hand; her free hand spins the pendant in the opposite direction from last time. A sickening heartbeat later, I am on the ground beside Sammie. Denver and Serena are talking. But this time, she glances at me, her steadying look and subtle nod letting me know we are both where we need to be.

"Can't you wake her up with your blood?" she asks for the second time.

I shake my head.

Denver frowns, his brow lowering.

"You may not have a choice, little brother." Somehow, hearing it the second time is no easier than the first.

"I will not make that choice for her!" I growl this time, and heat seethes through every inch of me.

Shuffling in the snow. The three of us turn. Too late. The flash of a silver arc through the air above us penetrates. Serena and Denver collapse into the snow. An evil smirk slides over Anjelica's face. "Oh, don't worry, they're not dead, only knocked out."

She staggers toward where I kneel in the snow by Sammie. "You and your little witch, however, won't be so lucky."

I inch closer to Sammie, as if my proximity can save her. Anjelica raises both hands. Silver threads snake through the sky, rising high before plummeting toward us. Sammie wakes, gasping for breath. I turn back to find her face. Her eyes widen and she throws a hand up. Anjelica's silver threads burst into tiny sparkling pieces like confetti. She tracks their source with her gaze, pushing off the ground to sit up.

"Why can't you just stay down, you *interfering* little witch!" Anjelica screams.

Serena murmurs and rolls over, pushing to her feet with trembling limbs. Sammie shifts her gaze to her friend.

Anjelica strikes.

Two shards of silver fly into Sammie's chest, disintegrating into nothing as they penetrate their mark.

Serena screams. "No!"

Sammie falls back into the snow.

Her golden curls lying on the soft white around her.

This is the moment. Six seconds is all I have before healing turns to turning.

I bite my wrist roughly, ripping the skin open for a good flow. The frigid air around us has turned even my blood to molasses and I grip above the bite mark trying to entice it to spill. Parting Sammie's mouth, I hover my wrist above her.

Five seconds.

The blood is slow, welling into small droplets on my skin.

Come on!

Four seconds.

A crimson drop splashes her face, missing her mouth.

Fuck.

I lower my wrist to above her lips. Another droplet hits her top lip.

Three seconds.

I squeeze my arm in a downward motion, forcing the flow through the open wound.

One, two, three, five, seven drops land on her tongue. She doesn't move. Her breathing slows.

Two seconds.

"Hell's fury, don't you dare think you're leaving me, Sunshine." The words are rough.

Vigorously squeezing my arm, a cascade of blood splatters into her mouth, over her teeth and lips.

One second.

"Sammie?"

I close her mouth with a gentle touch and kiss her lips, the coppery taste filling my senses along with her scent. I wrap her face in my hands and will her to respond to the blood, pressing my forehead to hers.

Time is up.

Nothing.

Her chest rises and falls and stills.

"God, Sunshine. Don't you dare!" I growl, loud and low.

Serena hits her knees beside me. Her hand touches mine. She shakes her head as tears cascade down her pale cheeks. Denver stands with his head hung behind her, despair etched over his face.

My throat is thick as short, thin breaths struggle to pass. "What have I done?"

CHAPTER 28

SAMMIE

Warm, endless white light surrounds where I stand. Nothingness fills every sense. No touch of the cold breeze from a heartbeat earlier. No sounds of Lewis by my side. No sounds at all. No tang of blood, snow, and desperation. I take a tentative step. It echoes through the space. I freeze, not knowing if walking —or any movement, for that matter—is a good idea.

"Sammie."

My breath stops. A yearning in my center turns to warmth, and I spin back. "Grandma?"

She is standing in her favorite button-down blouse and long forest green skirt, her grey hair twisted and pinned up. Her kind eyes connect with mine, a soft smile pulling over her face. Heat prickles behind my eyes. I slap a hand to my mouth, and she extends her arms to me.

I close the space between us, and she wraps me in a

tight hug as sobs spill from my throat. She rubs my back, the way she always did when I was upset as a little girl. I compose myself. Whatever this is, I am not wasting the chance to see her again with self-pity. I push back, holding her at arm's length. "How is this possible?"

"This is limbo, sweet girl."

"You have been in limbo all these years?"

I look around. The place is the definition of nothing. Like somewhere insanity would go and thrive.

"No, I haven't been here since I left you."

"Then why are you here now?"

She brushes my cheek with the back of her hand, and her chin wobbles. "I'm here for you."

"What?"

"This is the place souls go when they have not decided a final destination."

"Oh."

So, I'm dead.

I lose my hold on her as my legs give out on me. She kneels in front of me and tilts her head. "You did it, Sammie. You broke that heinous woman's curse on that poor boy. I am so proud of you, honey."

"Lewis is okay?" I choke out.

"Lewis is fine. You are one powerful witch, my girl."

I huff out a breath. So much for power—I still ended up dead. When Lewis gets here, he will kill me all over again. I huff a strangled laugh. "What happens now?"

She holds my chin with her thin hand. "Now, you choose."

"What, like heaven or hell?"

A laugh vibrates in her chest, and she shakes her head. "No, sweetness, you can choose to rest or to live." She nods her head, eyes sparkling with pure love and wonder. I place my hands on her shoulders and press my forehead to hers. I don't want to leave Lewis, my family, or Serena. I still have so much left to do. So many things to experience and places to explore.

"I know you do, darling."

She heard me. I lean back.

"Yes, I did." She smiles, crinkling her nose.

"How?"

"I have always had the gift of hearing other's thoughts when they are close. The thoughts of those I love dearly come through the loudest."

"I never knew . . ."

"We all have different gifts. Yours appear to be strictly elemental. But believe me, your powers are like nothing we have seen for centuries. A witch who can command and survive all four elements at once is not only rare, it's almost impossible. Don't let people take advantage of you, Sammie girl."

"I won't."

"Right, now you are up to date. It's time."

"Time to choose?"

She nods.

As much as I want to get back, I don't want to leave her. We have been living without her for over a decade, and it has felt like a part of our souls is missing.

"I miss you, Grandma; we all do."

"I know my sweet girl, but I made a choice and I had to accept the consequences."

"What was your choice?"

She is quiet for a moment; I can see the indecision in her eyes. Looking at me squarely, she grabs my shoulders. "You must know, this was my choice, and nobody else is to blame for the outcome."

I nod and try to steady my breath.

"I tried to help your Lewis. It is what I was doing when my magic became too much for me. I was not able to harness all four elements as you did. Three was a stretch, but I didn't want to give up. That poor boy had been hounded by that despicable witch for centuries. If I could stop her, I would. As it turns out, not only was I unable to cure his curse, my powers imploded on me. That was the last day I practiced. I wish I could have helped him. I wasn't strong enough."

She stares into the white void. I open my mouth to say something, anything, but nothing comes. She was trying to save Lewis when she died.

Holy Goddess . . .

No wonder he was so reluctant to let me try. He watched her die. There is no doubt he knew my connection to her. I sob and fall into her chest. She rubs my back, her hands circling through swirling motions. All this time, I thought he was being stubborn. He was protecting me, again. Trying to protect me from the knowledge of how my grandma died.

She had died helping a sworn enemy to witches. The depth of her kindness has always been known, but now I truly understand what it is to wield a power no other can match. It is to serve those who need to be served, defended, or protected. It is so much bigger than vampires and witches. Enemies and friends. If only the world would think like my grandmother had. Imagine the effect of unfiltered kindness.

"Sammie, you can choose whichever way you want to go. It is yours to make, no other's."

For a moment, the space of one heartbeat, I wonder what it would be like to stay here with her. To be in a space where kindness trumps everything else. To be in heaven with my grandma.

To never want. Never feel fear, sadness, overwhelm, annoyance, anger, or jealousy. To be at peace. No more bad witch, good witch. No more putting other people at risk because of who I am or who I love. Lewis would be safe. Serena would be free of her burden.

But how do I say goodbye to my parents and Jackson?

How do I leave my mate? We just found each other.

I ponder both ways.

Every thought is heavy. Too heavy.

"Sammie?"

I look up at the face I have loved all my life. Her eyes search mine.

I step closer to her. "I have made my decision."

She kisses my cheek.

Tears fall, burning their way down my skin.

Her thumb wipes them away, and she tilts her head, offering a soft smile. "Good."

I close my eyes and step into her space. Her lips press to my forehead.

"I love you, my girl."

"I love you, too, Grandma."

She releases my arms, and I smile, letting warmth spool from my center outwards. The whiteness brightens before crumbling to darkness.

I suck in a sharp breath.

I know in my heart I made the right choice.

Continue the story with *Tethered Fate*.

TETHERED FATE

GRACIE STONE

ABOUT THE AUTHOR

The fantastical has always fascinated Gracie Stone. So much so, that she spends most of her days living in worlds other than our own.

She plays with mystical creatures, goes on journeys with imaginary people and loves places and people that will never exist.

As a reader, it is easy to escape to these places too. And it is Gracie's greatest wish to help a reader to be sucked into a place that doesn't exist. To befriend magical creatures and characters...

You too can find yourself in these pages, or you can disappear into them entirely.

That, friends, is up to you.